Arabella

by
Anonymous
(1890)

LOCUS ELM™

find more by typing
Locus_Elm_Press
at:

Amazon United Kingdom
Amazon United States of America
Amazon Germany
Amazon France
Amazon Spain
Amazon Canada
Amazon Australia
Amazon Brazil
Amazon Japan
Amazon Mexico
Amazon Italy
Amazon India

*

Arabella

by

Anonymous

(written 1890)

All rights reserved. No part of this publication may be reproduced, stored in retrieval system, copied in any form or by any means, electronic, mechanical, photocopying, recording or otherwise transmitted without written permission from the publisher. You must not circulate this book in any format.

This paperback edition - Copyright: Locus Elm Press

Published: April 2015

TABLE OF CONTENTS

CHAPTER I..6
CHAPTER II..13
CHAPTER III...21
CHAPTER IV...34
CHAPTER V..44
CHAPTER VI...54
CHAPTER VII..63
CHAPTER XIII...72
CHAPTER IX...82
CHAPTER X..93
CHAPTER XI...101
CHAPTER XII..110
CHAPTER XIII...120
CHAPTER XIV..128
CHAPTER XV...137
CHAPTER XVI..150

CHAPTER XVII..161
CHAPTER XVIII..166
CHAPTER XIX..177

*

CHAPTER I

I am not - as I trust shall become clear - a woman given to bawdy talk or mere faithless, wanton ways. I have never indulged in the loose and immoral speech which nowadays cloaks so many novels. I find such productions crude and tasteless, lacking entirely in finesse and given to unlikely descriptions of equally unlikely behaviour by characters who are no more than cardboard people.

Even so, I am not a prude. Prudery is for those who fear the consequences of their own desires, however errant such desires may be. Neither will I countenance hypocrisy. There are always to be found a number of mealy-mouthed and self-inflated persons who would suppress all references to the most satisfying of physical pleasures. It is not my intention to do so here, but neither will I proclaim that they should be widely copied unless such art and sophistication is brought to them as I have been fortunate enough to be able to engender.

For I must make no bones about the fact that the comforts of wealth have provided often enough the wherewithal for many of my amorous luxuries. I call them that since they appertain to such voluptuous aspects of good living as the less well-to-do must mainly do without.

I am told by some that this view is false. All views to some are false. One can do no more or less than hold to one's own. I have known some quite pretty and adorable girls of the working classes. I have known, too, some doughty young males from the same milieu who could be counted upon to dispense with the normal crudities of their behaviour when in the presence of ladies. Removed temporarily from their drab surroundings and mean streets and brought into an atmosphere of luxury, their amorous abilities improved vastly, though ever requiring tuition.

But I must not delay my narrative too long by philosophising and shall commence with the many secret diary entries I have made throughout my life - beginning when I was seventeen. It was the year 1882 - that selfsame year when our dear Queen gave Epping Forest to the nation and the British Fleet bombarded Alexandria. I was proud to note such events in my early years, but as wisdom grew and the world progressed even more, so I devoted my immediate recollections to more personal events.

In the midsummer of that year, I was staying for a long weekend at the country house of one of my uncles. I needed not therefore to be accompanied by a chaperone, for my aunt played that role, or would have done had she been more alert to what was afoot all about her. The dear lady lived in dreamland, however, and this perhaps was all to the good insofar as it concerned my immediate education. The world is made up for the most part of fools and knaves, as the second Duke of Buckingham remarked. He was a writer indeed upon whose pleasantries I would have much cause to ponder in those next few days for it was he who first coined another phrase which was to become commonplace among those who neither knew nor cared about its source: "Ay, now the plot thickens very much upon us." This - for those whose learning would extend as does my own - occurs in the third act of his play, The Rehearsal.

Among my cousins was one Elaine. Six years my senior, she possessed my own medium height. Her ankles and calves were slender, her thighs well-fleshed as befits a woman. Her development otherwise tended to the 'bold', as we called it, for she more than amply fulfilled her dresses in respect of her breasts and bottom. Her eyes were large and her lips of medium size but slumberous - a delicious peach of a mouth to kiss, as I was to discover. Infinitely more knowing then than I, she was to teach me much.

I should say that in the grander houses of the time, two distinct types of weekend parties were held. The most general was that at which up to sixty or even seventy people might be invited - invariably during the shooting season. On the whole I found these boring. There were too many people to encounter about the house at odd hours-and sometimes to embarrass one.

The other type of party was arranged only in more knowing circles. The guests were fewer and more selectively chosen. Discretion was total, for all knew that the merest buzz of scandal beyond the porticos of the mansion would eventually ruin other such occasions. Within this understanding, certain delicious licence was permitted and orgies were not unknown. I am speaking of gatherings, of course, of no more than a score of guests, including the host and hostess.

Perhaps I should say also that these were country gentry whose morals had altered not a wit from those of their immediate forebears. They preserved their traditions. If a young woman was to be"trodden," it was accepted that she should be. She was expected to return the virile salute of the lusty penis with the same passion that it was accorded her. Many a fair bottom have I seen wriggling for the first time on a manly piston while murmurs of encouragement spurred its flushed possessor on.

Often if a girl were shy, she would be coaxed and fondled by several of the ladies into receiving her injection. Flushed cheeks and snowy breasts were exposed - an apparently burning anguish showing in the eyes as her skirts were raised - all such were salt to the occasion. Girls too bold in their ways provided little sport for an expectant assembly, and such as might have been were given sufficient hints in private to bring them to struggle and sob with great realism while they were laid open-legged upon a dining room table or a waiting divan, there to receive their first dosage of ardent sperm.

But I digress - a habit I must in these early stages of my memoirs avoid. It is of a late hour that I speak and I would not have wandered from my room on that Saturday night, so far past midnight, had the servant not forgotten to fill my bedside carafe of water.

Wine had made me thirsty. Believing all to be asleep, I opened my door quietly, padded in my nightdress along the corridors and began to descend the wide, curving staircase. At mid-point, however, I stopped. There was a light below. It shone from the dining room where the door stood half open. I heard voices - a faint laugh.

"No, Harold - not here!" I heard, and recognised the voice immediately. It was that of Mrs. Witherington-Carey whose husband had been newly summoned to his regiment. Of less than fully-matured years, she was about thirty-seven, as I fancied - a brunette of some distinct charm.

Crouching down behind the railings of the bannisters then, I saw her. There was it seemed a playful chase going on. A hand seized her arm as she made apparently to flee. Her long dark hair appeared already tousled. There then came into my view the owner of that hand. It was my uncle. His evening jacket, tie and collar had been cast off and his braces dangled from his waist. In a moment, with no more pretence of flight, his victim was seized and thrust back over the table.

"Harold, no - please!" she begged, though I noticed that in so pleading her hands gripped his arms in such a manner that she appeared not to be thrusting away.

"Sweet devil, it has been too long," he replied. Bending over her so that her feet skittered on the carpet, her shoulders laid well back upon the polished surface of the table, he accorded her a kiss of such passion that I wondered in my naivety at their capacity for taking a breath, so long did their lips merge. Then, rising, he drew her up with him.

"As before, Helen - you must!"

In my comparative innocence, I did not then note the state of his breeches which in fact were thrust out alarmingly by the most monstrous protrusion.

"You hurt me!" came the lady's response, though I divined the words to be an invitation rather than a refusal, so coyly were they spoken. So also, apparently, thought my uncle for without further ado he spun her about and groped up her skirt at the same time.

I could scarcely believe my eyes. In every fleeting second I feared discovery by another guest wandering from their room, or worse the appearance of my aunt or one of my cousins. Fate was kind to me, however, for there came no interruption to the proceedings. Despite her fiercely protesting whispers, Helen's skirts were raised up high.

Ah, what a voluptuous spectacle presented itself! In the fashion of the times her stockings were richly patterned and of a dark blue shade. Sheathing the curving columns of her well-turned legs they rose to mid-thigh and there were ringed by broad garters. Above, the vista was even more enticing, for in affecting split drawers, as she had done that evening, the victim's posture showed in all their appealing nudity the two plump cheeks of her bottom which the broadly-separated halves of her garment exposed.

A last febrile attempt by her was made to rise. I know now of course that it was but a token movement. My uncle's hand had in any event fixed itself strongly upon the back of her neck while, with his other, he groped at his breeches.

Heavens! I confess that it was not the first time that I had seen the male organ, though the few I had glimpsed hitherto had been limp and soft. The upstanding girth and length of this one was beyond all my previous experience.

I judged its veined majesty a full nine inches in length and some five of circumference. The ruby head was full swollen, gleaming beneath the glittering light from the chandeliers. Full rigid, it menaced the deep crevice which presented itself so lewdly to him.

A muffled cry - quickly choked back as if by practise of discretion - sounded from her throat as the crest of my uncle's staff inserted itself within the inviting valley. The lady's hands clawed for a brief moment at the polished top and then her face sank sideways - fortunately in such a manner that she could in no wise raise her vision to mine, even had she been able to discern me up on the dark stairway.

"Too...too...too big, Harold!" she moaned.

A grunt came from her inamorata. Further fumbling ensued and then his breeches slid down his trunk-like thighs, betraying to my gaze the sight of his large testicles in profile beneath his manly organ which had but nestled its head twixt her bottom cheeks.

"Nonsense, Helen, you have taken it before."

His knees bent slightly and he seized her hips, relinquishing at last his grip upon her neck. A further moan came from her. The table trembled visibly, heavy as it was, the surface shimmering in the light.

"OH!" moaned she, though it seemed scarce a complaint but rather a petulant utterance of compliance.

With that the thick shaft urged in and evidently sank some three inches within her puckered rosette, causing its recipient to screw up her eyes and bite her lower lip. I knew not then of course whether she was in agony or in the throes of sweet enjoyment. Her large bottom endeavoured to wriggle sideways, but was held.

"Ah, dear love, what a bottom, what warmth, what tightness! You are as fetching as you were ten years ago," my uncle growled. His features strained and grew ever redder. A tall, bulky man, the power of his loins was all too evident to me-not to say also to Mrs. Witherington-Carey who received inch by inch his powerful prodder. For a moment she appeared to grit her teeth. Her eyes had a look of anguish that might also, as I even then surmised, cloak an uprising feeling of passion. A little cry from both and the shaft was fully embedded.

Patting her flanks and caressing her stockinged thighs, my uncle thus held her, savouring no doubt the plump rondeur of her nether cheeks against his belly. Her shoulders hunched, relaxed, and then she uttered a whimper.

"Part your legs, dearest - straddle them - hold well. Is it not delicious?"

Helen's eyes and lips opened simultaneously. She was as one entranced. A gentle movement of her hips sufficed then to show me the pleasure she was evidently sustaining. A soft humming sound issued from her throat.

"Do not move it for a moment, Harold. Kiss me. Ah, you beast!"

Her neck slewed round, her tongue distinctly protruded. Bending full over her as he then did, their lips met. Words that I could no longer distinguish came between their passionate kisses. That they were lewd I doubted not for her bottom began to move in little jerks back and forth.

It seemed impossible to me then, of course, that she could receive and contain it there, but I was to learn myself of the particular pleasure of this mode. Small puffing sounds were uttered by both as my uncle in turn began to work his penis steadily in her most secret orifice. The distinct sound of the brazen smacking and slapping of her bottom to his belly came to me. His shaft emerged a full three-quarters and then rammed in again, the motion being repeated on and on while the most fevered twisting of her hips occurred.

Their breaths came faster, his balls swinging steadily under the lower bulge of her derriere. Their moans of pleasure rose. Thrusting one hand down beneath her belly, his fingers searched and rubbed. Immediately her shoulders and head lifted the more. Her expression was one of ecstasy.

"C-C-Coming! AH! I am coming, Harold! Faster!" The table creaked. Some instinct told me that my uncle, too, was attaining the peak of his desire. A trembling of his legs became apparent. His hands clasped her hips more loosely. Rising up from over her, he hung his head back.

"H-H-Harold! Oh, fill me, yes! What floods!" Her bottom thrust to him aggressively, receiving all to the very root while - had I but known it - the rich juice from his balls was already impelling its leaping jets within the sucking tube of her bottom. Groaning, he made a last effort to eject the final spurts and then collapsed for a moment upon her back.

Thus they remained still save for slight twitchings of their loins while the last tinglings of bitter-sweet pleasure surged through them. Then at last - as if gathering himself - my uncle rose and withdrew the soaked shaft of love with a positively succulent sound, causing his victim to tighten her bottom cheeks and huddle into the table until he drew her up in turn.

Swivelling about in his arms, she afforded him a final kiss of some tenderness.

"How wicked you are to do it to me thus, Harold."

"How wicked you are to let me," he responded with a laugh. Continuing to hold her skirts up as he did, I could see the well-furred bush of her mount and the gathering limpness of his tool against which it was lovingly pressed. I dared stay no longer. At any moment they might, I feared, turn to the door. Discovery would present such a horror as I could not face. Gathering up the hem of my nightgown so that I would not trip over it, I tiptoed to the top of the stairs, all thoughts of my earlier thirst having vanished. Fully dizzy with what I had seen, I felt a curious, warming moisture between my thighs as I neared my door and was aware that my nipples had risen, teased by the cotton of my garment.

I had left my bedroom door on the latch, but saw now even in the gloom that it was ajar. Some errant draught had disturbed it, I thought, though my mind was really too distracted for such matters and my pulses were racing still. Pushing open the door I gave a little cry which I endeavoured as best as possible to suppress.

Lying upon my ruffled bed was a white-robed figure that stirred and rose up at my entrance.

It was my cousin, Elaine.

CHAPTER II

"Oh, what a fright you gave me!" I gasped.

Quick as a flash, Elaine had bounded up from the bed and closed the door even as I faltered in the entrance.

"Shush! Do not make a sound! How you are trembling! Did I frighten you so? I could not sleep, Arabella. Forgive me, do, but I am so restless."

All this being said in a rush, and I scarcely having recovered from my double shock, she led me to the bed and drew me down upon it, passing her arms about me so to comfort me for my aroused fears, as she thought. Indeed, I trembled violently, though not so much from the scare she had given me as from the aftermath of what I had witnessed. Alas for feminine intuitions, I was not long to remain guardian of my secret.

"What have you been doing? Where were you?"

All such questions being thrown at me, I knew not how to reply for a moment. Her body being warm to mine and pressed thighs to thighs against me, I do not doubt that she could feel the risen perkiness of my nipples against the firm gourds of her own breasts.

"I, too, could not sleep - I went to get some water," I muttered.

At that, Elaine laughed and kissed me on the tip of my nose. "Oh, you have seen something - I know you have. What is going on down there?" she asked.

Fretfully I tried to stir from her embrace, but curiosity had awoken devilment in her and she clasped me the tighter, I becoming aware of the silky feel of our bellies together through the cotton of our nightdresses and the fact that my nipples were stubbing against her titties.

"Nothing, I have seen nothing - what is to see?" I blustered.

"I know you have. That is why you are trembling, and beside I can feel your excitement," Elaine laughed. With that she insinuated one hand between us and so manipulated my breasts and felt my hard nipples that I gasped and twisted for the caress was more enervating than she knew and my burning globes swelled to her touch.

"I have not - oh, I have not."

I blustered fiercely and would have gone on doing so had she not then closed my trembling lips with hers. How sweet her mouth was! Never before had I kissed mouth to mouth with anyone, nor ever thought of doing so with another girl. Had my passions not been aroused by the lewd spectacle I had witnessed, I know not how I would have responded.

"I will make you tell, Arabella!"

Moist and full, her lips engaged mine more deeply. The sensation, coupled to the blatant wandering of her palm all about my thinly-covered breasts, caused me to surrender utterly. I responded. The tips of our tongues met. In that first moment of the true uncovering of my desires, Elaine knew beyond doubt - as she afterwards conveyed to me - that my heated mind held secrets that she was intent upon devouring. Knowing full well even then her capacity for seduction, she commenced easing up the hem of my nightgown while I all too feebly attempted to obstruct the effort.

"Come, darling, come, for you must be longing for it. Did you see them at it?"

"I am not - no! Oh, Elaine, what a naughty thing to do! St-stop f-feeling me-AH!"

Of a sudden I was bared to my hips. The tip of her forefinger engaged the oily lips of my nest and found my button. I twisted, writhed. I absorbed her tongue. My protestations fled. At the first ardent rubbing of her finger I was lost. Or rather, I should say, found. Oft since have we talked about that moment and how the net of fate ensnares us by the most casual of events. I refer of course to the fact that Elaine had caught me in that moment. My hips wriggled even as Mrs. Witherington-Carey's had done. My legs parted, enabling Elaine to slip full-length upon me. Withdrawing her urging finger as she did so, her furry nest sidled moistly against my own. I felt the rubbing of our love-lips, the tingling merging of our pubic hairs. Coiling her arms under my knees and raising and thrusting my legs back, she caused our honey-pots to meet and rub fully. I gasped within her mouth, I clasped her shoulders. Our bottoms squirmed in mutual delight. In a moment a violent shuddering seized me and my belly felt as if invaded by bursting stars. Lashing her tongue wickedly all around my own, Elaine sprinkled my bush in turn with her own spattering lovejoy and then kissed me tenderly all about my hot face.

Alas, that one can never come within distance of such moments with mere words. Long have I practised such in my diaries, yet ever despairing of describing even the touch of lips to one's own in a manner that will communicate to the reader - even to myself. I who hold the dear memories of a thousand such moments of ineluctable bliss can frame them more closely in my mind than mere words can draw. The words provide but a sketch, the frailest outlines of reality. I trouble myself too much about it, perhaps. To Elaine I appear to possess a mastery of prose such as she can never attain to. Time and again in the years that have since passed after that first night of voluptuous discoveries, she has asked me again and again,"What did you write about it?" - referring of course to whatever event had last occurred. She has been party to almost all I have written, her eyes positively glowing as she has perused my diaries, while for myself I have fretted openly to her that I have failed to capture the fleshly bliss.

"Oh, if I could but write like you, I would write very naughty books," she has oftimes declared.

I have never been flattered by her praise, however. I know my faults, my shortcomings, the midnight wrestlings with words upon which I afterwards gaze with disappointed mien. However, I digress again and must return to the first ruffled bed in which we found ourselves alone and palpitating.

My nest throbbed. Our bodies were sticky together. With a sigh Elaine rolled off of me, though still continuing to cuddle and caress me. That I made no bones about letting her do so - and even returned her lascivious touchings - was the full sign that I had been drawn at last into my future realm. Hot-nippled as our breasts were, they rubbed together where our nightgowns had been drawn up to our armpits.

"Tell me now. What did you see? Who was it?"

I giggled foolishly, still somewhat naive as I was. That long night was however to temper me much in my attitudes and ways of thought. I recall not what I replied for I durst not tell her - as I then thought - that her own Papa was one of the participants. Indeed, in my own ridiculous fashion in those first moments of aftermath, I thought she would not believe me or would be shocked. Such veils of unknowing were soon to be rent from me. Persistent in her questioning and never ceasing to keep me thoroughly aroused between my thighs, Elaine at last after many hesitations and denials on my part, drew from me by simple methods of elimination of names the identity of Mrs. Witherington-Carey. Indeed, I bit my tongue and hid my face upon uttering the name. However, to my uttermost surprise, my cousin remarked with a charming laugh,"She is quite a beauty, is she not? How did he have at her? Were her drawers full down?"

"Oh, she had none on," I replied, realising for the first time that the lady had worn no such garment. Even as I spoke my breath was bubbling out again for upon Elaine's wicked forefinger as my dell was, I was yet about to come again.

It was over the table, I said. Who was the man, she demanded to know. Do not make me tell, I begged. At that she laughed and rolled me under her anew.

"I know - it was Papa. Oh, he has a big one!" she declared, to my perfect astonishment.

"Oh, it was Papa, then. What a big one he has!"

"Ah, Elaine!"

She had me exactly as she wanted. I was lost to her entirely. Raising my legs of my own accord, I wound them round her slim waist. Her words sang in my brain even as we kissed and rubbed and rose anew to a peak of bliss.

"How-how do you know?" I gasped, for all manner of thoughts were now raging in me.

"You sillykins, you do not know much, do you? Oh, you naughty thing, you are making me come again - is it not lovely?"

I could not but agree. The word painted but a ghost of the sensations I was prey to. The thorns of our nipples seemed to spin about one another's. Our lips indulged in the most lascivious kisses. The curls of our quims became matted with our merging spendings.

"We will do everything together, shall we not, Arabella?"

"Yes," I choked, though I knew not then the full import of her words nor to what scenes of libertine delights they were to lead us. Quietening ourselves at last, we lay quiet. In the milky gloom, Elaine bent over me and regarded me solemnly. Then, rising, she discarded her nightdress and bid me do the same. There being a flask of liqueur such as was kept for all guests in a side cabinet, we indulged ourselves by drinking from the neck of it. I knew not the time, nor cared.

"Shall we be naughty together?" Elaine asked. We sat up, our legs curled under us, hips touching.

"What can we do?" I asked naively.

"Everything, Arabella. I have long thought of it. Have you not wondered that I am not yet wed? It is of my own choosing. I may do so in a few years time, but for the nonce I do not mean to fetter myself to one man and one bed. I have learned too much for that, how utterly boring it would be! I am certain now that you share my feelings, or will soon do so, therefore I mean to confide in you. Do you know how many ways there are in which pleasure can be taken?"

I shook my head. I was all agog with wonder and so tremulous from the experiences of the night that I was ready to follow her in all.

"Let us consider, for I have read many naughty books that I filched from Papa's study, though he knows it not. Were all the things therein to be brought together, what exquisite pleasures one could have! Firstly, there are joys between ladies, such as we have just had and which are ever renewable. You were very easy to seduce, my love, for you were already in a fine fever for it. Supposing, though, that one seduced a girl who was not. What fun!"

"Oh, but she might hate it and make a fuss, Elaine!"

"Of course she would not - not for long. Girls are very understanding among themselves you know, and if she were a novice her delights would be threefold and we could teach her much. Then there is the mounting of a girl by a man. What a delight it is to watch!

Supposing we could bring it about!"

My mouth parted, I could not believe what I was hearing, yet Elaine spoke not in a coy fashion but a very plain and practical one that stilled the amazed response I might otherwise have given. Indeed, I was dumbstruck, which she - perceiving my silence to be halfway towards assent on my part - took quick advantage of.

"It is perfectly possible, you know, for I have heard about it being done at hunt balls and such. It is called being put to the cock and many a fair young lady has been initiated thus during the revelry. Alas, Mama is very prim and proper, you know, and so has never let me attend one, nor my sisters. I have endeavoured to wheedle Papa into letting me accompany him on some pretext of going elsewhere, but he has resisted. For my part, of course, I have pretended ignorance to him of the goings on, merely saying that I wished to attend a grand affair, but he will not have it, saying they are by invitation only. All the world knows that, of course, but it would trouble him nothing to arrange our presence."

"But in that case you would see nothing, for surely it is not done before the whole company and your Papa could scarce be present when you did."

"You see how I have to educate you, my pet! Did it bother you a whit that Papa was not putting himself to his wife? Of course not! Did it bother Papa or Helen? Not for a second, Arabella. The pleasure is all. I mean to bring you to my way of thinking on this."

"You said he had..."

I could not finish the sentence no more than I could stop myself from uttering it.

"A big one? Well - has he not? How I know this I do not intend to tell you as yet, which I know will tease you much and therefore to listen to me ever more carefully. So you see, as to bringing a girl to the penis, that is more easily done than you would think, although the moment and the atmosphere must be right. I have witnessed it once, as you have, and found a perfect pleasure in doing so. What more could be gained than by gazing upon the intimate conjunction of the parts, by listening to the sighs, the moans, and seeing the rolling of the eyes and the passionate merging of lips."

"Yes, that is true," I exclaimed, for the more I then thought upon it, the more I wanted to see it again.

"Well, then, and so is much other than one can think and read of. What a waste were we to let it all pass by us, Arabella! What utter boredom to find oneself too early wed and the doors of adventure closed. Listen now, for there is much more than I have already said. To birch a girl is quite delicious, for instance."

"Oh, but that would hurt her!"

"My tender one, it would sting and burn her, yes, but if wielded properly - as from all I read - the ensuing pleasures are a perfect delight and not by any means to be scorned. The twigs burnish the bottom, cause it to become fervently heated and the cunny to moisten, and so all is well prepared for the amorous assault that needs follow."

"Is that true? Oh, I suppose I can imagine it a little! Papa has never birched me, though. Has yours?"

"No, my pet - he has been too busy on other ventures with other females to think of baring my bottom. But wait, for we have not by any means reached the end of our lists. There is riding, for instance, when the man - mounted on the same horse behind the female of his choosing - may put himself to her easily enough as she raises her bottom to the jogging of the horse. The reading of such an event much excited me, as I'm sure it would you. There is then also the binding of a girl by ropes or straps when she may be made to take the cock. I have heard it said that some girls are well held by other ladies to the same end at such rumbustious occasions as I have mentioned, so I see little difference in the matter save that by more elaborate means of bringing a girl to her fate one may take more time and have more enduring pleasure in it. But I see you are looking doubtful about it," declared Elaine, taking another swig from the flask and passing it to me.

Whether it was the headiness of the liqueur or that of her words, I knew not, but found myself shaking my head in denial. I averred only, and rather weakly, that it seemed a trifle cruel.

"That is because you have not thought about it, my pet, as I have. The girl would be well prepared beforehand by being tickled and kissed and teased, just as you have been this very night. Did you not surrender and willingly? I have no doubts at all that any sporty girl put to such mischief would soon enough take as much pleasure from it as you did. Think you now of other things, however, that one might do, as for instance entertaining two gentlemen at once."

My exclamation at this was such that she burst into laughter.

"I forget, Arabella, that you have not even been threaded yet and know only of the real pleasures by proxy. I must warn you though that they are not always brought forth with such voluptuous skills as you have witnessed, and indeed that bout itself was of brief duration from what you tell me. This is not to say that one might not sport briefly oneself of occasion - out of a sense of mischief, perhaps, if nothing else. We must ourselves enjoy all that we speak of, and more, or we shall remain as novices. What say you, cousin?"

What could I say? To venture her a negative reply would have been ludicrous, yet I teetered on the edge of all such wickednesses as she had spoken of, though a continued tingling in my cunny surreptitiously announced my pleasure at the thought of them. Nor was that all, for as Elaine had told me she had garnered many very naughty ideas from her father's secret store of books and had memorised them all.

Making not too much of my wondering silence, she stroked and fondled me, well seeing that I was all a-quiver still to receive her tongue and her fingers. Ere dawn broke, Elaine had tasted my honey-pot with her mouth and I hers. We trickled and spurted our pleasure between each other's lips. After doing so, we coiled our tongues together so that we might take a further taste of all that was mixed.

"Is it not more delicious than the finest of liqueurs? Come, leap with me into a divine course of wickedness. Say that you will!"

"Yes!" I assented. The die was cast. Never would I turn back.

CHAPTER III

"First you must be threaded, darling, and have your cunny filled to the brim," Elaine murmured to me before departing for her own room. The sheet was long twisted under me from our rompings, yet I felt no discomfort from it. My passions stirred upon all the things of which we had talked. Amidst my musings I saw ever again and again the sturdy shaft that had reamed dear Helen who unexpectedly was later to become a dear and knowing friend. The vision of it enflamed me still. I toyed with myself and fell into the most vivid dreams wherein all earthly cares are cast aside. Upon waking at the entrance of a housemaid bringing tea the next morning, all churned up again within me, yet I could scarce believe it had all come to pass. The fevers of the night seemed to my drowsy mind but tattered emblems of a wild imagination. Indeed, a certain morbidity would, I believe, have seized me, had not Elaine once more entered upon the scene.

Attired in a pale pink peignoir adorned with lace, she looked perfectly lovely. Her legs, elegant as they were and full womanly at their juncture, twinkled palely through the gap in the fine, silky material. Her eyes were warm. Seeing my expression, she gave a loving smile and sat beside me, taking my hand.

"I meant all that I said, be not in doubt of it. Long have I waited to have an accomplice such as you," she declared. "You have such an air of angelic innocence and prettiness as will disguise many of our escapades. Your passion will know no more bounds than mine. Say that you are still of the same mind, Arabella, oh do!"

Such was the pleading in her tone that I laughed almost in relief at being lifted from my cloud of doubt. Taking this for all the assent that my expression was intended to reveal, she kissed me warmly.

"Repeat now the final lesson I taught you," she demanded. While I hesitated, she tapped my lips playfully with her fingers, saying that if the words did not come out she would tickle me to distraction. "Cock must come to... Come on, Arabella!"

I hid my face but could not suppress a grin. Her hand moved to tickle me beneath my armpits and I jumped.

"C-c-cock must come to cunny," I whispered.

"Yes - go on!" The excited impatience in her voice was evident.

"C-c-cock must come to bottom - lips must come to cock - pussy must come to pussy - lips must come to pussy... oh, Elaine, I forget!"

"Oh, you story, you do not - but that will do for the moment. But you have forgotten one thing: it does not matter whose they are so long as they are nice! There, you see, it sounds like a little song! But listen, for I have a most wonderful idea. You remember that I told you that I wished to attend one of the private gatherings and that Papa would not take me? Of course you do. Well, we shall exercise our devious powers, my pet, and to the advantage of us all. Papa is much smitten with you, as I happen to know, for 'tis always he who ensures your invitation here. Yes, you may well blush, but that is the truth of it. Now, as to my plan it is really very simple. I shall make it known to Papa - indeed, we shall do so - that you are much taken with the idea also. Of course, he will believe us innocent in the real affair of things, but no matter. The idea will come far more fetchingly from you and I feel certain he will not then resist."

I became almost pettish at first at the idea which I thought merely hot-headed, I confess.

"Elaine, we dare not, for whatever passes there will be seen by your Papa as much as we, and I would have no face to put upon it, let alone you."

"Have I not thought of that, my darling muddlehead? It will be known, of course, that Papa and I are kin and so discreet arrangements will be made to ensure our separation. I shall be whisked away - I have no doubt of that - but hence will still enjoy myself and, who knows, with the help of one or other may yet still peep in upon the proceedings. As for you, 'twill be quite other, for Papa will be discreet enough to withdraw from you, I know."

"Oh, Elaine, what boldness! I could not!"

"Ha! See how you scurry to your rabbit hole as soon as we begin!" Elaine jeered and made to rise, which reaction from her caused me to seize her wrist, for then - as now - I would never be taken for a coward, however bizarre all seemed to me then.

"I do not! I will do it, you will see!" I blurted, much to her satisfaction, for she embraced me and declared that she had really known it all along.

"Really, you have no need to bother about Papa any more than I, Arabella. He knows perfectly well what is afoot at such gatherings and will be well apprised when something naughty is about to begin. At that he will no more be able to face you than you him and so will take to one of the bedrooms with some lady of his choosing. To put not too fine a point upon it, the occasion will give him fair opportunity to do so."

"Yes," I countered, "but he will know that we know."

"Make not too much of that, my sweet. Papa may then see in you and I accomplices of a sort - already compromised by his own lights - and may see us well out of the affair. It would not come amiss were he to buy me the pearl necklace he has long promised!"

"Oh, you wicked one!" I declared, but could not help laughing at her boldness and her quaint determination. I have long thought that innocence was upon her in some part even then, and knew not the trepidations - which she afterwards confessed to me - which she experienced in embarking upon her course. My own uprising sense of mischief and daring gave strength to her. We were as wall and ivy, the one complementing the other in our upward reachings.

Reflecting upon the affair now, as I often still do - for it is as well to know our own motives in all things - I perceive that one or other of two qualities would have carried me through. I refer to naivety on the one hand and the full knowledge of experience on the other. Either would have done to decide me upon the path I trod then. Had I veered between both states, as many foolish women do, I would in all probability been too utterly shocked to entertain such ideas, or on the other hand would have wavered feebly and come to nothing but inertia. Thus naivety is put to good purpose while experience finds its own. Elaine had divined this instinctively during all her readings and daydreamings. Males who invariably consider themselves the lords of the universe could never have done as we. Nor could even the most determined of young women contrived on her own what we accomplished.

That I was destined to pleasure myself as I have done has long been clear to me. It will be seen however that none suffered in the process and many gained enduring delight from my precepts. That I occasionally surpassed her in my daring fretted her not. Hedonism is all. In the beginning we shared all, whether by our mutual presences or by our confidences afterwards. Each of us in a sense was the other's fervent disciple.

Our first plot - which I confess made my heart palpitate madly - proceeded with an ease born of the self-same fate which directed our footsteps.

"We shall stroll a little in the garden, Papa, will you not join us?" Elaine asked him after breakfast. I had not until then thought of my uncle in any sense of being an admirer of myself, but now that the thought had been put into my mind I perceived with what interest his eyes passed all over me. He had been minded, I believe, to do something other, but as it chanced this proved his first opportunity to converse with me beyond the hearing of my aunt.

Upon his approval, therefore, the three of us took to the sward whose green and springy surface floated comfortably beneath my feet. Elaine seemed unduly quiet to a point at which I thought she was regretting her idea. Once out of sight of the house, however, she quickly broached the point, saying that I was much minded to enjoy my first festive evening with dancing and company.

At this a shadow passed across my uncle's brow. He hesitated much before replying.

"I fear, my dear, that your Mama would think it very strange were I to take you both. No, I do not think it can be thought of. Moreover, there are Arabella's parents to be consulted."

One quick glance from Elaine and I knew that I must speak. Somewhat to my surprise I then heard my own voice declaring that Mama and Papa would make no ado about the matter and indeed were minded that I should enjoy myself.

"Ah yes," my uncle replied. He was clearly in a dilemma. Walking on the other side of him, Elaine took his hand playfully.

"Will you not, Papa? It is a trifle deceitful, I know, but we could always tell Mama that we were attending some other function. After all, no harm will come to us for you will be there to chaperone us. Dear Papa, say yes!"

Her apparent innocence was perfectly judged in tone and manner, while my own could equally be in no doubt. My uncle, glancing at me as we made our way through a shrubbery, appeared flushed of visage. I would have given much then to read his thoughts. He was most obviously at a loss, since he must either forewarn us of the consequences or simply refuse. The smile that I afforded him appeared to swing the balance.

"I do hear," he declared, "that there is to be a small reception at the Eastwoods on Saturday evening. I must mention, however... well, that is to say... they are very lively." His voice appeared hoarse, his visage strained.

"I have so heard also, Papa, but that is to the good is it not; for we mean to enjoy ourselves," replied Elaine who could scarce conceal a smile of victory.

"Yes, my pet, but..."

"Then it is settled, Papa. Besides, I have a topping idea. We will apprise Mama that we are attending a seance. You know how such things fret her and that she will have nothing to do with such events. Oh dear, I have no kerchief about me and must fetch one. Pray excuse me!"

With that she was gone, leaving me in full knowledge of the fact that it was but an excuse whereby I might wheedle the more into her Papa's favours. Alone with him, however, I knew not what to say and felt my tongue quite twisted. He for his part appeared ruminative and frequently on the verge of saying something which he could not bring himself to speak. I surmised, of course, what was on his mind and finally found voice as we came upon a rustic seat outside a summerhouse where he seemed as pleased to rest as I.

"As to the-er-reception, my dear, I fear that neither Elaine nor your sweet self know of the nature of such-er-functions," he observed hesitantly.

"Oh yes, we are fully apprised, Uncle. There is dancing and

music and general merriment such as perhaps may not take place at more formal gatherings. Be certain that we are fully prepared to enter into the spirit of things."

Had I spoken too boldly? His eyes searched mine - his hand encompassed mine where it lay on my lap. So far from imagining it, I felt his knuckles graze not unpleasurably against my belly where I had inadvertently parted my thighs a little. Wearing as I was a light summer gown with naught but a chemise and stockings beneath, the warmth of my body in such an intimate region communicated itself to his hand immediately.

"Yes, my dear, but there is a certain-er-freedom..."

He appeared to have difficulty in finding words. I interrupted him sweetly.

"Society puts upon us, does it not?" I replied. Keeping my lips parted I gazed at him with such lustrous innocence that he knew not how to answer and indeed made no attempt to do so in words for with the swiftness of a swallow his mouth came upon mine, causing me at first to hold my breath.

"How young you are - you know not what you are at," he murmured, though appearing to do so himself by passing his hand up until it all but encompassed my left titty. Responsive as my nipples have always proved, he was in but seconds in no doubt of their springiness which made itself apparent through my gown. I gulped, I swallowed. Even so I made no attempt to avert either my mouth or his hand which wandered first from one mound to the other and weighed the gelatinous hillocks amorously.

"Oh, you must tell me what you mean, please," I begged as our lips parted.

Appearing then to realise where his hand was, he placed it instead upon my upper thigh where his fingers savoured the ridging of my stocking top through the fine cotton of my dress.

"I meant not to kiss you - yet how delicious you are," he muttered. His desire to be encouraged was obvious.

"Dear Uncle, if you mean to kiss me, you shall, for I see no harm in it. It is not a very wicked thing to do, is it?"

"Nor this?"

With something of an eager grin he replaced his cupping hand, this time upon my other breast, allowing it to swell in his grasp as had its neighbour. Glancing swiftly down at his breeches I saw that he was well-armed for an amorous conflict but felt certain that he would not attempt one at this time.

"I cannot call it wicked, Uncle, for it feels pleasant. Do wicked things feel unpleasant? There will not be unpleasantry at the reception, will there?"

"One may gauge it so or one may gauge it not, Arabella. The most wicked things are invariably the most pleasant. Even so, I hesitate still to take you there for your innocence will be confounded and undone, I fear."

"Oh!" I ejaculated and pursed my lips so prettily thereby that he could not help but lavish more kisses upon me, all of which I received with a certain coy pleasure while wondering muchly whether Elaine intended me to draw him out upon the subject or not. I could find no words, however, to frame a question in such a way that would not betray my foreknowledge. Making great play of being petulant and sulky, I pushed his hand away. "Then I shall not let you kiss me, for if we do not go we shall not have any fun," I exclaimed, leaving him much in the dark as to what I knew or did not know. Seemingly, however, he was satisfied since, having made several attempts to dissuade us both from our course there would be no one to blame but ourselves. Thus guile did win the day, and thereupon also did Elaine reappear.

"How flushed you look, Arabella! Has Papa been at you?" she asked merrily in a manner that could be construed by two meanings. His pego stuck up so visibly in his breeches that she could no more fail to see it than I. At her remark he flushed heavily and told her not to speak nonsense for he had - he said carefully - no need whatever to upbraid me.

Coming then, as I felt it tactful to do to his support, I averred that we had been talking together very nicely and that he had finally given his full assent to our attendance on the Eastwoods.

"Why then, we shall all have fun," Elaine said as she smiled artlessly. "I have told Mama, so there is no hindrance to the matter. We may even be late in returning if we wish for I have had her believe that the spirits do not rise well before midnight."

This remark causing us all to laugh, though not in an unkindly manner, eased the atmosphere much, though a certain agitation evidenced itself in my uncle who upon some excuse soon made his departure, walking with a rather curious gait. I had no doubt that he would have been pleased to accompany me alone to the Eastwoods' private party, but was anxious at the intended presence of his daughter. Indeed, the matter appeared to have played upon his mind for that selfsame day he succeeded in cornering me in a passageway upstairs close to my room, saying that he would have converse with me. A nearby linen closet being unattended I allowed myself to be escorted within, my uncle closing the door with solemn mien.

On either side of us were shelves upon which sheets and towels and other necessities were stored. The space between was such that we were brought to stand close together, I making no demur when he passed his arms about my waist and drew me against him.

"My dear Arabella, my sweet child, there is a matter of some import I must convey to you. It concerns the reception which you and Elaine would have us attend."

"Yes, of course, Uncle, what frets you? Oh, what a pretty kiss! Have you brought me in here only for this?"

"No, my pet, but you are truly irresistible and therein lies the crux of the affair, as much also as it appertains to Elaine who is as thoroughly excitable and carefree as yourself, but knows not the consequences thereof."

"Pray do tell me, then, for naught shall pass my lips of what is said here," I replied with great solemnity while he, passing his hand down from my waist, made bold to caress the rondeur of my bottom.

"There are country pleasures of which you know not, Arabella. The guests on such occasions are given to great frivolity. I hesitate to say to what extent. Suffice perhaps to tell you in all confidence - and such of course must never reach the ears of my dear wife - that the ladies are given to doffing much of their attire, as also are the gentlemen. There follows much amorous play, of course, for in select and well-chosen company such is accepted as a pleasurable pastime and no ill is thought of it. You see my dilemma?"

I feared at first to speak, not so much out of modesty but because in speaking he had slowly gathered up my skirt at the back and - first fondling my bared thighs and the sleek silk of my stockings - succeeded in cupping my bottom cheeks which protruded boldly upon his hand. Appearing much confused I pressed myself as if protectively against him and hid my face. My drawers being of fine batiste permitted the warmth of my derriere to exude over his hand which searched the hillocks somewhat feverishly. It was an amusing situation, for I swear that the poor man was struggling twixt desire and the need to advise me of my future fate, as also that of Elaine whom clearly he knew little despite her occasionally bold manner.

"Shall we then need to take our drawers off?" I asked while not permitting him a view of my expression.

The question being so put caused his penis - which had already thickened - to rise measurably against my belly through our garments. The proud rod strained. I felt its anguish.

"Those and much else," he replied thickly, whereat his febrile fingers loosed the ties of my drawers and caused them to slither slowly down my legs. "It will be so, you see," he went on, raising my chin with his free hand and passing his lips across mine. I quivered and strained, for the seeking of his hand beneath my bottom cheeks caused me to rise up on tiptoe. A sweet, sickly sensation invaded me. By passing his forefinger under my derriere he was able to touch the soft warm lips of my quim which moistened instantly. The impress of his mouth upon my own grew stronger. My lips parted. I received his tongue. Roaming his hand all about, he then brought it to the front between our bodies and fondly cupped my pulsing nest. "It will be so, my love, while you in turn will be required to grasp your partner's cock and frig him. Feel my own for it has grown mightily for you."

Thereupon he rapidly unfastened the flap of his breeches and passed the monstrous organ into my hand. So lusty in girth was it that my fingers could not hold fully around it. It throbbed like an engine. I felt the veins outstanding against my flesh. My belly swirled. I could not help but widen my thighs as much as my fallen drawers would permit to allow his finger to seek up between the lips of my love-nest. I know not what words passed between us in those brief moments save that on his part they were lewd and on mine excited. I moved my hand gently up and down his shaft. My senses reeled. Second by second I could feel my cunny moistening the more. Our tongues flashed together in such utter yearning that the moment clearly could no longer be delayed.

"You must know how it will be, Arabella, must you not?"

"Yes!" I assented, though I scarce recognised my voice as my own. I felt myself being borne back. We fell together upon the floor, he taking care that I would not harm myself in doing so. Without more ado my drawers were ripped from my ankles. With a certain roughness that thrilled me exceedingly, he thrust my legs apart, raising himself a little above me on one hand while with the other he fumbled his enormous cock against my slit.

"You will be put so upon the floor, or upon a couch, and fucked, Arabella."

"OH!" I moaned. His knob was at the portals. I felt the huge bulb of it press into my wetness. For a second or two our hot eyes locked together and then with an ineffable groan he inserted two inches of his meaty shaft and was full upon me. Our lips meshed. I was in such an ague that I wriggled my bottom to obtain more of his prick, though to my uncle the movement must have appeared evasive in intent for he seized me strongly about the waist and embedded his throbbing peg the more so that in some magical wise my cunny expanded to receive it.

"You will be thoroughly fucked, Arabella - do you wish to be?"

"HAAAAAR!"

I could not speak. I was filled with him. His huge balls hung beneath the lower bulge of my bottom. His lips savaged my own. With a passionate jolt of his loins the peg was fully inserted and then all but withdrawn so that I near cried out for its return. His face appeared haggard and flushed. I saw the ugliness of male lust and desire that soon enough melts into fiery passion as two bottoms begin to work in unison.

"You wish to be - you wish to be!" he exulted.

"Oh, Uncle - oh!"

Some inner wisdom in me told me not to respond directly, though I would have fain have cried out that I wanted his prick to work me strongly. Some measure of modesty must be present at all times in the first moments of erotic bliss. Such draws the male on to excite one the more. They would have us all be whores in bed.

"You do, you do - confess it! What a luscious little cunt you have - how tightly it enclasps and sucks upon my prick. I shall come in you ere I mean to. Ah my god, yes, work your bottom!"

In my fever, I was doing so without knowing it. It mattered not. We were lost in that world wherein fulfilment is all. The selfsame cock that I had seen pistoning back and forth in Helen's bottom was now in my own enamoured possession. I gloried in each powerful stroke of it. My spendings sprinkled his balls. I implored his tongue the more by twirling my own in his mouth. I was as one who drowns in passion and seeks to do so. Cupped now upon his broad palms, the tight cheeks of my bottom rotated savagely, though it was then to my gain that he thought me endeavouring to fight free from under him by so doing and hence his tool rammed in and out the more lustily.

His questions poured upon me. It was my first lesson in discovering how a man will try to draw the lewdest words and phrases from his mount, seeking to find beneath her apparent innocence the hottest pits of desire. I answered not except by chokes and sobs. Advised by instinct that he would think me otherwise a schemer, I held back the lascivious responses that would fain have come to my lips. It is no folly to use them when one knows one's stallion, though all should be spoken haltingly and not in too great an efflorescence of words, for such would render the female common. The lure must always be that all is not said which it is wished to be said by one's partner. Thus is he kept in thrall, ever convinced that he will finally succeed in drawing one out to confess all one's innermost desires and - indeed - prior adventures. One is not so foolish, however, as to disrobe one's mind fully in front of, or indeed underneath, others.

My legs lay limp, my knees slightly bent. He was nearing the end of his course, as I sensed by the roughness of his panting. His praise for the tight sleekness of my cunny was ever expressed. I continued to moan. I evaded his mouth from moment to moment as though in inner conflict at what I was permitting. His kisses rained upon my cheeks and neck. I felt the throbbing of his cock increase.

"It will be so, if you come," he croaked.

I AM coming, I thought, but told him not. I bucked, I clung, my soft cries grew ever wilder. All that had been promised to me by Elaine was true. With a last rattling cry he flooded me. His effusion pumped into me, a veritable leaping of thick gruelly sperm that I received with joy. Our mouths fastened together again, for I could refuse him not in that moment. With every inward thrust a fresh jet spattered me. The strokes of his cock grew shorter. Panting, he thrust it in to the full and lay all too heavily upon me for a long moment until he stirred. I felt the slow withdrawal of his weapon with infinite regret. Had another taken his place upon me then, I would have welcomed it. Drawing me up, his eyes searched mine. I hid my face and affected great confusion. Thick and limp, the big worm of his prick dangled against my thigh.

"You will not tell her?" he demanded hoarsely while caressing my long brown hair with a certain tenderness. I quivered and pressed in. My skirt being caught up still, the warmth of my belly stirred his doughty weapon.

"No," I comforted him softly, "yet what of the reception? Oh, pray say that only you will do it to me if I have to take my drawers off."

The apparent naivety of my words - tinged as they were with eroticism - struck exactly the right note, as I had intended they should. He laughed and mussed my hair, awarding my yielding lips a long kiss.

"Only I, my pet, but you must pray warn Elaine. Would that I could take you alone."

"She may not believe me, Uncle, but I will try. How am I to say that I have come upon this knowledge, though?"

His brow furrowed. "That is true. I had not thought of it, for there is scarce a guest here who would venture such confidences even if they were to know of them. I know not what to say."

I had expected him to proffer the name of Mrs. Witherington-Carey, whom I suspected knew much of such things, but discretion in him obtained. It was a small but pleasing sign that he had become not so flustered as to completely forget himself. One must beware ever of the possible indiscretions of lust.

"Say naught, Uncle, for whatever will be, will be, and it is too late now to dissuade her or she will think it my fault. We may hide ourselves away there, may we not, so that whatever else passes happens not before our eyes."

"By Jove, yes, that is the only solution to the matter. What a delightful and resourceful girl you are! Did you like what we just did?" he asked as if in apparent anxiety.

I giggled. I pressed my cheek to his. "I believe so. If you do it to me again at the reception, I shall know better and tell you. But haste, we must not stay here or a servant may discover us. Pray go first and then I will follow."

"You minx, I truly believe there is more to you than anyone could imagine," he chuckled and thereupon - fastening his breeches with evident regret - made his way out. I had not long followed when Elaine appeared as I was about to enter my room.

"I have been looking for you. What have you been at?" she asked curiously.

"Oh nothing. I am about to find a book to read," I replied. Perversely no doubt I did not mean to tell her of my amorous engagement on the floor of the linen room. Later on we would exchange all such secrets. With a strange expression on her face she shrugged and passed on. It occurred to me only afterwards that she had probably similarly encountered her Papa on the stairs in his descent.

CHAPTER IV

As might be imagined, I dreamed much that night of what had passed and became restless for more. My cream puff had been well filled, but sought extra dosages. I was not to be lacking in them, as will be seen, nor was Elaine. That which we immediately ventured upon was wicked in the extreme and I doubt not that had I demurred in the linen room and been of lesser daring, my Uncle would have sought some excuse not to take us, for it was apparent to me that he saw in his daughter a mischievous but innocent girl who knew as little as I had seemed to him to do about the ways of the world.

Time floats and passes, however, and soon enough the hour was upon us, I affecting a dark red dress and Elaine a blue one. Our stockings matched our gowns, for we had decided upon that in terms of appearance, were we to be disrobed. I had no doubt now that we were to be and told my cousin so.

"What will you do, then, if your Papa sees you without any drawers on?" I asked. I had not forgotten what she had said about his implement and was still very curious about it.

"Well, he must not, for you must divert him," she answered and I am sure quite believed herself. "Besides, Arabella, I am sure that there will be quite a crowd there and in all the bustle and gaiety no one will notice what others are at. If Papa does see my bottom I shall be careful to keep my face hid and he will know not who it belongs to, for I swear I will not dance about without any clothes on – and neither must you," she added with remarkable solemnity.

"Oh, as to that, I am sure excitement will overtake us if it is all that you say, but what a lark it will be if all is rumour and nothing happens!"

"You silly, of course it will, as soon as everyone is in their cups. Be sure that you see to Papa if anyone lifts my skirts."

"Of course," I replied demurely, though it seemed to me even then that Elaine was containing herself too much and I already thinking ahead of her. It was scarcely to be imagined that the three of us could attend such a rumbustious event without several untoward events occurring. As I had learned even briefly in the linen room, the fevered imagination quickly rises to a pitch at which all things are possible. In the immediate aftermath they drain away and become dissolved, for there is a momentary peace and a delicious sense of floating. Soon enough however the imagination soars again and no bars are to be put then upon such enticements as enter the mind. Thus I thought and most curiously in so doing was a step ahead of my cousin who but hours before had been my mentor. A desire arose in me to see her being exercised, as we were prone to call it. Had her Papa not weakly conceded to her wishes then all would have been different and mayhap fewer opportunities would have arisen to put her philosophy to the test.

We affected no gaiety upon our departure at eight of the evening in question, for it was to be seen by my aunt that we were upon solemn business. By good fortune she was a rather vague lady and would no doubt have forgotten by the morrow what the purpose of our outing had been.

The house of the Rt. Hon. Edward Eastwood and his family was one of the grandest in the neighbourhood. It was said often enough in joke that all looked up to them, for their mansion stood upon a slow rise among many rolling acres. The jogging of the carriage as we made our way there did nothing but encourage my now passionate temperament, for my bottom bounced up and down all the while as did Elaine's. It being dusk already we could see little enough of her father who accommodated himself on the seat opposite, but I did not doubt that his thoughts of the advancing night were as much as mine.

The house was well lit as our carriage at last approached the entrance. But a single aged servant appeared to be about the place, though the reason for this soon struck me. All others had been dismissed for the night, perhaps locked in their rooms with their supper or packed off to an inn. Thus there were to be no witnesses as to what followed other than the assembled gentry.

As Elaine and I had already surmised, they were not many. I counted as many ladies as gentlemen and found the score not greater than fourteen. Among the former were several beauties of local distinction. By good fortune I knew none of them. All were perfectly polite and utterly discreet, as I discovered. Mrs. Eastwood was a lady of remarkable charm, approaching then her fortieth year, who herself met us in the hall and took our cloaks without the faintest hint of embarrassment.

"You have come well provided for," she said with a laugh to my uncle while gazing both Elaine and I up and down most approvingly. "You have advised them well, Harold, I trust, for there are to be no misunderstandings."

Such boldness took me as equally by surprise as it did my cousin. We exchanged the most furtive glances. A purplish hue spread meanwhile over my uncle's features. The doors to the drawing room being closed, we all stood alone.

"Ah, as to that, perhaps we might converse privately," he said. His voice sounded exceedingly strained. I stared at my feet as did Elaine.

Mrs. Eastwood shrugged in a languid manner."If you wish " she declared and led him into a small side room, though leaving the door ajar of a purpose, as I surmised. A muttering came to our ears and then a faint laugh from our hostess.

"My dear Harold, discretion is all here. You above all should know that. I make no demur myself about the presence of Elaine and nor will anyone else. What? I cannot hear what you say, and really I cannot keep the others waiting. She must be put up to the gentlemen as needs be, as we all are. That is the sport of it. You had no need to bring her, my pet. Let me speak with her for I do not wish her to enter upon the proceedings in total innocence, though should she wish to make play upon struggling a little that will be all the more fun. As to the other very pretty young lady who accompanies you, I will have her no more in the dark than Elaine."

"Oh, I say! But Mavis..."

All was lost, or all was gained, depending upon one's philosophy, for my uncle's interruption was itself interrupted by the emergence of our hostess who clearly was determined to have no break in her evidently smooth affairs.

"Elaine, my dear, there will be much pleasantry tonight for which you must forgive us, as I am sure that - Arabella, is it not? - will also. Within half an hour or so when all have been well warmed with wine we shall call upon the ladies to present themselves, by which I mean you will doff as gracefully as possible such outer attire as you have, including of course your drawers."

A gurgling sound came from behind her as these words were spoken. My uncle stood in the doorway of the side room as might have Hamlet or Macbeth. No sooner had this sound struck softly upon us than Mrs. Eastwood, persuading herself between us, took us both by the elbows and steered us towards the drawing room, talking as merrily meanwhile as if we had been attending a fete.

Within was such a bubbling of voices and laughter as immediately warms the senses. Though the hall had been well lit, the drawing room was otherwise. A single chandelier had been lit in the centre of the ceiling, the gas mantles being dimmed so that while the middle of the room was sufficiently illumined, pools of shadow lay all about around the sides which gave a cosy atmosphere. The room was naturally commodious, there being some five large sofas and divans placed about the walls for such comfort as would be required. A huge sideboard accommodated piles of tiny sandwiches and canapes together with an impressive number of bottles and glasses.

"You, my dear, are one out, for we have an equal number of ladies and gentlemen, but as such you make a piquant addition to our party. You will not be put out if you are attended to simultaneously by a lady and gentleman? Of course, you will not, for there are many couples here who like to dally with a young woman together before disporting themselves," our hostess said calmly enough to Elaine.

Before Elaine could gather herself to reply - though I know not what she would have said - we were surrounded by admirers of both sexes and drinks placed in our hands.

"All are known by names other than their own, of course, so you may use any pseudonym that you wish," remarked Mrs. Eastwood helpfully and then disappeared to the other side of the room the while that my uncle made his hesitant entrance and stood regarding me. I moved towards him upon instinct and stood by his side. Elaine, throwing me a somewhat frantic glance, found herself sandwiched between a gentleman of some forty years and a young woman scarce older than herself. Even as we watched I heard the girl declare, "Let me kiss you, for you have such lovely lips."

At that, and while others watched the trio as fondly as might parents observing their children at play, Elaine was embraced by the looping of the girl's arms about her neck. I believe she might have started back, but all happened so quickly that there was naught for her to do but surrender to the moment. As if to encourage them a beautifully attired couple standing by merged to one another as if they had waited long for this moment and exchanged the most lascivious kisses which all then fell to partaking of save for my uncle and I who stood apart as two who enter a room and see no one but strangers before them.

As may be thought, this state of immobility lasted not long. Moving swiftly behind Elaine, the gentleman whose female partner was impressing ever more passionate kisses upon her lips, raised her skirt so quickly that she had not time to retreat - nor any space to do it in - before her shapely legs were fully bared and her proudly-filled drawers were displayed to all. Giving her no time to wriggle from between them, he then fumbled his trousers and thrust his erect penis between her thighs just above her stocking tops.

"Down with their drawers!" a voice cried, whereat several of the ladies made great play of shrieking and endeavouring to run all about, though not with such energy that they were not quickly made as captive as my cousin who could be seen moving her face agitatedly from side to side while the gentleman into whose stomach her bottom was pressed, held her waist tightly and so allowed his companion to further her endeavours by unfastening Elaine's corsage. Isolated in a corner as I seemed to be with my uncle, I could but watch dry-mouthed as my cousin's lustrous firm titties were brought into view while the gentleman's sturdy penis moved to and fro between the backs of her bared thighs.

All was now as a scene painted in one's own erotic dreams. All about were to be seen suspendered stockings, corsets, arid emerging breasts and bottoms as the females everywhere were being disrobed. Some fumbled for their partner's cocks at the same time while others pretended a ridiculous coyness which however did not abate the strippings. A cry from Elaine announced that her own drawers were being descended. Quite without thinking I sank down upon a sofa in company with my uncle whose arm stole about my shoulders. I turned my flushed face to his. Our mouths met in the wildest of kisses. Scarce knowing what I was at, I felt for his prick which stood as a bar of iron under the fine dark cloth of his breeches.

Moans, cries, laughter, squeals, came to our ears while blindly our tongues met and whirled. Feverishly he fondled my breasts and then, dipping one hand into my corsage, sleeked his palm over the silky swollen surfaces to taunt my stiffening nipples. I fell back, encouraged by the seeking of our hands, unbuttoning him as I did so. The long thick prong of his penis came into my hand. I was as one possessed. Forgetful that he thought of me as naught but a novice, I rubbed the great shaft fervently. His hands sought my gown and threw it up, tearing at the waistband of my drawers.

"Let me kiss her. How pretty she is!" a voice sounded dimly from above. My uncle moved from me, allowing me to see who had spoken. Above us, legs astride and with a well-puffed mount displayed, stood a beautiful woman of about thirty whose attire consisted solely of a fetching black waist corset, stockings and shoes. Lying half beneath my uncle as I was, I had not time to stir nor rise before she lay down alongside me and captured my lips in a breathless kiss. Therewith my uncle stirred and must have slid to his knees so that he knelt beside the sofa and, pressing back my legs, applied his mouth to the succulent haven of my cunny.

"What is your name?" she asked amid fervent tonguings.

"Rose," I gasped for want of anything else to reply, while her hand dipped as freely in my gown as my uncle's had. My bottom being cupped and slightly lifted now on his broad hands, I wriggled madly at the invasion of his tongue between my love-lips.

"Harold, let us have her things off," the unknown murmured, causing me to feel somewhat like a piece of property, though all was such and I so feverish by now in my responses that I made no demur as I was drawn up between them and quickly bereft of all save my shoes and stockings. My titties, bottom, thighs and cunny all being caressed the while, I was in a perfect fever to be fucked as was evident in the way I rejoined our triple embrace once more upon the sofa. Even so, I had not failed to glimpse Elaine and neither, from the rubicond hue on his face had my uncle. Having surrendered to the opportunities of the moment as quickly as I, she was upon her hands and knees on the floor receiving a sturdy penis from the rear. All about us indeed were such scenes of libertine delights, the gentlemen being by then in as great a state of nudity as the ladies and all cocks rampant.

"I adore kissing young girls while they are being fucked," my female companion declared, and so it seemed, for while we pecked amorously at each other's lips and caressed each other's breasts, my uncle made ready so swiftly that his bulky, naked form pressed against my quite tingling nipples, Davina - as she appeared to be called - breathed teasing words into my mouth even as the lusty shaft drove up into my cunny.

"Is he your first, or have you been a truly naughty girl?"

"My f...f...first," I stammered. All my senses reeled. The selfsame cock that I had but once enjoyed now plugged me again to the full. I felt the brushing of our pubic hairs together. Our three tongues joined. My legs being drawn up, I wrapped them about his waist. We jogged, we writhed. His prick sluiced in and out, causing me the most exquisite raptures which were all the more enlivened by the caresses that Davina and I lavished upon one another. The triple kisses in the very midst of being so manfully pleasured added to our bliss.

"She is coming," breathed Davina who with seeking fingers could feel the rippling in my belly. Her tongue plunged into my mouth anew. My uncle's fingers sought her bottom, causing her to churn her hips, bending as she was then with one knee on the edge of the seat. I came, I sprinkled, I melted, I urged his thrusts with sensuous movements of my bottom. Our moans resounded, mingling with those all about us, though in my lowly posture I could see naught.

Frothing then all within me and labouring like a shire horse, my uncle offered me in turn his libation which pulsed jet upon jet within me while Davina announced her own delirious pleasure by tonguing our mouths in turn. Febrile quivers shook us. My tight cunny seemed to suck upon his embedded penis, imploring every spurt and drop until, in withdrawing at last, his well-soaked knob smeared my thighs with our mingled juices. I floated. Warmth and satisfaction spread in easy waves throughout my uttered charms. With a soft gurgle, Davina eased herself off of my uncle's probing finger and sat up languidly to look all about.

"Ah, Elaine is having her dosage," she declared to my full surprise at having so casually uttered my cousin's name. With something of a satisfied grunt my uncle removed his heavy weight from my body. I drew up my knees and swivelled on to one hip, leaning into a corner of the sofa. My uncle's thick pendant cock oozed its last pearl. His eyes were transfixed as were my own for a moment on Elaine who now lay with her head and shoulders beneath a large oak table, couched beneath a second stallion whose balls swung under her bottom, her ankles crossed about his waist.

"How well she takes him," Davina murmured, having seated herself on the other side of my uncle so that he was between us. Her hand stroked his trunk-like thigh. His eyes appeared glazed. Kneeling beside Elaine was the young woman who had first kissed her and who was now entertaining a rigid penis in her bottom. But a few feet away - and all at the centre of other heaving couples - our hostess was being steadily fucked.

The scene blurred, came clear, and then blurred again before my eyes. Stealing my right hand sideways I mischievously stroked my uncle's prick the while that Davina dandled his huge balls. His cock stirred almost immediately, thickening to my touch.

"See how she wriggles her bottom," Davina said of Elaine who, while she could not possibly have heard and indeed must have been utterly lost in her sensations, appeared at that moment to twist her lovely face all about and gaze directly at us across the carpet. At that my uncle's jaw literally gaped for he sensed that their eyes were locked even though I felt certain Elaine would have seen nothing but a swirling of bodies and faces. Rock-hard as it now became, his re-erected penis stuck up in the half encirclement of my fingers. Elaine opened her legs wider by letting her feet slip to the floor. A species of snorting moan escaped my uncle. The man's cock was clearly to be seen pistoning in and out between the lips of her love dell whose well-furred fringe looked utterly enticing.

"Oh pray, Uncle, dear Elaine will be much confounded at your seeing her," I uttered. The words seemed to bring him to himself.

"Shush, Rose, for we may all do as we wish, do not spoil the sport," enjoined Davina who obviously knew clearly enough my cousin's identity yet batted not an eyelid about the matter while all about us bodies slapped together, tongues writhed, and pricks worked steadily in such orifices as were freely offered to them.

"No, no-oh, do not look!" I burst, for while I knew the situation to be truly bizarre yet I feared lest Elaine might think I had turned traitor to her. Rising and throwing myself against him between his legs so that the crest of his tool rubbed against my bush, I pretended even greater alarm than I felt and urged that he must carry me out. Momentarily embarrassed perhaps at all that was about - though I confess to knowing less about human nature than I do now - I was borne in a moment from the room into a smaller reception room where with scarcely a word I was fucked again upon the floor as lustily mayhap as I have ever been.

"The naughty girl, ah the naughty girl!" he groaned with every stroke, yet I will pass over now the fevers of the rest of that night which in many senses were but a preamble to all that followed. Others entered upon us once we had spilled our liquid pleasures. My uncle took himself upon Davina while I, mounted successively by two gentlemen, could do naught but swim in lost passions until my cunny literally bubbled with sperm.

By midnight all were as exhausted as could be. A strange quiet fell as various assortments of clothing were recovered and the ladies made haste to dress even before the gentlemen. A little simpering, some final kisses, and all was concluded. I, entering not upon the main scene until caution apprised me of the right moment, found Elaine huddled in a corner, fully dressed.

"Oh, I cannot face Papa!" she entreated as quietly as possible.

"What nonsense, he has seen nothing, we were in the other room," I said.

Her relief was evident, asking me again and again if it were true. Most tactfully he was nowhere to be seen. With furtive mien and not a little blushing she made her way out with me into the hall where my uncle was bidding adieu to our hostess. Impeccable and unsullied as she again looked, we might well have been leaving the most sedate of gatherings.

"You will come again? I trust you will for it has been most pleasant," she murmured as though to all three of us at once. Seeing that neither Elaine nor her Papa appeared ready to answer, I gave a polite nod of my head. Despite my relative youth and the positive whirlwind I had been through, I found to my pleasure that I was perfectly in control of myself, admiring also as I did the exquisitely civilised manner of our hostess.

"I doubt it not," I replied and shook her hand. From the expression in her eyes I gathered that her interest in me had increased threefold. A few more polite murmurs and we went out upon the dark drive to the carriage where my uncle had to shake the coachman to awaken him, poor fellow. Then within did we settle ourselves. In a way, all had been briefer than I thought it might. Had it not been for the presence of Elaine, we might have greeted the dawn there.

Moving into a corner seat, Elaine sat constrained, peering out upon the dark. My uncle perched opposite, coughed several times, but said nothing. Utterly dark as it was in the lanes through which we drove that we could barely see one another. The silence irritated me, however. Elaine had clearly got what she wished, as I had, but evidently regretted it in the aftermath. I twirled my fingers in my gloves and gazed at her huddled form.

Matters could not be left like this.

CHAPTER V

I have long learned that what seems bizarre, reckless or strange to the world about us appears full otherwise to those who are involved in such events. Too often have I heard both men and women utter in tones of apparent shock,"Oh, I would never do that!",only to find that they are perfectly ready to do so when an opportunity arises and the loose cloak of social conventions is cast aside.

Curious indeed was the situation in which I, my uncle and Elaine now found ourselves upon our return, for as often as my cousin asked me what her Papa had seen, I gave her increasingly little comfort. I meant not to be harsh with her, yet it was she who had inspired the occasion and she indeed who had put forth much philosophy on such matters to me. It may be well imagined that such encounters as we had together with her father on the following day were in part constrained and in part expectant, for each of us seemed to wish to speak, yet all held our tongues.

A touch of fate occurred but two afternoons later which was to prod our destinies, for I at least was surprised by the arrival of the selfsame lady who had assisted my uncle in fucking me. Her true name was Pearl and the nature of her visit showed me much of how things were veiled, for my aunt was well acquainted with her, as was Elaine.

Naturally I showed all modesty in greeting her and, while my aunt was otherwise occupied - for Pearl, it seemed, was too old a friend to require formalities - the three of us repaired in feminine fashion to Elaine's room. Quite astonishingly Elaine had been unconscious of Pearl's presence at the orgy, but this was to be accounted for by the dizzy eagerness with which she had succumbed to several amorous assaults.

Whether Pearl - or Lady Mathers, as she was properly called - was aware of this really mattered not, for she was plainly intent on broaching the subject, first complimenting me upon my"performances," though being discreet enough not to mention the names of my partners on that particular battlefield of love.

"Oh! were you there, then?" Elaine asked her.

"You did not notice me? Ah, but, my dear, you were rather too occupied. I know not who was the more agile and passionate of you two. You are both much to be congratulated on your entry into the lists, for all spoke of you with high praise and your return is looked forward to. Praise be it that your Papa was not backward in bringing you."

"Oh, but say nothing to him, I pray, or he will discover all," begged Elaine, causing me thereby some hidden mirth which Pearl shared more openly.

"Really, what a silly you are for I swear he thought you looked quite adorable," declared our companion who was obviously able to speak of such matters as if they were everyday events. Seated about the bedroom as all three of us were, Elaine duly became the focus of attention for such dismay was spread upon her face as could not be disguised. I need not however repeat her expostulations, for they were as quickly swept aside as is a cobweb, Pearl declaring that if Elaine were to play the hypocrite then her true nature had not been as her actions had revealed.

Seeing my cousin's confusion and feeling not a little sorry for the way she had vainly endeavoured to cloak herself in illusions, I made what best of it I could by falling upon her and tickling her, this having been done many times to me in the past by my Mama when I was in poor salts. In vain did Elaine endeavour to fend me off, for I think she would sooner have affected misery than pleasure. Pearl watched at first with amusement, thinking us - as she said - quite like two kittens at play, but no sooner had I got my cousin to giggle at last than Pearl declared the best place for such amusements to be upon the bed.

Elaine then became - not too unwillingly, I should say - our victim. Being duly raised up and hustled upon the counterpane, she was trapped between us, I attending to the waving of her arms and her increasingly weak protestations while our companion raised up Elaine's skirt and set about to tickling her between her thighs.

Being as susceptible as I to such a caress, Elaine succumbed, though saying that she knew not what devils had got into us as I unbuttoned her corsage and set to teasing her nipples with lips and tongue while Pearl, thrusting up Elaine's legs, began to gamahuche her deliciously.

"Oh, oh, Mama will come!" protested Elaine who could not help working her cunny against Pearl's mouth.

"That she will not, for your Papa is diverting her," replied Pearl in a very muffled voice. Giving Elaine's quivering clitoris a final lick and having made her spend already, Pearl then clambered up upon her and lay belly to belly with her, having raised her own skirt for the pleasure. Then in a triple embrace while I lay beside the pair did we fall to exchanging tongues and lips. Pearl's hand roamed about my naked bottom which I presented to her. A fervour of pleasure seized us. Pearl's lips passed from one to the other of us. The lewdness of the moment was all. We exchanged as many hot words of pleasure as we did kisses.

"Ah, that we might be naked," I murmured.

"Soon, my pet, we shall, for all will be arranged," said Pearl, dipping her long tongue between my lips as she spoke while at the same time rubbing her quim fervently all around that of Elaine who was as lost as I.

"Tell me, what then are we going to do?" I begged her.

At that, Pearl rolled on to the other side of my cousin who lay panting between us, uncovered to her belly with her silk clad legs responding ever to our joint caresses.

"Now that we have Elaine in a better mood, I shall tell you. Your uncle has diverted his dear lady in order that I might apprise you of future events, for I fear he is a little shy to do so immediately himself. Pray, no more exclamations, Elaine, for he has seen and admired all, and there need be no more hindrances between you."

"Oh! Papa saw me!" ejaculated Elaine.

"Saw and enjoyed, my dear, and what harm is there? You are not the first nor will be the last to be furrowed in sight of your kin. The sport is accepted within our circle, for a young lady is nourished by having as many cocks as possible. We have but one bar to our pleasures, which is that a girl shall not be mounted until she has attained the age of fifteen when her cunny is fully able and willing to absorb the male juice as well as to spill her own. If, as I suspect, you are late in starting, then you have much to make up for."

At that, Elaine fell silent and indeed could do no other since with one accord Pearl and I lavished her with so many kisses and caresses that her spendings spilled again, to the great joy of all.

"How easily you oil the route, my sweet, but let us have an end now to recriminations and hypocrisies and lend ourselves only to pleasure. What say you?" asked Pearl.

"Elaine has been my ardent teacher and has told me that one must never refuse a stout cock to the cunt, so I make no ado about the matter," I responded slyly, thus allowing my cousin no room to refuse. Nor was she in a mood to, being as ready for the spouting of a prick as she would ever be. Profusely flushed, she hid her face as best she could and yielded such a silence as in the case of young ladies ever indicates assent.

"So be it, for you are both ripe now for whatever adventures befall. Yet we must ever be circumspect in our affairs. The Eastwoods and their friends will rut with you freely, yet I think them not so polished in their ways as to give them free rein. Hence we will to Paris, my dears. You, Arabella, must seek the permission of your parents, I know, but I will assist you in this, for it will be apparent to them that you are well-chaperoned and will be able to advance your knowledge of the language much. I shall advise them that we are to visit the Louvre, the Tuileries, and other places of cultural interest."

"But what of myself and of Papa and Mama?" asked Elaine whom I perfectly well knew - as did Pearl - was putting on a pretence of ignorance, since she had surely guessed, as I, what was to be.

"Your dear Mama inhabits a world of her own, my dear, wherein she is thankfully perfectly happy, for she is a sweet woman at heart and so delightfully vague that all happens about her without her knowledge. As to your Papa, what think you? Did I not say that he had encouraged me to bring you this intelligence? He will join us, having the perfectly good excuse to conduct some business there."

"Oh!" ejaculated Elaine and succeeded in covering her face, this gesture bringing an amused sigh from Pearl who rose from the bed and made herself tidy and proper, as I also sought to do. Scarce thirty minutes had passed in all since we had entered the bedroom, and yet as so often the pleasures seemed as of an eternity. Elaine followed more slowly which caused Pearl to nudge me in a manner I well understood.

"You do well, my pet, to appear a little reluctant, 'tis ever a good pose, for the gentlemen appreciate it more and get the stiffer cocks thereby," said Pearl to her, passing her hand back from where she sat at the dressing table and running it slowly up Elaine's legs.

"Yes, she is very good at that," I assented eagerly.

Passing my arm around my cousin's waist, I hugged her as if in compliment upon her deliberately coy attitude. "Remember all you told me," I whispered to her.

"Oh, I do not know what to say. I am all of a dither now, it has all come about so unexpectedly," said Elaine, though not looking at all displeased at the thought of our new venture.

"Say naught, Elaine. Just extend your tongue, wriggle your bottom and feel for a hard prick," laughed Pearl who made no bones about anything and was truly as Elaine really wished to be.

"Very well, I shall, but if I am very naughty then it is you who will have made me so," replied Elaine without any malice whatever. Seeing no retreat, she obviously wished to make the best of the situation and I could tell indeed by the changing expressions in her eyes as she brushed her hair that she was as prepared to accept the greater openness of our acts as I, and with as much amused mischief. "Who else shall be of this party?" she asked then with such self-possession as made her previous behaviour about it seem but a game.

"None but the most civilised, and none that you will otherwise know, which will make it all the more intriguing, will it not? Arabella, what say you that I ask your parents while you yet remain here?"

To this I eagerly assented, though even in so doing I questioned how Pearl was to manage it, being unknown to them.

"I am acquainted a little with your father," replied she to my surprise. "I met him by way of business several times in the sale of some land and a few other matters that you would not have concerned yourself with. He, I believe, can be perfectly persuasive with your Mama, so I anticipate no problems about it. I have a mind to venture that way and so will call upon them. For the nonce then I will leave you two angels - for such you really are - to pass the time together and will return on the morrow."

At this an interruption came as a maid knocked and Elaine went to answer.

"The Master says as are you coming down, Miss?"

"We shall ALL be down," called Pearl, at which the maid disappeared and we all gave a final touch to our attire. "He is anxious for news, you see, for we must reserve our cabins upon a steamer," Elaine and I were told, which caused me quite a tingling feeling of excitement.

Descending, we found my uncle awaiting us in the morning room while Pearl made immediately ready to depart, affording each of us a swift kiss upon the cheek before doing so, much as any maiden aunt might. Seeing her departure made so soon, my uncle made bid to follow her, but she being accompanied as was proper by one of the servants, he evidently could not say what he wished to and so returned. I had no doubt then that he wished to know what she had told us, and indeed whether she had told us. Putting therefore a bold face upon it, I said without further ado that Elaine and I much looked forward to our forthcoming trip.

An expression of relief spread over his face. His eyes searched Elaine's which dropped. She appeared to busy herself with a loose thread in her dress. Offering such complicity as I thought was needful, I ran to close the door and then returned. The morning room gave out upon the conservatory, but there was no sign of my aunt about nor anyone else. The former was engaged in conversations with the gardener into which my uncle had inveigled her. Knowing her interest in all matters horticultural, I guessed that she would be some time about it.

"If Papa but agrees that I may go, oh, but I am sure he will for Pearl is very persuasive," I said familiarly. Elaine standing uncertain, I approached him so that he stood between us. "How she flattered us, did she not, Elaine? Why, Uncle, she said that we were two perfect peaches and must be ready for a lot of mischief."

The expression clearly startled my cousin who made as if to step away, but at that my uncle chortled and placed his arm about both our waists.

"So indeed it may be, Arabella, but what is life if it may not be lived without care. What say you, Elaine? Shall we sport a little there and enjoy ourselves?"

Releasing a giggle, Elaine glanced across him at me and bit her lip."Oh, I know not, Papa," she responded.

His grip about us tightened. He was clearly emboldened. His eyes sought mine. The faintest smile came upon my lips. I appeared, I believe, to nod. At that, his right hand slipped down to caress my bottom while his left accommodated itself similarly under Elaine's warm bulge.

"Peaches indeed you are, and withal as firm as melons," he averred, feeling all about our lightly-clad nether cheeks while Elaine blushed to her eyebrows and compressed her lips. Giving her no leeway to escape the moment, I sighed and leaned my head to his shoulder. The incident was one of the utmost wickedness and yet all so lightly done that his soothing hands seemed but to compliment our bottoms. Gathering up the material of my gown in his fingers a trifle, he cupped me tightly and patently did so also to Elaine who emitted a little gasp which was thankfully swallowed as quickly as it was uttered.

"A kiss upon it then, for we are as one," he murmured.

I permitted him to attend to me first. Making no bones about it, I clasped my arms about his neck and returned lips to lips the while that he continued to caress my nether charms with one hand and Elaine's with the other. Sighing not a little I impressed my belly to his and felt the risen nature of his sturdy tool from which I had thrice now drawn his sperm. My tongue protruded a little. I allowed it to touch his own. Averting my lips from his, I murmured fondly against his cheek.

"We shall have a lovely time. Elaine, it is for you to kiss now," I averred.

She would have stepped back, I do believe, if he had not turned and grasped her immediately. Twisting her face in some confusion, she allowed his lips to fall upon her neck, staring blindly the while through the glass-panelled doors that led into the conservatory. In releasing me, both his hands were free to seek her bottom, which they did fervently.

"Come, dear, be not shy, give me your mouth," he husked.

The moment, I saw, was one of intense passion on his part. Elaine could not but help feel the considerable protrusion of his cock through his breeches. I saw her distinctly tremble. Her face dropped and was hidden to his shoulder. Very delicately then his hands played all about and beneath her bottom cheeks, causing her hands to press against his chest.

"Shall you be so coy in Paris?" he asked and therewith lifted her chin so that she was forced to return his gaze.

"I know not, Papa," Elaine trembled. Giving her no respite, he then brought her mouth to his. She would have escaped it had he not cupped the back of her head much as he was doing with her bottom. I held my breath, for there seemed to me no more stirring a sight. Her lips moved petulantly but then was taken again. As subtly as one playing a violin, he fingered all about her bulging nether cheeks again, kissed her more deeply until her knees distinctly bent and then released her with as gay a laugh as might have been managed in such moving circumstances. The state of his erection being obvious, I wagged my finger playfully at him.

"Dear Uncle, you must not be naughty with us too soon," I laughed and, taking Elaine by the wrist, guided her out.

"Oh, what have you done?" she asked, "really, Papa is too wicked!"

"'Twas but a kiss and a caress, you sillikins. We shall have enough of that soon. Come, we must look to our wardrobes for I am sure the ladies of Paris will try to outdo us in all respects and that we cannot allow!"

So cozening and teasing her, I finally overcame all her reluctances, for seeing that I treated the matter so lightly, Elaine thought to do the same, being reminded by me of her earlier remark about her Papa's tool.

"Oh, but I did not know. I was but jesting to make you think me the more daring, Arabella."

"Well, whether that is so or whether it is not, the truth of the matter is not to be denied," I declared, whereat she could not help but ask if I had done it with him.

Of course she knew well enough what I must have been about, yet was intent on making it appear that I now was more wicked than she, though not in an unkindly manner but one which most slyly encouraged me to urge her on, thus changing the positions in which we had first found ourselves when I was seemingly under her tutelage.

"As to that, you will see well enough in Paris, for being divorced as we shall be from troublesome eyes and ears then I am sure nothing at all will be hid and we may make as free as possible. Do you not think Pearl a most delightful lady? I am sure she means the best for us," I added quickly to divert her.

"Well, indeed yes, though until now I never suspected it of her. Do you think she might now seduce your Papa and encourage him to venture with us?"

"No, for that would be most improper," I said without thought and with such quaintness, such as I least intended, that we both fell to hugging one another in our laughter, this proving as great a release as any from the sense of excitement we both sustained. All seemed most natural by now, though had the shoe been on the other foot and I in Elaine's place, I know not how I might have comported myself. My father, being as chalk to cheese in respect of my uncle, was a studious man of quiet manners and with a very fine sense of the conventions, though he displayed no stuffiness in such matters.

Mama, on the other hand, was more frivolous, and perhaps they complemented one another. It was she who for the most part encouraged my freedoms, saying often that a young lady must find her own way in the world. To this Papa had only once or twice mildly objected. I, being the apple of his eye, he wished no harm to come to me. Nor had it, as I deemed, for I was sensible enough to know that what a female enjoyed in bed with her husband, she might also enjoy elsewhere. Such women who see the delights of copulation as a sin rather than a blessing are to be pitied rather than scorned. Some may be led to it, as I was to discover. Others, being frigid of nature, forever dwell within their own consciences and apprehensions as to what is right and what wrong. Such is called morality. I am thankful that I have never abided by it, for it is as if one scattered precious seeds on barren ground in the sun and left them to dry until the husks fall apart and the seed itself is left to wither, forlorn.

A girl who is well and frequently fucked may be seen by her bright complexion and her general merriness to be so. This is not to say that she is too open in her favours, nor that she is boisterous. To the contrary. I always comported myself with the selfsame discretion as Pearl had wisely spoken of. I have refused males who were too ruttishly eager. By doing so I have cloaked myself in a certain exclusivity that may yet unwind at will. Those who raise eyebrows at my behaviour with my cousin and uncle should well give pause to consider the utmost privacy in which such things occurred. In truth, our foray into the party of the Eastwoods had carried with it a scent of indiscretion, yet such must befall all newcomers who then learn thereby. Tongues knew better than to wag lest others be wagged back at them.

Thus did my philosophy grow, albeit that it is a simple one. I make no claim for cleverness. Fortunate it was that Elaine and I were of the same mould. Our cunnies, once having tasted cock, pouted for more. The divine pleasures of seeing one another in rut were yet to develop.

CHAPTER VI

Tout le monde were in Paris when we arrived some ten days later, for it was well past Easter and the season was in full swing. To be seen in the Bois de Boulogne around noon was essential if one were to be counted among the Upper Ten Thousand of France. Before we did so, however, Pearl was insistent that we clothe ourselves a la mode, being none too pleased with the gowns and hats we had brought, for Paris fashions change so rapidly that one must ever keep up with them.

My uncle's purse suffered much depletion as a result of this, but the outcome was so much to his taste that he averred it well worth while, being thankful perhaps that we had not gone to Monsieur Worth but to a smaller salon where decolletage was accepted as a sine qua non of revealment, which Monsieur Worth evidently abhorred, having decreed with a woodenness that came, I am sure, from his English origins that he dressed only ladies. Being told this, Elaine responded that we were not ladies but were enjoying ourselves. Both of course were true, but I admired her for her spirit which had so risen that she seemed to care not a jot what she did, provided it was not in public.

For my own part I was as a bird released from a cage. All about us were strangers and it was indeed in this sense as if we were attending a perpetual masque. Pearl had done her work well with my parents, for neither made any remonstrance upon my going, Papa warning me only to take care of all that I did.

As to our accommodation, there could have been none finer. Elaine and I possessed a suite of our own in a hotel close to the Champs d'Elysees while my uncle modestly had a separate one from that of Pearl. That we would not long suffer the privations of isolation was made clear to us by our official "chaperone" upon conducting Elaine and I on the first morning to the coutouriere.

"You must be seen at your finest not only fully adorned but in great part unadorned. This is to say, my pets, that your lingerie must be of the finest and the most seductive," she declared. Being of the same mind, we acceded to her every wish, the perfect undergarment - as she explained to us - being a guepiere or waist corset which constricted that part of our bodies tightly and so gave the most alluring prominence to our bottoms, hips and breasts. The latter remained uncovered, for the frilled top of the guepiere supported them beneath. At the lower extremity the glossy black corsets were cut and trimmed in a subtle upward curve so that the pubic mound was equally left revealed. So attired, and wearing naught else but stockings and shoes, Elaine and I paraded ourselves with many an admiring giggle in a commodious back room of the salon before tall mirrors.

"Are we not then to wear drawers?" asked Elaine of Pearl who with the proprietess of the establishment had seen to our fittings and chosen different colours for us, ranging from pink through blue to purple, and finally black.

"Why no, for how the effect would be spoiled you might well judge by trying drawers on, Elaine."

Indeed, it was seen to be so, for drawers were ever large and would conceal the pretty lower portion of the corsets, so rendering the appearance bizarre rather than attractive. All colours were tried until Elaine and I wore the black corsets which with matching silk stockings gave the most fetching effect that might be imagined. Pearl indeed appeared to think so, for she made no bones about standing between us before the mirrors and cupping our brazen, naked bottoms while giving praise to our charms.

The constriction of the corset first made me quite breathless, but finally pleased me.

"You must continue to wear them now in order to become accustomed to them, for all the most forward young ladies of Paris wear them," declared Pearl, turning then to the proprietess who herself was dressed most elegantly. "Is that not so, Madame?" she asked. Agreeing that it was, the lady then bade us be seated as we were in order to bring us refreshments. Being all females together, nothing was amiss in this and so we quaffed the wine she brought while warming our bare bottoms on the velour of her chairs.

Having a taste for such a good wine as came to my palate, I drank well as did Elaine. It warmed me exceedingly and so much so that I began to feel drowsy. The crystal lights around the room verily danced and seemed to glitter even more brightly than I thought them to. Finding myself somewhat in a daze, and being dimly conscious that Elaine had rather slumped in her chair, I heard whisperings by my side between Pearl and the proprietess.

"Comme elles sont jolies! Il va les sodomise maintenant?" I heard.

"Oui. Leurs cons ont avait deja etc lubriques. Il faut qu'elles etudient leurs lecons Grecques, Madame. Il veut bien bourrer son pine entre leurs fesses," came Pearl's response.

Clouded as my mind was, the purport of her words came to me but dimly. I commanded little enough French, but sufficient to comprehend that our bottoms were to be put to pillage since - as Pearl had so graciously announced - our cunts had already been lubricated. Who"he" was I could only guess and my bottom cheeks fairly tightened at the anticipation of receiving my uncle's considerable pestle in my derriere. My head swam. I endeavoured to glance at Elaine and succeeded in only half doing so. She sat beside me, her eyes glazed, mouth open. Even then she looked remarkably attractive. It was impossible not to do so in our little corsets with our titties bulging out over the tops, our bushes well displayed, and our legs made all the more attractive in their black silk stockings which peaked to fine points where the suspenders from the corsets drew them taut.

"Alors, il faut preparer la route," declared the proprietess then.

I had noticed upon our entrance to the room two padded bars which stood supported on either side. I had thought little of them, fancying them for the odd pieces of apparatus that adorn such places and over which cloaks and other garments might be put. In an instant, however, it came clear to me that in all probability it was we who were to be put over them in order - as the lady had said - that our "routes" might be "prepared." I had not time to stir, however, before a young man entered upon some signal he had evidently been given. His years could have counted not many more than my own and he was naked. Even more noticeable than this fact, however, was his penis which stood upright, long and extremely slender, having almost the appearance of a church spire. So small was the knob that it was less in circumference than the root of his penis which was evidently strong enough and stout enough for what was intended.

Elaine being less in her senses than I was then lifted up by the lady while Pearl attended to my rising and led me tottering to my fate.

"Wh...aaaaart?" I asked foolishly.

"Come, darling, you are about to be initiated in a way that will serve you well, for Phillippe will see to you both.

He has opened many a young lady's bottom to pleasure, as he will yours."

"Oh!" I cried, or at least I believe that I did, for at that Elaine's voice rose above my own, but were there to have been any protests they would have arrived far too late. I being bent over by Pearl, my cousin followed suit. The bars, being made for the purpose, as I have no doubt, saw to it that our bellies were not constrained - being pressed down upon thick velvet pads - while our bottoms rose in offering.

"No! What is to do?" cried Elaine, albeit in a somewhat drowsy fashion, her shoulders being well bent down by "Madame" as my own were by Pearl. So close indeed were my cousin and I that our hips touched warmly and so provided what little comfort we momentarily had. Being thought perhaps to be the most recalcitrant, Elaine was taken first. Advancing upon her with solemn mien, Phillippe took her hips and thus prevented her from waggling them too much. Thereat, "Madame" with her free hand sprinkled his spire-like prick with a little oil, some of which proving surplus he proceeded to rub around Elaine's most secret aperture.

At this she moaned and bumped her hip to mine, I being just able to see by virtue of inclining my head sideways.

"Hold her well, Mama," exclaimed then Phillippe to Madame, to my uttermost astonishment.

"Of course, cheri, do I not always? Put it to her slowly and she will take the pleasure of it. Ah, what a good boy you are to do it so nicely!"

This ludicrous remark having been made, there came a shriek from Elaine at the first touch of that virile young organ to her rosette. Being patently well accomplished in the art, Phillippe made no ado about then sleeking in his knob, which accommodation, due to his slim size was - as I found for myself - by no means difficult. Elaine, however, cried out again and would have risen had not Madame held her down more strongly.

"Is she tight, Phillippe?"

"Superbly, Mama. Oh, but it is not too difficult, I am almost half in."

Indeed, so he seemed to be from Elaine's wild contortions. Her breath rasped from her mouth, I making then to wriggle up but being firmly constrained by Pearl from doing so. Having then my head pressed further down, I could see naught but could hear well enough from Phillippe's soft panting and Elaine's cries that the dire deed was proceeding. A small, sharp screech from my cousin and he was full embedded, whereat he held her thus, her moans bubbling out the while.

"Hold well, dear, you have parted the cheeks and her bottom is filled. She will learn soon enough the delightful sustenance of it. Move now a little," abjured Madame.

"Yes, Mama," Phillippe gritted amidst ever-rising moans from Elaine whose hip bumped to mine at every stroke. I could not conceive what it felt like for her, but was soon to know. Evidently very well schooled in his art, Phillippe gave her a dozen long thrusts and then, upon command, withdrew. His organ, as I felt, must have been literally steaming, though I suspect that such ideas came to me in aftermath rather than then.

"Do not tighten yourself, Arabella," Pearl murmured to me. A finger came to my rosehole that I knew was Phillippe's. Artfully he guided a thin film of warm oil all about my bottom-hole and then within, by means of his fingertip, making me jerk like a young filly, as indeed I was often to be called when in my skittish moments. I tensed myself but to little avail. Phillippe was evidently hungry for this second assault or perhaps thought my bottom even more attractive than Elaine's. I felt his knob. I yielded, I succumbed, knowing perhaps that resistance would but prolong the endeavour. Ah, what a sensation! It was as if a long warm cork were being impelled within me. The breath flooded out from my lungs. I made to squeal but could not. Holding my back down with one hand, Pearl stroked my hair with the other.

"Good girl, press your bottom out to him," she murmured.

Even though loathe to show myself doing so, I obeyed. The slow entry of his cock at first brought with it a strange stinging sensation that however quickly passed away with every persuasive inch. I choked, I cried out. Feeling the movement of my bottom cheeks towards him, Phillippe grew emboldened. He had some four inches to go. In one upward lunge I received all. The sensation was momentous. My head shot up - unimpeded then by Pearl's hand - and then sank again. My back rippled. I felt my nether cheeks drawn tight into his belly. I was corked. I was the recipient of that which I had surreptitiously viewed at my uncle's house. I squeezed, I tried to eject him, but in vain. The constrictions of my bottom-hole but served to heighten his pleasure.

"Ah, Mama, je t'en prie!" he exclaimed.

"Yes, Madame, let him for he has toasted the one and may now inject the other," exclaimed Pearl who, as she said afterwards, could not hold herself in at the delightful vista of seeing me so upon his prong.

"Let me hold his balls then, for he likes that, do you not, Phillippe?" the lady purred. At that Elaine who had remained curiously motionless, slumped sideways, but falling upon cushions did herself no harm and no doubt had a fine view of the proceedings, looking up as she was between Phillippe's legs.

Such a scene then occurred as I only afterwards painted fully in my mind. Raising her skirt and taking hold of his balls in a light cupping gesture (which I afterwards learned from Pearl), the lady massaged her son gently while he in turn groped her own bottom, whereat no doubt he had learned his art. Not being minded to remain spectator, Pearl then leaned sideways over me and seized Madame's lips. I, being bent over beneath all, felt only the slow shunting of

Phillippe's prick which, inserting itself rhythmically back and forth, impelled by his Mama's hand, made my passage seem suddenly freer.

I confess to more pleasure in the act than I at the time allowed myself to feel. All above me were gasps and the moist sound of kisses the while that my bottom was urged back and forth. A hand groped my cunny. It was Madame's. Her fingertip cunningly sought my clitoris. I moaned the more. Her own was being assailed by Pearl's long-reaching hand, while her own bottom-hole was in turn titillated by Phillippe's finger. All of this being visible to Elaine who described it to me vividly afterwards. I was yet the recipient of the best. The initial stinging I had felt turned decidedly to pleasure. The gentle massaging of my clitoris assured all. My knees buckled, thus pressing my bottom ever more eagerly to Phillippe's assaults. I rendered my love juices, not once but seemingly endlessly until with fervent groans from he who was corking me, and much luscious kissing and fondling above, I received the fine spurting of his come which warmed and lubricated me deliciously until my bottom and loins all but melted.

Thus did my initiation advance, all being conducted with such ease and grace as if we were performing a gavotte. Elaine for her part pretended to faint, but was soon brought around. No doubt she was surprised to find me not in tears nor writhing torturously. Phillippe then discreetly disappeared, his cock dripping not a little.

"Come, what a sport we have had, we must return now," announced Pearl gaily as if we had been at a ladylike tournament of archery or such like. I indeed had received the arrow, so may have felt that the simile was well placed. My bottom burned within, though not uncomfortably. Elaine made more of it in the carriage that transported us back, declaring that she could not sit for a week, although she was doing such right then.

"That was but a prelude to your fuller pleasures. You will have larger there and in not too short a time. It is known as the Greek or Turkish method, though others more crudely call it buggery or sodomy. Your bottom has as much elasticity as your cunny and the pleasures of receiving tongues and cocks in that way are infinite," declared Pearl.

"A tongue? Would that be so pleasurable there?" I asked.

"Why indeed so, if it is done properly and the tongue neatly curled to tease your rose. It is called indeed feuille de rose in Paris and is a delicate act of l'amour much sought after. One lady does it to another before the cock is put in, for then the route is nicely moistened," said Pearl.

"Phillippe came in her, I know he did," Elaine said and evidently knew not whether to laugh or not though she continued to wriggle more than I. Such an effect was to be expected at first, Pearl told us, but would not last. Our bottoms being accustomed to receiving the male plunger would soon settle. Moreover, she added, there were certain advantages to be taken of it since a young lady could not become enceinte in that way and so could absorb as much of the male sperm as she desired.

"Could you really feel it, then?" Elaine asked, wrinkling her nose as though she were not certain that she liked the idea or not.

"Oh yes, it bubbled and entered deliciously in me. I felt it even more than in my cunny," I said, which remark caused me to realise the truth of it, as saying things often does.

"So then, you have both learned a little more," laughed Pearl who knew us to be greater novices than we then liked to believe.

"Ho! I do hope Papa is not to learn of this, though I cannot imagine that you could tell him," said Elaine.

At this Pearl laughed, for she was as much aware as I by now of how my cousin's moments of hypocrisy came and went like grains of dust dancing in a sunbeam.

"All shall be for the best in all possible worlds, Elaine, as Voltaire said, for we are in Paris now and enjoyment is not counted here a sin. Bottoms must buck to cocks and pussies must come to pricks," Pearl replied, thus unwittingly echoing the selfsame sentiments that my cousin had uttered to me when she felt safe enough out of sight of a rearing penis. I indeed nudged Elaine at this and she had the grace to blush. Being more open in our talk with Pearl, more could be said and our tongues became ever bolder as we spoke of what had occurred and what might be yet to follow. It had been a signal adventure, both elegant and yet bizarre, the two elements meeting so pleasurably as to make the whole affair more piquant. To be taken by surprise, I found, was somewhat to my taste, as it was to be to Elaine's. Putting up every appearance of fretting, as she often did to disguise her desires, made it the more engaging to see her put to a cock. Such moods added salt to the flavour of our adventures.

Upon returning to our hotel we were pleased to find that other male company had now joined us in the form of two well-attired gentlemen. The one, being a few years younger than my uncle, was introduced as the Comte d'Orcy. The other, a most handsome man, appeared to be his nephew, Roald, though I was never certain of this and such things little mattered. We were to dine it was said, Elaine and I having been much admired and complimented upon our fetching new gowns beneath which our corsets hugged us alluringly. Being of an extremely decollete nature, the gentlemen were able to peer well down between our titties which they did with much pleasure and as little embarrassment as I myself felt.

So far from entering into an orgy, as might have been thought, we enjoyed a most civilised conversation, which I was to learn as part of the art of good manners before settling down to amorous combats. I listened and learned much, all of our discourses being in English as a politeness to Elaine and myself. There were many cocottes, or really naughty girls, we learned to be seen parading in the Bois de Boulogne and at the races at Longchamps and elsewhere, but these were to be distinguished from ladies, by careful observation, through the slightly more gaudy nature of their attire.

It was not ever so, however, the Comte advised us carefully, for there were a small number of mondaines - the wealthiest and most attractive of the whores - who would spend small fortunes on their attire and jewellery and so only could be distinguished by name or reputation.

"How then shall we be taken?" I asked with some daring, though at a stage when I felt we had come to know each other well enough.

"As you may wish to be," the Comte replied. "By your delightful attire you will be taken as no other than you are - as true born ladies. By your deportment in the boudoir, however, you may well - I suspect - outdo such as are of more common blood."

"Then we are complimented, are we not, Elaine?" I laughed though she, being more cautious still in the presence of her Papa, but ventured a smile.

Two hours and much champagne having passed in this pleasant discourse, our guests took leave of us upon a promise to meet at eight for dinner. The lull that then ensued did not last long. I was loathe to stir, as was perhaps Elaine, being seated as we all were in my uncle's suite. It was put then upon Pearl to break the pleasantly somnolent spell, for - seeing the doors to my uncle's bedroom open - she rose and beckoned us.

"Come, my dears, you must show your corsets," she said.

CHAPTER VII

There could be only one spectator of our charms apart from Pearl, and he - being my uncle - rose to view them.

"Oh, no, for I wish to bathe!" declared Elaine, all of a dither at the prospect. The hour was but five-thirty of the afternoon. The sunlight glowed pleasurably through the windows which, being French, were large and imposing. In a society which normally takes tea at four and dinner much later, it is a pleasant hour, whether in summer or by the early light of a coal fire in a dusk-laden bedroom in winter. I have frequently flirted with a cock - as oftimes a woman's lips as well - at such times, then rose refreshed to enjoy yet others later. Such is my nature. It may not be that of others.

Having already received Phillippe's penis in my bottom, I was stirred for further adventures and had no doubt that the advancing night would be a meritorious one. Perhaps my eyes spoke of this to Pearl, for she smiled and gave me a little nod. Elaine curled herself up in her chair, undecided whether to rise or not.

"We have no drawers on. Will it not be unseemly?" I asked. I could not prevent myself from saying such. I provoked. I had the devil in me. Fully prepared to indulge me, Pearl responded in kind.

"In the best bedrooms in Paris, young ladies do not wear drawers. They make themselves ever ready for what might befall, Arabella. As to your both having no drawers on that will provide an even more piquant pleasure. You wish me to speak more frankly? There are no other gentlemen here save your uncle, by whose grace we are present."

"Oh! we must not talk like this in front of Papa. You shame me!" burst out my cousin.

At this Pearl compressed her lips. She was clearly not in a mood to be crossed.

"My dear, you have much to learn," she replied coldly, bringing my uncle's eyes and my own to bear upon her. "You think yourselves perfect little adventuresses, do you not? Well, it has yet to be seen if you are or aren't."(I knew myself to be included in this remark more as a courtesy to Elaine rather than as a rebuff to myself.) "There will be entertainments tonight, Elaine, in which we will all make free to join. You will be bereft of your drawers then. Why dither now?"

At that, Elaine uttered a little cry, rose up from her chair and was gone. The door slammed. I heard the adjoining one of our own suite open and close. My uncle assumed a mournful visage.

"You put too much upon her, I fear," he remarked to Pearl who in quite a boisterous manner then got up and opened another bottle of champagne with a very loud explosion as if it helped to give vent to her feelings.

"Nonsense, Harold, she is younger than Arabella here, yet puts airs upon herself when it comes to matters of tingling pleasure. We know we have come here to enjoy ourselves and I for one make no bones about the matter. What say you, Arabella? Come, sit on your uncle's lap and give him a kiss or we shall all be forlorn."

I laughed and did so. My bottom moulded warmly into his lap. Having kissed quite demurely I accepted a proffered glass, as my uncle did, while Pearl seated herself on the arm of our chair. Reaching one hand down she toyed her fingers lightly about my breasts, so encouraging him to in turn caress my thighs.

"Perhaps you were too hard on her, though," I murmured, albeit without reproof. The champagne was but a preliminary to our adjourning to the bedroom, as I knew. The thought enervated me. A cock in my bottom frequently now makes me want another in the more conventional manner, and vice versa. My uncle's was not slow in making itself felt under the roundness of my derriere. I wriggled upon it until the crest was nicely settled between my cheeks.

"Do you think so? You know I was not," Pearl said teasingly. "The Comte has a taste for birching, you know. It would do no harm for Elaine to be warmed-up to the proceedings once we are gathered again."

"Oh, you would not do that!" I exclaimed, though I must confess that the idea caused me a certain inner merriment.

"Be sure that I will if she displays such awkwardness as she had just exhibited. Harold, you should have seen to her bottom ere this!"

"True!" groaned my uncle with some feeling which was in great part impelled by the subtle movements of my own upon his rod. "My dear wife, though, would have misunderstood the matter."

"Well, she is not here now," said Pearl with great practicality and then smiled and said, "Come!"

Bound for pleasure, we made into the boudoir. The large bed lay covered in a grey silk eiderdown. The long velvet curtains were half drawn, veiling all in a pale light. Their tassels hung limp in marked contrast to my uncle's prick which stood as firm as a pole. In a trice he was naked, I in my corset and Pearl similarly attired. Standing upon the thick carpet by the bed, our clothes tumbled carelessly upon it, he embraced us both fervently. We sought to massage his prick together. The carefree atmosphere of the moment was delightful.

Even as he palmed our bottoms, Pearl wriggled and laughed.

"I must pee first," she declared and drew a gold-rimmed chamberpot from under the bed. Thereupon my uncle drew me upon the cover beside him, murmuring much of my beauty and the charm of my guepiere. I clasped his rigid shaft, we kissed. Together then we looked down at Pearl who had half squatted over the pot so that her bottom and her hairy love-purse hovered over the receptacle. Her mouth opened, her eyes half closed. A beauteous smile appeared upon her lips.

"He likes to watch. All men do," she whispered and thereupon released a fierce rain of golden urine that splashed down heavily into the china pot and all but gurgled as it settled, only to be rained upon again as her stream continued. Feeling then my uncle's balls which seemed to swell at the spectacle, I observed the flushed excitement in his face as Pearl's love-lips. continued to gush their offering. I frigged him. Our mouths meshed wildly, then we looked again to see Pearl rising.

The sight made my belly sparkle. I wriggled.

"She wants to as well," laughed Pearl, and indeed I did. I had no need to contain myself. She indeed helped draw me off the bed, saying she had a splendid idea. I was soon to know what it was. Her ingenuity is ever great. "This is called 'feeding the little girl'," she said and brought me to squat over the chamberpot as she had done save that, arranging herself behind me and bending to hold me beneath my armpits, I was more comfortably accommodated, as in a sling. "Wait, darling, do not piss yet. Harold, put your cock to her mouth!"

I could not resist. My uncle was off the bed in a flash. He had not even to bend. Mouth open, I received the plum of his knob over my tongue. His penis slid in a full four inches, causing me for a moment to choke until I had accommodated myself to the fleshy shaft. At that, Pearl cupped my breasts. My back rested against her. I held myself in, as I sensed was required.

"Piss now," she murmured, "ah, we should have made Elaine do this."

The words excited all. My uncle's cock began moving sturdily but cautiously in and out between my lips. In such matters he was ever a gentleman. By leaning forward he was able to engage his mouth with Pearl's. I began to suck. The sensation was delicious, coming as it did as my rain splashed in turn. Electric sparks seemed to explode in my belly. I was beginning to learn the true nature of sensuousness. I pissed more vigorously. His tool throbbed violently in my mouth.

"Come, darling, come, let her have the taste of it," I heard Pearl mouth.

He groaned. I cupped his balls and was allowed to sink down fully on to the pot. The two, following my movements, bent the more. I sucked the harder and persuaded another inch of his divine shaft into my mouth. All visions and sensations of wickedness were mine. I heard his anguished puffing, the liquid sounds of their mouths and tongues. The pulsing of his veins increased. The first jet of his sperm hit the back of my throat in a cannonade that was soon enough followed by its eager fellows. In a trice my mouth frothed with his gruelly substance. I found the taste to my liking. A sense of power possessed me. I would have sucked him dry had he not withdrawn it, declaring that he wished to put it in my cunt. Few men could have sustained himself as he, for with those very words I found myself upon the bed, wet as I was withal. Falling heavily upon me, his spouting cock plunged in. I held him quivering. Pearl's cries of pleasure at the spectacle seemed as my own. One single divine shudder and we were done. The last shoots and pearls of come spattered my cunny within. I clasped him tightly, quivering in our bliss. I knew no greater heights of pleasure.

All being done and to our immense satisfaction, the limp worm of his penis slipped regretfully from within my velvet sheath. Rolling upon his back and quite depleted, he thus permitted Pearl to come upon me in turn. Between my open thighs she lay, rubbing her cunny madly to mine and exchanging such a torrent of erotic phrases as I returned in full.

More sensuously than can any male, she squirmed upon me, full knowing that I was ready as never before to spill my excitement anew. In this she was right. The rubbing of our love-lips. and our pubic curls made me soar again to heaven. Blind in our hungers we mouthed and tongued. I felt her wetness. Yet again she trilled out her sparkling juices as did I until the hairs of our cunts meshed oiled and wet together. Uncaring of the condition of the eiderdown which would betray our pleasures we then lay still as might two babes. Murmuring gently we exchanged kisses as soft as doves.

"Ah, you are well fitted for it," Pearl sighed. A laugh escaped her as then my uncle stirred and came upon her, thus bearing his weight upon us both. Few things stir a man so much as the sight of two lovely women at play, as I have long learned. His cock, stiffening again, moved in the furrow of her bottom. Her belly bumped to mine. I was all but squashed beneath them.

"Let him put it in you," I murmured to her.

"The beast, I cannot stop him - oh, he is getting it in!"

I felt indeed that he was. Albeit that he was not then fully erect, his knob found its path between her love-lips. The rolling of Pearl's eyes and the movements of her lips upon mine told me that it had. I raised my legs the better to allow them to proceed. With quite a jolt he was full in her and there stiffened completely, a most pleasant sensation, as I was myself to learn later, for the male member swells up between the walls of the vagina which by their subtle clenching and sucking motions encourage the affair.

Pearl clearly wanted it badly, for she began to puff and moan, her face full flushed. By devious struggles I got out from beneath them. I wished to watch; Drawing up her hips and bottom, my uncle began to plug her in earnest while her face buried itself in the pillow. His face had a sheen of lust upon it. The vision of his big male shaft easing back and forth between her pouting lips quite mesmerised me, though I did not but stroke her sleek back gently, as if I were needed there to encourage her lewdness. Her hips strove, working back and forth, her elbows bent so that her forearms were placed flat on the bed. I have seen many photographic likenesses of such since, but none to rival the reality. Her tits swung with every inward thrust of him. Of a sudden I rose, mounted her back and - facing my uncle with my legs straddled on either side of her waist - afforded him my lips and tongue while rubbing my quim along her spine. I was careful not to put too much weight upon her and did so by placing my hands on his shoulders.

His movements quickened, making her bottom slap and smack to his belly. In his second course, as he was, his ejaculation took longer."Oh! oh!" Pearl gasped in pleasure beneath us. I felt proud of my initiative, which had come by instinct.

"Fuck her, fuck her, fuck her!" I babbled to his lips.

"Yes! Oh, what pleasures!" he groaned. Hearing the words from my lips brought him on. He clenched her hips the tighter and gushed, as well I could tell by all the signs of both. Ramming her to the full, he expelled his sperm while I received his tongue, his groans, his cries.

All then was peaceful. For the nonce we had taken our fill. Our stallion had proven worthy of the event. His cock, thick and heavy, spumed its last as we lay down. Being between them, I rubbed my thighs sensuously against theirs. Moving our fingers across to one another, Pearl and I twiddled each other's spermy split. Not a word was said. We lay in such beatitude as follows a fair and lusty bout, our breathing coming softly.

Visions of Elaine danced through my mind. Most oddly I felt a certain guilt that she had not been there, or - if not that - then that I was. How strangely the mind works in such moments. Yet I did not care. The haze of satisfaction was upon me. I could have taken another prick and another, and knew it well. Pearl stirred and pushed the covers down with her feet. Her movements were charmingly petulant and almost sleepy. Being then of one mind we all ruffled ourselves between the sheets and slept the sleep of love. A full hour passed before we stirred. I awoke to find myself pressed between them, my uncle's penis rampant against the hot cheeks of my bottom. Feeling around me by instinct for it, Pearl laughed as though to admonish me.

"He must conserve his forces. Oh, my mouth is dry. Let us get up and call for some lemonade," she decreed. This we did, staring at each other's unclothed bodies with a certain curiosity. My uncle's balls were full and pendant. They promised well for the night.

Having dressed - which was a simple enough matter for I wore only a silk chemise and gown over my corset - I fretted anew about Elaine and said that I had best go and see to her. I saw then to my hair, as did Pearl.

"Oh, she will come to it soon enough," said Pearl, adding that we were to the Comte's house after dinner and that Elaine would not be permitted any hesitations there. Even so, I could not leave her in isolation and so excused myself, this being done as politely as if we had been upon any normal social occasion. Such niceties ever please me. Pearl was clearly delighted with my comportment.

Elaine I found huddled up on the bed, as I expected to.

"Oh, what have you been at?" she asked crossly. Evidently she had slept, for her hair was all array and her skirt up. I suspected something of that and, before she could rise, threw myself merrily upon her and reached my hand so far up her thighs until I could feel her quim. There was such a stickiness there that I knew well what she had been about.

"You have enjoyed yourself," said I.

"But not as much as you, I am sure," she replied pettishly. Blushing deeply, she pushed my hand away, got off the bed and went to her dressing table. Determined to break her mood, I bent over her from behind and, sliding my arms beneath hers, cupped her breasts.

"What naughty thoughts did you have?" I asked, whereat she had the grace to giggle.

"None, and you have not told me what you were doing. I suppose you were conversing again," she said sarcastically. I turned her face - moving my free hand all about over and beneath her proud titties -

and kissed her. She felt my fervour, my affection. Her lips returned the compliment.

"Yes, it may be called that," I murmured. I had no cause to blush, nor she. "It was nice to have it in your bottom, was it not?" I asked", my lips continuing to brush her own while her neck was turned about to me.

"No," she said softly, but I knew the word not to be taken at its face value nor indeed any value. I told her then what I had heard the Madame say to Pearl before we were put over the bars. At that, Elaine's hand clutched mine and held it over her left breast.

"Is that really true?" she asked.

"Of course. Why else do you think it was done? Phillippe's prick was divinely formed to open up our furrows so that the larger ones might follow. It tingled me at first, but it was nice. I am sure you felt the same."

"Oh, then have you...?" she asked, referring of course to my absence and well imagining, I am sure, that her Papa had breached the same route.

"You have not told me whether you liked it or not," I countered. At that I raised my head and pressed her face to my breasts while feeling for the little velvet buttons of the front of her dress.

"Yes, all right, I did, though not at first. I wished he had kept it in longer. You had the best of it," Elaine confessed.

Little by little I had freed her breasts as she spoke. My fingers roamed now over their glossy swollen surfaces. Her nipples, quickly risen, stubbed against my fingertips.

A little awkwardly I drew her up, but she following easily, we moved sideways together back cross the room and fell pellmell upon the bed. Her mouth was moist and hungry. Licking at her nipples while she sighed and let her arms loll above her head, I raised her skirt and dwelt my eyes with pleasure upon her mount. The dark hairs were crisp and well-fluffed up. The lips were oily with the excited thoughts she had apparently sustained. Working my tongue into the whorl of her navel, I caused her to giggle and double up her legs. Upon her doing this, and having her bottom half hanging over the edge of the bed, I dropped to my knees and - holding her without resistance - plunged my pointed tongue back and forth in her pussy.

Elaine squirmed and moaned, but pressed into me, quite mushing me with her pubic hairs.

"Did he fuck you? Tell me, oh tell me," she quivered.

"Of course, as he will you tonight."

She hid her face, enjoying my tongue muchly as the sly movements of her bottom showed. Rolling her upon her back and forcing her thighs askew, I plunged my mouth in deeper. She was on the point of coming as I could tell by all the little febrile movements of her body. Her stockinged legs stirred passionately, waving this way and that. The slurping of my tongue sounded.

"Oh, no, I cannot!" she moaned.

Gliding my luring tongue without, I rubbed my chin all around her clitoris, this coming as an inspiration to me and proving most effective, for she bucked the more and let me feel her tricklings.

"You silly, you must, for else you will be birched and your hot bottom put up to them one by one. Many a girl is so treated at the Comte's, I hear."

"Oh - woh!" Elaine's knees spread themselves over my shoulders, the heels of her shoes digging between my shoulder blades. Her back arched. She came again, this time in a fiercer spurting whose fine rain spattered against my chin. Her legs slumped down either side of me and remained open. Her eyes stared at the ceiling. I was upon her like a tigress. Our stocking tops rubbed together.

"Say yes, for I would not have you birched," I begged.

"Yes!"

Whether she even heard herself speak, I know not. She kissed divinely. Our quims rubbed together as sensitively as the strings of violins. So wriggling and squirming together we released our juices which mingled in the oiling of our thighs. Quiescent then in the pale mists of fulfilment, we lay panting. Moving half off of her I toyed with her slit. My left leg lay across hers.

The night would soon enough come upon us. I whispered to her of what must come to pass. She hugged me, answering me not, her eyelashes fluttering against my cheek.

CHAPTER VIII

The maison of the Comte was luxurious in the extreme, as might have been expected. Gildings, decorations and large mirrors were all about. A huge winding staircase gave promise of what was to follow above. That we were to stay the night was tacitly understood. At dinner the Comte arraigned himself at my side - his companion acting as escort to Elaine while my uncle sat with Pearl. All looked most seemly. Waiters whose quietness would have flattered the Savoy in London went back and forth with an endless array of dishes. The wines were so numerous that I almost lost count of them.

"We will, with your permission ladies, take liqueurs at table," the Comte announced at the end of our repast. The suggestion was curious, but in a moment I saw the reason for it. The doors opened and a most divine young maid appeared, bearing glasses and bottles upon a silver tray. These attracted our attention but little however in comparison with her attire which was such as a Greek princess might have worn in olden times.

Her sole garment was a robe of white which, being translucent, allowed one to see the proud orbing of her breasts, the dark circles which surmounted them and - below - where the material wafted out with every step, the brazen triangle of her bush.

Her limbs were slender, her hips finely curving, and the rondeur of her marbled bottom announcing itself boldly beneath the white mist. Being tallish, she carried herself regally, her feet shod in silver slippers whose heels gave perfect rise to her legs. Unblushingly and with her long dark hair moving easily about her shoulders, she served us one by one, my uncle being sufficiently discreet and well-schooled not to appear to take overmuch notice of the pendant breasts which nudged his shoulder as his glass was filled.

The liqueur was Benedictine, one that is ever my favourite. It has a perfect bite to it yet is smooth as velvet and does not clog the throat. Its headiness is insidious but pleasing. One becomes not so much tipsy from it as floating around it.

Expecting as I did, the young beauty then to retire, I was duly astonished to see her place her tray quietly down upon a side table and then with feline grace slink down upon her knees and disappear beneath the table. The purpose of this however soon became clear to me. A faint gasp came from Pearl but then was hushed. Simultaneously my uncle spluttered for a moment into his glass but then was quiet in turn.

The Comte turned not a hair but continued conversing with us, asking me whether I did not like the paintings of Renoir whose delineation of females was, he said, the finest ever to be viewed.

"No, for I think Renoir's ladies are too fat," I replied to his amusement, keeping as I did one eye upon Pearl and my uncle who were moving about most curiously and for good reason since the maid, having plunged her face up between the lady's thighs, was also attending to my uncle's prick with her hand. Their expressions were amusing, for each strove to act as if nothing at all were happening and indeed might well not have been so far as the Comte was concerned. Both drank more quickly than they would otherwise have done and 'twas my uncle who reached for the bottle and refilled their glasses, which I considered quite a feat considering the trembling of his hand.

The pair having thus been lubriciously readied, the maid most obviously turned her attention next to Elaine whose mouth opened in a wide aperture of surprise while a blush flooded her from neck to forehead.

"Are you not well, my dear?" the Comte asked, feeling well up my thigh as he did beneath my gown. I stirred and assisted his endeavours, being not uneager to taste the maid's tongue myself, or rather to afford her a taste of my cunny, for I thought her tongue to be well coated already.

Elaine bubbled. I can only describe it as that. Raised as it had been to her mouth, her glass chattered against her teeth and then dropped limply to the table, almost causing the precious liqueur to be spilled. Pearl was meanwhile smiling and more at her ease, having - as I was afterwards to know - my uncle's prick in her hand beneath the tablecloth while he prettied his fingers about her bush. Elaine's companion, Roald, was doubtless suffering a similar assault, for he rolled his eyes and worked his body, the two appearing to perform St. Vitus' Dance.

"HAAAAR!" gasped my cousin - most indiscreetly, for I was yet awaiting my turn, though I needed it less now that the Comte's fingers were at me. Having parted my thighs well and shifted my bottom forward on my chair, he was enabled to tease me to distraction by turning his wrist about and playing with my clitoris.

"She should be upon the table, for she has been but lightly seen to today," then said Pearl who clearly wished to hasten matters and, I have little doubt, had been primed to do so by the Comte.

"Indeed, has such a delicious young lady then been so neglected?" inquired our host in the most courteous manner. Gurgling all the more and with her head hung back, Elaine was meanwhile being even more closely attended to. I knew then how little all had been arranged, but sensed that what was to follow did not come about by accident or the mere fervour of the moment. Clapping his hands, the Comte then caused the door to open and a seeming twin of the Grecian maid to appear. Wafting across the room silently while her robe billowed out to display the delectable nudity beneath, she moved immediately behind Elaine's chair and to only the feeblest beating of hands of my cousin all by ripped the front of her gown open so that the milky gourds of her breasts were fully displayed. Reaching then beneath Elaine's armpits, she drew her up and sideways so that her chair faltered and fell.

All was then to be seen, her open legs, the lower fringe of her black corset, the muff of her quim, her silky thighs whose whiteness was made all the more sensuous by the black of her stockings. Therewith also the first maid slithered from beneath the table and grasped the ankles of Elaine who squealed and cried out much as any virgin might who was displayed to the assembled company.

"Come, we shall take our pleasure now," called the Comte who rose with his penis as well displayed as did Roald and my uncle. I being drawn up with him allowed myself to be fondled warmly twixt my thighs while Elaine, being carried bodily into an adjoining room wailed her protests.

"Yes, let us to cocks and cunts," laughed Pearl, "for each of us is to be threaded and your balls had best be full for the task."

Such a bussing and rumpling then occurred in all the heat of passion that in no time were she and I down to our corsets, shoes and stockings, and the men naked for the battle, their prongs well upstanding. Elaine's moans being heard, though now more muffled, we followed in, Pearl holding my uncle's cock and I the proud possessor of both Roald's and the Comte's. The room was one we had not entered before but was clearly furnished and designed for the sport. All about were broad divans covered in black or crimson velvet. Brocaded cushions of silk were strewn discreetly so that any who wished might fall upon them.

Two chandeliers glittered their greeting discreetly. Upon a sideboard glasses and bottles awaited the moment when we might require rejuvenation. Most remarkable of all was the further wall to which long mirrors were affixed, side by side, so that all that occurred, whether upon the divans or the floor, was faithfully reflected.

Feeling the twin throbbing of my companions' penises, I saw then to what delights Elaine was being treated. Her gown was thrust up to her waist and her corsage, as I have said, fully opened. Laid upon a black velvet divan which complemented the dazzling whiteness of her skin, though at the same time echoing the hue of her stockings and the dark bush of her quim, her legs were splayed to the tongue-twirling of the second maid while the first massaged and sucked at her swollen titties.

Whether she saw us enter or not, I do not know, for my cousin's eyes alternately opened and closed, her mouth grimacing in pleasure.

"Let us observe. It is a pretty sight indeed," murmured the Comte who, having advanced closer under my excited guidance, could not resist fondling the bottom of the nipple-sucking maid.

I rubbed him but gently, as I did Roald, well knowing that either might come before their time was due. Elaine puffed, snorted and moaned alternately. Unable to resist, I bent and kissed her mouth, so quietening her a little while, with my arms stretched back I continued to hold what I might call the horny reins of my steeds. I wanted both, I was greedy, yet no more so than to see Elaine at pleasure.

Taking advantage then of my position, the Comte neatly drew his penis from my grasp and, taking hold of my hips and bending me further over my cousin, deftly inserted his knob at the portals of my love-pot. I wriggled. Two inches slipped within. Holding Elaine's chin I drove my tongue in her mouth. All three of us were now at her and the rising delirium of her pleasure was obvious from the excited stabbing of her tongue around mine.

Sheathing himself fully, the Comte took full possession of me, bringing my bottom to mound into his belly while his balls hung beneath.

"Elaine! He is f...f...fucking me," I moaned. My legs straightened, my back dipped. I knew well how to present myself to such a lubricious assault. His cock tingled in my velvety depths, clamped as firmly as in a baby's mouth, as afterwards he was at flowery pains to tell me. He worked himself, I moved my hips in response. Roald, having been released from my hungry clasp, fell to having his cock sucked by Pearl who - bending forward for the task - then received my uncle's prick in her cunt.

Thus were we arranged, in as lewd a tableau as might be imagined. Naught sounded but the soft hissing of our breaths and the combined smacking of our bodies. Spreading his legs and with his balls swinging gently, Roald made the fullest of offerings to the mouth of Pearl who was not loathe to take advantage of her double offering. I, who had thought to do the same thing, raised my mouth from Elaine's and watched the pair through bleary eyes while the Comte pumped me sturdily. His hands held my hips in a manful grip which I liked, occasionally descending to caress my thighs or titillate my clitoris.

In the very midst of our transports, however, a new fancy took him. That he was so in command of his senses to effect it, I much admired. Withdrawing his steaming prong but briefly from my dell, he motioned the maids aside and set me astride Elaine in such fashion that my cunny came over her mouth, though an inch or two above it.

My cousin stirred not, nor could. Gazing down into her hot eyes, I smiled, though my expression was not long held for the Comte then inserted his penis again so that Elaine was brought to suffer its contact with her mouth. Surging into me as it did, not much was then left of it for her to attend to, wherewith the Comte gruffly commanded her to lick his balls.

Whether or not she did, I know not for I was then bent further forward until my hands came at the end of the divan. Truly I could feel movements beneath me, but by then our course was already almost run, as were those of the other combatants. I had come already several times and well splashed the Comte's balls with my offerings. Now, with a satisfied groan, he afforded me his due. Pressing the warm orb of my bottom back into him so that we seemed as if glued together, I received every long shooting of his sperm in the selfsame moment that Pearl was inundated front and back. Therewith I seemed to feel Elaine's tongue gently licking, but my sensations were too overwhelming for me to judge. The lips of my cunt oozed along the steaming tool of the Comte as he injected me thrice and fourfold until the bubblings of our liquid treasures merged and I turned my neck about to meet his mouth.

The last quiverings seized us. I balled my bottom deeper and absorbed the finer spurts of his sperm which then as always I was greedy to receive. So enraptured we stayed with our warm, pulsing bodies close-pressed until the gradual weakening of his tool in my grotto announced the regretted finale. In withdrawing he spilled his pearls upon Elaine's chin, as I also doubtless did, though so heady was the scent of sperm and the finer feminine odours in the room that it mattered not.

Being drawn off of my cousin, I took to the cushions on the floor and lay there as might any Eastern princess. For such I felt, well knowing that I was to receive two more libations at the very least. About us flitted the two maids. Wine glugged into glasses and was well received. Elaine lay as one who cannot help be perceived but who wishes not to be. Of a sudden she curled up and turned over upon her hip to the wall, so presenting an ardent bottom to view.

I knew her well by then. She was"presenting," as we say, though would have denied it. Being flaccid of organs, the men said little save by way of desultory conversation that was but lightly sprinkled with lewdness. We were not, after all, whores, but ladies with gentlemen. The two maids, having seemingly performed all their duties, went out and closed the door upon us, perhaps regretfully, as I thought, though in aftermath I realised that they were the fortunate participants at many such entertainments, as Pearl was always pleased to call them.

Elaine, as I say, lay as if upon a soft platform, for we were all by then seated at our ease amid the cushions, or rather, lolling upon them. Most hopefully Pearl and I both kept our legs open. For what we were about to receive we would be duly thankful. The night had but begun.

"Recount us your adventures, for you must have many in this very room," invited Pearl of our host. So began our first session of "Parisian Nights," for that was the name I gave to them and how I duly recorded them in my diaries and notebooks. In vividness of narrative, the Comte was never failing, for this was one of several evenings we were to pass there during our sojourn in Paris. He spoke of virgins and cocottes, of mature ladies and of younger ones. The pleasures of the birch came readily to his lips for he avowed that a sweeping of green twigs across a recalcitrant bottom was the finest method by which to prepare a maiden for the cock's entry.

Much was the badinage that occurred of course during his discourse, and not few the questions on my part, he delighting occasionally in what he deemed my naivety, though much complimenting me on the sweet way that I interjected.

The birch, I suggested, was a fearful instrument. This I announced for the ears of Elaine who lay still and was mainly disregarded by us, though her round bottom and the partly-offered fig of her slit looked most toothsome, being well seen from our lower vantage point.

"Ah, but the English have not the art of it," the Comte replied, "they think to birch their girls into submission whereas we perform the finer arts of inducing their bottoms to rise to the occasion by the more gentle but insistent sweeping of the twigs which naturally must be well softened for their task. Thus is heat slowly induced, causing the hips to wriggle not so much evasively but in full concord with the tingling which is induced."

"Is that not also done to males and would it not have similar effect then?" I made bold to ask.

"Why indeed that is so with some men, though I would say few. It depends, I believe, on the subtle conformation of the nerves beneath the skin. In rampant youth the effect is more marked and many a boy's pego has been made to stiffen agreeably when under the maternal hand. Thus does he learn to grope while being spanked and is perhaps smacked the harder thereby. However, this little game continuing and the promise of his stiffened penis being felt upon the maternal thighs, the spanking eventually becomes other than a disciplining and resolves to more licentious acts, as also occurs with young ladies whose drawers are down."

Seeing the twinkle in his eye, I laughed, for he would have me confess - I knew - that I had both suffered and enjoyed such, but I was loathe to make up stories of that nature for Papa had never put his hand to my bottom nor indeed any other part of my person.

These discourses having lasted some forty minutes or more, the arousal of the males again became evident. In some part this was secured by Pearl and I asking ever more licentious questions which caused the Comte to expand upon every detail of events that had occurred in the mirrored room.

"Would you then force a young maiden to take the cock?" I asked, fingering his own rising tool as I spoke.

"If I know she will be the better for it, yes. There are many signs to be followed in such circumstances, for their eyes are to be watched more than their lips should be listened to. A young girl say of fifteen or sixteen is often more easily brought to it, however, than a spinster whose longing for the manly prick has become too well submerged in false shyness."

I raised my eyebrows and asked whether a spinster might be sufficiently attractive to warrant such attentions.

"A few. They are rare and yet as jewels, for if well-formed of figure their bodies are exceedingly ripe for it. The ladies take as much pleasure in converting them as do the males. I might instance, for example, the daughter of a cure, a vicar, as I believe you say. She was in her thirtieth year and deemed by many to be as warm-bottomed in bed as any, though that exceedingly attractive part of her anatomy had until then encountered naught but her own hand. Being brought here, she was duly courted and flattered, much to her surprise, I might say. The wine then took effect on her, unfairly perhaps, though she was put to her trials more fully the next day when out of her cups. Even so, it took much to encourage her to raise her dress so that, as was said, her legs might be admired. At first she would display only her knees, but then by persuasion conceded to mid-thigh. Her legs were superbly fashioned, even as are your own," the Comte said gallantly. "Several other ladies then showed their garters and invited comparison with hers. I fear I bore you with such a recital, but being slowly enacted and with much deliberation, all proved most exciting. Her drawers and a finely-curved belly were seen at last. Assistance was then given, if I might so put it, to holding up her dress, while she continued to tipple. At what was deemed the right moment, her drawers were then descended. Being a trifle inebriated - which I regretted, for a woman must know what she is about - she was then laid back upon the table and fucked by several of the gentlemen. Each she received dumbly, as if it were a great surprise, which I am sure it was. I then saw her put to bed, my maids acting as chaperones."

I guessed in what wise the two delightful girls had "chaperoned" - no doubt having kept the tempted lady busy thereafter.

"You spoke of the morrow," I said. His penis was now fine and glowing. I bent and gently sucked the knob for a moment.

"A lust had come over me for her, I scarce know why, save that she had one of the finest figures I have ever seen, firm and round in all its aspects. Having been bathed and breakfasted in her room, I had her brought to me. She was dressed but without drawers, for they had been confiscated. In my nightshirt, I lay upon the bed and spoke to her gently, holding her wrist the while. I spoke to her of pleasures. She listened for a moment, but then would have tugged away. I grasped her more firmly. I know well how a woman who has been in lust succumbs to the lure of erotic words that are not too crudely spoken. I apprised her of what I intended, that my prick was to enter her bottom. She cried out at that, but knew in her heart that I would have her, or so I do believe. The maids entered and the birch was brought. I had little doubt that her Papa had oftimes basted her bottom, if only to see her knickers.

"So it proved, for though her struggles were at first gallant, she yielded finally. Held by the two maids as she was, I brought her bottom to a fine glow, having cast up her dress. Her squeals and cries were at first loud, but she finally settled, as I knew she would. I twitched the twigs more gently, noting every movement of her hips and every tightening of her bottom cheeks. She should have been finished off long before this and perhaps knew it. Her bottom yearned for the final assault that I afforded it. Parting the richly-fleshed cheeks, I inserted my knob in her orifice, telling then the maids to release her. She beat then at the counterpane and moaned, but made no attempt to delay my entry which was slow and deep. Within the passing of a minute she was fully cleft. Her bottom worked to me, she sought the forward movements of my prick. I said naught, but continued working her, causing her buttocks to urge back and forth against me. Her effusions wettened the bed long before I came. The sleek interior of her rosehole sucked my sperm in. All was well and all was done. Twice more I had her that day before she departed, laden with gifts and more glowing of visage than she had been for years."

"This then you called bringing her to her trials?" I asked, moving my hand gently up and down his shaft as Pearl was doing to my uncle and Roald, for they had listened as entranced as I.

"Why, mon chou, I believe it to be a useful phrase and in many respects a correct one," he replied. "Why do you ask?"

My gaze wandered across to Elaine who seemed to have huddled up ever more tightly.

"There is one here who has not yet been put to her trials," I said. "Or, at least, not in that respect," I added with a smile.

CHAPTER IX

Poor Elaine, she was the subject of my mischief that night, but it could not be helped. Her benefits, however, were considerable and so mollified the wrath she might other wise have poured upon me.

We have argued about it since."You were sulking," I have said. "Oh, you story, I was resting," would come her reply, though said with a smile she could not conceal.

Had we been in less civilised company, our host might have demanded or at least enquired why my cousin was not party to our merriment. Being of great experience, he knew her predicament to be one of seeming shyness which, like an egg, but waits to be cracked open. It was for me to spring the hare, so to speak, and this I duly did since all were again ready for the fray. All eyes then being fixed upon the reclining beauty, I rose and tiptoed across to her, quite certain that she had absorbed every word and was as ready for her dosages as I. Placing my hand under her bottom, which she had left uncovered, I whispered to her that she must now take her choice of the men's pricks.

"I want to go home!" she whined, this being heard by Pearl who hastened across.

"What nonsense is this?" she demanded merrily. Then, giving me a wink, she reached beneath the divan and drew out a small birch, the bound handle of which was prettily decorated with a blue silk ribbon.

"This young lady must be warmed for the feast, and who else to give her bottom pleasure but her Papa? Come, Harold, to your duty."

"No!" shrieked Elaine, becoming thereupon quite lively, though at the sight of her father rising and advancing with his cock waggling eagerly, she sat up and hid her face. "Oh, Papa, you would not!" she implored, by which time however he had reached one arm beneath her knees and the other under her armpits, so lifting her that Elaine uttered a wild cry and appeared to faint. That she did so was partly to her undoing for she was carried easily enough to a convenient table, at the sight of which she abandoned pretence of swooning and sobbed and kicked to such effect that my uncle, all but persuaded by her, would have put her down had it not been for Pearl.

"None of this, now, put her over!" she cried whereupon the Comte proved his worth yet again by demonstrating that the table was designed for such recalcitrants. Positioning himself to the side of the table as Elaine was lowered from her father's arms, he took one of her wrists and so drew on her arm that she was bent over the further edge, screeching the while that a strap - fitted to the underside - was snapped about her wrist, Roald, acting as his accomplice, saw to the other so that my cousin was as well secured as could be with her toes just touching the floor and her bottom perfectly poised for action.

"No, Papa, no!" Elaine squealed unendingly until Pearl - securing my cousin's gown well up above her hips - afforded her such a resounding smack on her pert nether cheeks as made her howl with outrage and then sob more quietly. Flushed with pleasure, anticipation - and doubtless many other emotions - my uncle then took the little birch from Pearl's hand while we, easing away from the table became enraptured spectators of what was to follow. Save, that is, for a piece of advice that the Comte thought fit to offer.

"Monsieur, if I may so suggest, a dozen firm strokes would be most fitting upon this occasion - the first to be applied from the right - sweeping right across her bottom, the second to be given from the left, and the third coursing a little more lightly up under her bulge. Spare her not, for she will best be brought on to your cock in this way."

"And time it is for her indeed to be," murmured Pearl who then began massaging his cock while I attended to Roald's, the pair of them holding us about our waists while we leaned against them and

Elaine's sobs and cries of despair echoed all about.

"Oh, Papa, you shame me, you shame me!"

"Take no notice, Harold, the little minx's quim will pout even more appealingly once you have warmed her bottom," chuckled Pearl. "Let us take to the divans, Arabella, for if we kneel upon them on either side of the table we can then receive our partners' cocks from the rear at the very moment that your uncle presents himself to her."

"Oh-ho-ho-NO!" sobbed Elaine who looked perfectly adorable, I thought, for her enforced posture showed well the curving lines of her stockinged legs, the pale orb of her bottom, and the coy peeping of her slit beneath.

The marvel was that my uncle did not breach his daughter's offering then and there, for his knob was but twelve inches from it and Elaine's cunny was most succulently poised to receive it. What her real state of mind then was, I would love to have known, for her outward protests counted as nothing to me.

Having taken up postillion at our rears upon the two divans, as Pearl suggested, and all being comfortably if teasingly placed, the feting of Elaine's bottom began the while that the crest of Roald's tool waited menacingly poised towards the cheeks of my derricre.

Tentative in the raising of the birch as my uncle appeared to be, yet the determined first swish that he rained across Elaine's out-thrust orb seemed to presage all the earlier frustrations he had doubtless felt.

"Yooooh!" my cousin screeched. Her hips waggled wildly, her feet teetering this way and that as the spraying twigs sparkled their points of fire into her globe. I was yet to know - though much later - the sensation myself. It burns, it stings., it taunts, causing the bottom to rotate and so offer itself ever more invitingly to the male prong. Should it belay the bottom too hard, then the very purpose is lost, for one cannot sustain too deep a stinging and pleasure at the same time. Of this I thought little at the time, for the pink streaks that began to appear in contrasting hue upon the pale bulb of Elaine's bottom were exciting in the extreme. Twice, thrice, and four times did she howl to the searing strokes, the third of which - coming up beneath her bottom in accordance with the Comte's instructions - caused her to reach beguilingly up on her toes.

"NOOO-NOOO-NOOO, Papa!" screeched my cousin whose wild entreaties appeared to soften his heart, for with that he began to belabour her much more lightly and by instinct appeared to begin to know what might draw her on and what might not. The gritting cries that had sped from her mouth then began as if by magic to diminish.

"Ah, superb - magnifique! - he has learned the trick of it," murmured the Comte who I swear would rather have birched her himself.

"OOOOH-HAAAR!" came then from Elaine, the pink of her bottom now assuming a slightly deeper hue that made me wonder muchly at the streaks of fire that must be coursing through her. Swish - swish - swish! sounded the birch again, though ever still as light in its application as my uncle had adapted himself to. Afterwards he said that in truth he could not at first bear to birch her bare bottom, but then taking a liking for the sport vowed to himself that it would not be Elaine's last.

Such noises Elaine continued to make as I never could interpret. At one moment she emitted a long hissing sound such as might be expressed by"WHEEEEEE!" At another a bubbling sob would ripple up from her throat, her smooth belly pressing into the edge of the table as the twigs impressed their urging fire into her every crevice. Whether my uncle was counting the dozen she was to receive mattered little to us all, save perhaps my cousin whose cheeks were well pearled with her tears which trickled saltily down to the corners of her mouth.

A surging of remorse that was yet mingled with an excitement of pleasure coursed through me, for I sensed her well to be at the gateway to uncountable desires that the thought of her Papa's rigid cock and swinging balls could not help but evoke.

"NEEE-YNNNNG! Oh, oh, oh, Papa!" she gritted. The sound merged with a sob of waiting pleasure that rose from myself as Roald - who sensed that the divine denouement was at hand - eased apart the springy half-moons of my derriere and poised the knob of his pestle full against my rosette. I cringed a little. He felt the movement. He grasped my hips, my lips parted in a pretty cry. He was already entering. That which I sustained then was the sensation of a huge piston of rigid flesh and muscle urging itself remorselessly into my bottom. For a moment then I lost view of Elaine for I dropped my head, allowing my somewhat tousled hair to fall in part over my eyes. I gritted out a moan. I tensed my knees, feeling as I did as though all the air were being driven from my lungs as inch by inch he probed within.

"WHOOOO!" I gasped even as Elaine was doing. Afterwards she said that she heard me, yet thought it was but an echo of her own cries. Endeavouring to resist a little, I drew my hips forward only to have them rammed back.

"Arabella! come - you must take it! What a divine bottom you have - what warmth - what tightness! Say I am the first!"

"Ah, yes!" I lied. "Oh, but you must not put it right in!" I moaned, though all by then was lost, or gained. Another thrust of his powerful loins and I received a full five inches of his jouster which throbbed exceedingly in my hot orifice. "HAAAAR!" I heard from Pearl at the same time, for the Comte was putting himself to her in the same wise. The room bleared before my eyes, entertaining as I was the first full manly prick in my bottom. Every vein seemed to impress itself against the sleek walls of my channel. The knob appeared bigger than it had done in my cunny, though doubtless my fevered squeezing made it so. I gritted my teeth. I wanted him.

The knob urged more. I had come to full womanhood, as then seemed to me. The sensation of complete submission to the lusting male was quite delirious. My moans echoed in my ears even as did Roald's, for with yet another tender push he had me to the full, my bottom balling into his belly. I was corked. I felt the nudging of his balls beneath my quim which added exquisitely to the curious yet divinely enervating sensation. No doubt the brushing of my curls there excited him equally, though all was contained in the delicious feeling of being fully sheathed and held, as might be any female animal.

But a minute or two had passed since my cry had merged with Elaine's. She it was now who was to receive her bounty, though instead of putting her forthwith to her Papa's cock as I had anticipated, he loosed first her wrist-straps, wherewith she would have slumped backwards to the floor had he not lifted her bodily and laid her accommodatingly upon cushions.

"Oh-woh-woh!" Elaine blubbered, feeling her hot bottom laid to momentary rest upon the downy supports. Her arms flailed, her stockinged legs endeavoured to close, but clearly my uncle would have no more of her hesitations. With a growl he was upon her, so levering her thighs apart that he was able to couch himself upon her belly and keep her legs apart by the doughty intervention of his own. Therewith at last I saw his cock throbbing upon her belly, the while that Elaine twisted her face from side to side.

"I shall tell...I shall tell Mama!" she blathered, but then - taking both her wrists and laying her hands above her head - he so held her, each tremulous jerking of her belly almost causing him to come no doubt, for her navel wriggled bewitchingly under the crest of his weapon. "OOOOH! HAAAAR!" Elaine choked. Her torso twisted, furthering his excitement.

Therewith Roald began to move his cock in me with a gentleness of purpose that betrayed well his desire to please me.

"Watch them as I bugger you, my pet," he husked.

"Yeh-eh-esss!" I moaned. I could do no other, nor sought to. Elaine lay full before me on the carpet, but a yard or two away. Her tremulous struggles appeared to be weakening. Her knees skewed sideways and relaxed, allowing Papa's balls to couch themselves lewdly against her nest. His lips flourished all about her ever-twisting face, flushed and tear-streaked as it was. Her bubbling cries diminished. In a moment her lips had merged beneath his own. Held by the wrists still in a position of utter submission, her hands opened and closed several times and then lay lax.

"Hold still, Elaine," he murmured.

"Oh, Papa!"

"Come - your legs wider. By heavens, I should have threaded you long ere this and well you know it."

"My b...b...bottom burns, Papa!"

"And the more it shall, my pet, if you move your hands when I release them, for I shall put you to the birch again and cork your bottom first, as I mean to before the night is out. Still now, you little devil! Lift your bottom a trifle that I might cup it and so bring your nest to part its lips to my knob. A little more - there, so!"

For a moment Elaine appeared dazed. Her hands remained limp where he had left them, one above each shoulder. The protrusion of her nipples from her white, swollen titties where her gown was opened was delicious in the extreme. Biting her lip, she raised her bottom a full two inches so that his hands, gliding beneath, allowed it to throb upon his palms. Withdrawing a trifle, he allowed his eager knob to oppose its lusting bulb against the pouting lips of her cunny.

My bottom moved more easily now upon Roald's shaft. Some subtle lubrication seemed to have eased his passage. My senses swam. Poised over me, he palmed my breasts, needing no longer to hold me for his game. I was accomplice to the art. The itching and burning sensations thrilled me to the core.

"Go faster!" I urged and then broke from me a further cry that no power could have stilled - "h, Uncle, fuck her!"

A moan from Elaine and he had already sunk in, a full four inches of his cock already being embedded. Victorious in that moment he raised himself above her. How moist and sticky her quim was I could only guess. For a moment her back arched as if she would dismount him, then with a frail bubbling cry she was submerged beneath him, her legs kicking mutinously until he was full within.

"NOOOOO!" she choked, but it was her last such dying cry to be. His lips settled upon her risen nipples, sucking at them strongly the while that she bucked.

"Yes, Elaine! Ah, what delights! Take him - take your Papa's cock!" I cried.

His balls swung heavily and he began to joust her. No longer then did she resist, though twisting her face to one side so that her mouth could scarce be taken, she allowed him to ream her, her bottom writhing ardently upon his palms as the spell of it took her. His prick shunted, thrust, emerged and then thrust in again. I saw the lips of her cunny distinctly swell and grip around it. Their breaths panted together. In a moment they were in full flight. Spreading her legs wider, he encountered no resistance now, smacking his receptacles against the under-swell of her bottom until with a moan of frenetic desire Elaine offered her lips to his and both made a merry dance with their tongues.

"Let me come in you, my darling!"

"HA! OOOOH! Yes, Papa, yes! Work your cock in me - how big it is!"

All blurred. The divine vision exceeded all my imaginations. Thrice and I come and now a fourth time spattered. Our cries resounded. Roald's panting grew louder.

"I must!" he cried.

"My love, yes, do it in my bottom - come!" I exhorted. Beside us, Pearl and the Comte threshed equally. The wicked orgy was nearing its peak. In but seconds I received the hot splashing of Roald's come, deep up my orifice, while in turn both Pearl and Elaine received their manly tributes until all lay soaking in the aftermath which so stirs the mind with pleasantries that might yet be to follow. Casting myself lazily forward at last, I so disengaged myself and lay with my face a little shyly hidden at our shamelessness.

Such was not to be for long, however. Pearl would not have it so and brought us all soon enough to the wine again. Elaine, having by then been divested of her gown, sat naked to her corsets, stockings and shoes, as did I. One arm around her, my uncle played with her titties which he weighed fondly. A tiredness that had entered upon our champions made itself known by the doleful limpness of their pricks, about which I much teased them, they taking it in good part.

"Let us all lie down, for all then shall be soon restored," countered Pearl who took herself to Roald and I to my uncle, while Elaine was made to lay with the Comte.

Pleasant indeed are such moments when an amorous langour is upon one, for the discourses flow softly and while many libertine suggestions are made, there is no hurry upon the matter. I have read long since many meretricious works - these being all however of fiction - in which the males have a nonsensical vigour and ever-readiness of purpose which in real life few if any attain. A woman may be fucked a dozen times in a night, yet a single male may be able to attend to her only thrice or four times while others take the saddle in his place. Enough however of the fooleries of itinerant male scribes who allow their imaginations to become overheated by vision of that which I doubt they would ever experience, having neither the time, the opportunities nor the wealth. Nor, I should say, the wit, for despite all the lasciviousness of our intent and our succeeding actions, scarce a crude word passed between our lips when discoursing in relative peace of such matters.

True it is that the French language softens much. Little by little Elaine and I were to learn such terms and phrases in that delicate tongue as were needful to us. Frequently also, to our vast amusement, we were able to employ them in the company of the less informed who had no idea, for instance, that pine means "prick" and les fesses the "bottom." Numerous were the ladies of our acquaintance who had learned only "polite French" and little enough of that. We were to play many merry japes by virtue thereof, though afterwards pretending with affected coyness and even dismay that we had been mistaken completely as to the true meaning of the words.

From Pearl on this memorable night I learned, too, the value of discretion, for while the Comte regaled us with such wicked tales as would have allowed him to compile his own Thousand and One Nights, she remained charmingly evasive as to her own. Thus one is most subtly portrayed as having less experience than others which, in the eyes of many males - as also not a few females - renders one the more desirable. A whore is not sought after unless by those who pathetically jingle sovereigns in their pockets for a mean two minutes pleasure.

An hour passed before we returned to play the game which Rabelais rather crudely described as that of the "two-backed beast." Elaine was to receive her Papa's accolade in her bottom, as had been promised, while I was to attend to both the Comte and Roald - the latter to put his penis to my lips while our host, having me kneeling before him, gave my cunny a fresh injection. Pearl, as she proclaimed, was to be the ring-mistress and to this end first made great play of drawing my cousin to the selfsame table over which she had been birched. No such punishment being due this time, however, Pearl placed a small blue velvet cushion upon the edge of it, upon which Elaine was to rest her tummy.

Her legs being well-spread and her bottom showing a perfect cleft orb, her Papa then toyed with her gently, bidding her be still and obedient in future as was his wish. To this Elaine gave no reply, affecting as ever some would-be shy confusion as first he eased his fingertips about her cuntlips, the better to moisten and excite her. I, being uncertain again as to whether in the final event she would endeavour to spring up again, held back my stallions until his rod had sought the tightness of her hole. Placing one hand in the small of her back and urging her gently to keep her bottom well poised, he oiled his fingers from a phial that waited accommodatingly for the purpose and caused her to wriggle much and to sigh and to moan as he then lubricated her puckered rosette.

"She has taken a young man's cock up there this very day and may now enjoy the paternal one," said Pearl who much enjoyed ordering young ladies about. So saying, she clamped her hand firmly upon the back of Elaine's neck and - bidding my uncle step back a little - began to massage and finger her all about her bottom and beneath while whispering to her what I had no doubt were all sorts of erotic fancies.

Breathing softly and keeping her face hidden in the crook of her arms which were folded upon the surface of the table, Elaine commenced rotating her bottom lasciviously while her Papa waited with urgently strumming cock to take his prize.

He was not long about it, for being "finger-dipped" - as Pearl called it - which is to say that she began working her forefinger in and out of Elaine's rosehole, the maiden's cleft was soon taken by her father's prick which rammed slowly into her until her quivering shoulders and whimpering sounds told of her pleasure. Not until his penis had all but emerged and then had sheathed itself again did I resort to my pair. At one end I sucked greedily upon Roald's prick with my mouth while my love-lips. pouted equally upon the Comte's stiff tool. Thus with many wracking cries - my own being entirely muffled - did we all glide down the hill of bliss.

Finishing his course first, my uncle withdrew his steaming weapon with an audible plop which left Elaine's bottom as well-creamed as I have ever seen one. Being not long in following, I loosed Roald's cock from my mouth for just sufficient time to call upon both to lather me equally which they did with more vigour than even I had hoped.

Thus wearied of our games, all finally dispersed to bed. It being well and tactfully understood that the men would require their rest, I took to the sheets with Elaine who had been too well pleasured for her now to deny it.

"I told you that Papa had a big one," she murmured triumphantly, as if all had come about by her own endeavours rather than by the urgings we had found it necessary to employ.

"As to that, you have neither seen nor felt the last of it," I replied, though cuddling her to me warmly. Our fingers sought each other's dells, for to reminisce about such without accompanying titillation would be as to eating strawberries without cream.

"What then of yours, for you have not been so venturesome as I," she declared as one might who has earlier lost much ground and will now recover it by whatever means possible.

"Papa?" I exclaimed in astonishment, for though it would not be entirely truthful to say that the idea had by now not crossed my mind, I had truly not given much account to it. "That is different, for I am younger than you," I replied with a remarkable lack of logic that caused me to smile in the darkness.

"We shall see, for what I have received you must also, else I shall be cheated upon. Come, say that you will be as bold as I."

I would not. I giggled and evaded her questions. Even so, the very thought of it made me part my thighs more eagerly to her caresses.

CHAPTER X

All was utter decorum the next morning when, in the discreet fashion of ladies and gentlemen who have partaken of mutual pleasures, we breakfasted and bid the Comte and Roald a fond adieu. This being conducted without any suggestive mannerisms or caresses pleased me. Being somewhat constrained as first with her Papa, Elaine soon fell into the ease of things when it came upon her that we were simply three ladies and a gentleman returning to their hotel and that not a whit of lewdness lay visibly about us.

I flattered myself not that the Comte had specially chosen us and had few doubts that the night would yet see others jousting in our place. No sense of jealousy or loss occurred to me. I was wise enough perhaps to apprehend that we had used one another, though not selfishly but in mutual accord. Elaine who had but long days before boasted to me of her knowledge of all things amorous, now betrayed a naivety that both amused and made one feel more fond towards her than ever.

"Have we not done all that could be done - I mean by way of being wicked?" she asked when, upon arriving, the three of us took by silent accord to Pearl's suite while my uncle absented himself. So saying, she then began to prattle on about what she had read in her Papa's books, hopeful perhaps that she might so impress Pearl.

"No, my dear," Pearl replied at last by way of answer to Elaine's first question. "Not to put too fine a point upon it, you have entertained a cock in your cunny and also in your bottom, but you have yet to have one in each at the same time."

My cousin's face was a picture and at the very thought she wriggled about upon her seat, pretending amazement that it might be possible.

"Indeed it is, and blissful it can be if the males are not too rough with one, though that is not a contingency I anticipate in our circles," Pearl responded and went on, "You are still but at the beginning of your adventures and indeed your tuition, for you are brought here for the latter as much as the former. Just as a fiddler may draw many melodies from his violin, so may we with our bodies and our ingenuity. The mind above all is the most marvellous instrument and can excite ideas which at the moment may be beyond your ken. Had Arabella, for instance, fallen at your Papa's feet last night and begged him to desist from his attempts upon you, you might still remain among the unconverted. As it is, you have let yourself go and have been deeply enriched both in sensations and emotions. It is they you must utilise as much as your fine forms, for the one will lead to the fulfillment of the other."

"You mean, to use our imaginations?" I asked, thereby coming to the rescue of Elaine who looked a little put out that she had not impressed Pearl as much as she had wished to do.

"Precisely, Arabella. No two things and no two events are ever quite the same. Both of you have now proven delightfully perverse and will I am sure remain so. Indeed, you will flourish, for it would be a poor outcome if either of you were to settle into marriage before having tasted all the fruits in the garden."

"Elaine has already had the forbidden fruit," I said mischievously, causing my cousin to squeal and shush me.

"It is as well she did. Such barriers put up by a hypocritical society are not for us. There are only two rules whereby we guide ourselves. The first is complete refusal to participate in the body's pleasures, for ultimately the proclaimed will of the individual must be respected. The second - as I need hardly say - is that the giving of pain must be avoided at all costs."

"Oh, but Papa stung me with the birch!" interjected Elaine.

"Stuff and nonsense, girl, he but burnished your bottom. You had not a mark to show upon it afterwards and naught but pleasure in the outcome. For the most part, young women of your age receive such admonitions of the birch through their drawers and conceal thereby their ultimate modesty. Many a girl at boarding school receives the birch, the cane or the strap before her Papa lays hand in turn to her bottom. Such as are brought to so-called illicit delights in that way may count the birching a part of the bargain, for it persuades the girl to a submissive posture and a readiness to succumb. Finding that the cock spouts pleasurably in her and that she is frequently afterwards fondled and rewarded for her compliance, all is then well. Such is far better than that she may be taken to the marriage bed in ignorance. Come, Elaine, sit upon my lap and tell the truth. Did you not like it?"

My cousin, obeying, found her thighs and pussy immediately prey to Pearl's caresses and thus answered in heat more quickly than she might otherwise have done that she had found it indeed to her liking.

"And the birching? It did not really pain you? You were not in torture?"

"Oh no. It stung me and bit me, for some of those twigs had awful tips to them, but once I was made to...to...to do it, the stinging became a lovely glow and I felt the better for it."

"You were held and plugged, my pet, that is how it should be after your bottom has been well-warmed. A girl must be taken quickly if she is to succumb, else she may entertain all sorts of doubts and wriggle her way out of it. Once the cock has found its niche in her cunny or bottom and she is so held, then the outcome is certain. A gentleman is one who will then fuck her lovingly that she might partake of the delicious sensations and so be brought to the full sport of it. Shyness has a certain charm, however, and I wish you not to lose it. Come, Arabella, the minx is coming on heat. Attend to her bottom while I make her spill!"

Thus saying, Pearl drew up the back of Elaine's dress and raised it to her waist so that my cousin's bottom bulbed out over Pearl's thighs. This allowing me perfect access to her nether charms, I threw myself down beside them and worked my forefinger delicately up into her bottom-hole while Pearl tickled her clitty.

"Oh, oh, what are you at?" gasped Elaine who jiggled this way and that but - being firmly held - could not escape.

"A little introduction, my pet, to what two cocks may feel like though I fear that our fingers are rather small for it."

"HAAAAAR! I c...c...could not!" my cousin moaned, though seeming to like the intrusion of my finger she weighed down upon it and so forced my finger in past the first knuckle while Pearl equally inserted her own into her slit. Then instructing me briefly, Pearl told me to feel for the sheathing of her own finger, at which I was to withdraw mine to the tip. At the emerging of hers, I was then to allow mine in turn to act as the "poker." Thus did I gain the art of it, and Elaine too, emitting an "OOOH-AH!" each time we deftly worked our digits alternately. Indeed, there were moments in my haste when I could feel the pressure of Pearl's finger through the membrane that divided the two orifices and from this I also learned the purpose of so pleasuring in this way.

Clutching at Pearl's shoulders, Elaine seemed unable to speak, though she several times attempted to. Her hips pumped and her breath literally whistled out.

"Ah! she is coming again!" cried Pearl whose fingers were already well lubricated while I sensed upon my own a filmy moisture such as in my own case had much improved my bout with Roald. This, Pearl said afterwards, was a secretion provided by Nature when sufficient titillation was provided, though in the case of male penises some warm sweet oil was always to be recommended, for then it afforded immediate pleasure to both parties.

After such enervating trials as she endured in the next few minutes, Elaine slipped from our grasp and lay quietly curled up upon the floor, Pearl nudging her playfully with her toes and winking at me.

"Her Papa shall not so have her bottom while another is in her cunny, for he would be too big. Young boys are the better for this sport, their penises being thinner and, besides, they may be trained to it. We females may be put often enough to our trials, but so must some men be, particularly when they are young and malleable."

Relieved no doubt by what she had heard about herself and what might have been playfully termed her future prospects, Elaine thereupon sat up and listened, saying not unwisely that while she was thoroughly prepared to offer herself up to the sport, she feared the shadow of indiscretions.

"Wisely said, Elaine," Pearl complimented her, "and hence two conditions obtain. The first is that one must beware of betraying oneself in indiscreet company. You may flirt, my kittens, as you wish, but that is an utterly different thing from showing that you are prepared to be pleasured. The gentleman who handles you rudely - that is to say one who fondles you upon early acquaintance as if you are his property - is to be spurned. He is surely one who will retail his exploits to others, in his Club or elsewhere."

"What did you mean by compromise?" I asked.

"You seize well upon the point, Arabella. Another term for it is 'inducing.' Let us take the example of a young lady - fair of figure and looks - who one suspects has within herself the seeds of mischief. She may be well chaperoned, or she may have been so ignorantly apprised by her Mama of all matters appertaining to sexual joys that she starts as might any nervous filly at the first touch of a hand. It may even be that she pretends to have moral scruples. In such a case it is as well for her to be seduced first by the ladies - two such as you," Pearl said with a twinkle. "That this might be easily accomplished we know from our experiences in boarding school where few of us have not got between the sheets eventually with another girl, or two. The skilfulness of the maiden's seducers is requisite, for she must be brought to a point of panting and frothing at which she will accept the cock of a male kept secretly in waiting. Her female companions, having viewed the bout with pleasure, now have her more at their command. However, she must be guided and not forced. Her own inclinations, stirred by what has happened to her, will bring her along in the end and so perhaps make her an accomplice in other desired matters. Thus is a chain initiated and all may be kept within a closed circle. Each relies upon the other, and secrecy is all."

"As with our visit to Paris, for dear Mama does not dream of what we are at," exclaimed Elaine.

"Precisely so, though I have known it to be the other way around, when the Mama has acted as the Messalina while her sons and daughters are kept in ignorance of the fact. It is never too late to induct even a lady of maturity, provided that her face and figure are of sufficient attraction. Sometimes this may come about without design and needs not the intervention of outsiders. Thus I have known of a high-placed Society lady who was inadvertently caught in the bathroom by her young son and his school-friends. Believing them to be safely playing in the garden, she had left the bathroom door ajar.

"When it fell upon her that they were watching her through the crack of the door, with much whispering and giggling, she felt exceedingly put out and called down her wrath upon them, saying that both were to be severely spanked. While clambering from the bath and quickly drying herself, she ordered them into her boudoir where, she said, they were to doff their trousers. Attired then only in a bathrobe, she entered to find the two penitents bent over with their ears thoroughly burning to think they had been so caught out.

"Making no bones about the matter, as she thought, the dear lady put their bottoms side by side - exposed as they were - and attended to the smacking of each, causing them to yelp and squirm. In the process, however, she could not help but note that their cocks had arisen, for not only were they stimulated by her spanking palm but also by the delicious perfumes that emanated from her. Saying then that she had never seen such a disgusting sight, she - ill-advisedly as might be thought by some - took hold of their stiff pintles in turn while continuing to spank them. At this of course they became thoroughly excited and knew not whether to sob or emit their natural sounds of pleasure.

"Perceiving this, as she was bound to, the lady felt well the throbbing of their slender tools, for they made perfect handles to hold, as it were. With each smack they moved their cocks more and more excitedly in her hand until she feared they would come. 'You naughty bad boys, I know not what to do with you,' she cried, whereat they were allowed to rise. Turning about and with their bottoms well smarting and their pricks lewdly displayed, they begged for her forgiveness. Casting himself against her, her son caused his penis to intrude between the folds of her robe and so press to her belly, saying that he felt most strange.

"At this a lewdness fell upon all three. Passing behind the good lady, the boy's chum raised her robe and impressed his cock in turn to the groove of her ample bottom. Thus all but transfixed, she knew not how to comport herself. The persuasive rubbing of their penises fore and aft soon quickened her senses, however. With much pretended remonstrance, she allowed herself to be tumbled upon the bed, there to receive her son's cock in her cunny while his friend pestled her bottom. In no time at all a throbbing course was run which put her into quite a delirium of pleasure, for both her orifices frothed to her entire satisfaction."

"As well as theirs, no doubt," I chuckled.

"Without doubt, Arabella, for she returned to the sport again and again thereafter, swearing both to secrecy while entertaining them in the same wise on her bed each afternoon. None knew of this, for she affected otherwise the airs of a saint."

"How then did you know?" I enquired.

"As to that, my dear, it came about by accident. Being on a visit to the house, I was changing in a small room adjacent to her boudoir when the boys - not knowing of my immediate presence - rushed in and began to tumble her with much love and jollity, upping her skirts and I know not what and declaring that their cockles were longing to be milked, as they put it. Being horrified that I was a silent witness to this, she chased them out and then fell to crying when I appeared. For she believed me, too, you see to be a model of propriety. I however comforted her and assured her that if there was such sport to be had, she must not deny herself."

"Oh, then, did you join in?" asked Elaine.

"No my dear, I did not, for I perceived that the lady required her pleasures to be taken alone. Such as are like that must be respected. Swearing myself to secrecy, I nevertheless gave her bottom a thorough whipping, saying that this would exculpate her from past and future sins. Truly she believed me and I have no doubt that she returned to the field of love as soon as I had left, for once such pleasures are begun they are hard to leave off."

"How I would love to do that," I said, as much to put myself ahead of Elaine as anything else.

"Why then you shall, for there are many fresh young cocks to be teased and put up to one, much as a young girl may herself be put up to an older male. A well-behaved couple of lads are required, for they must be taught discretion. They can be trained to be of service to ladies, rather as our young friend was at the dressmaker's. Another pretty device is to have a fervent prick in one's bottom while the cunny is being tongued by a pretty young lass. Ah yes, that is an extreme pleasure!" quivered Pearl whose eyes were positively reminiscent in their glowing.

"Tell us more," begged Elaine, for having heard all that she had, she felt not so much wicked herself as more of a comparative innocent who has but dipped her toes in the waters of passion.

"In time you shall both learn all that I can teach you. You did well to read your Papa's naughty romances, my dear, but such for the most part are rather simple in their ways. You will devise your own games, for there is half the pleasure in so doing. Be lewd or be shy in your taking of the cock, but be not in-between, for that is dull. Speak not of your amorous encounters to others lest you trust them implicitly, or they may make a mischief of it."

"What, though, if one is caught out? Have you never known such a contretemps?" I ventured.

"There are ever to be mishaps, Arabella. One must learn to deal with them. You might put on boldness, for instance, or you might fall to weeping and declaring that it was but your first slip, that is to say, as long as you are young enough to be able to aver that. Another course is to turn the tables if you can, which of course may be done by involving in one way or another - then or later - the very one who has thought fit to steal in on you."

I was to remember those words and put them to good account later. Pearl, I was pleased to find, deemed me more mature in many aspects than my cousin, despite that I was junior in years to her. This I learned when Elaine excused herself from the room for a little while.

"There are different roles to be learned, which you will come to more naturally than Elaine, for I believe you to have a finer instinct for such things than she. I chide her not for her behaviour in being put to the birch, for it was her first time. She will come to enjoy being spurred on as time progresses. One must know when to yield and when to command. There are as many joys in submitting as in conquering. But I mystify you a little, Arabella. Promise to place yourself in my hands for we are going to have a little adventure this evening. I wish to see how you comport yourself."

A quiver of excitement ran through me. Her eyes were both mischievous and kindly. Knowing that she would bring us to no harm, I acquiesced with a nod and a smile.

"What a delightful girl you are, Arabella. Come, be my little slave. Kneel down before me, burrow your pretty face between my thighs and lick me, for I am about to come at the very thought of what you are going to enjoy!"

CHAPTER XI

Elaine was all of a flutter at the news of a mysterious visit we were to make. Thankfully, perhaps, I could tell her nothing of it. Had Pearl confided in me more I might have let her wheedle it out of me.

"Don't ask Pearl too much or she will be put out, she intends it to be a surprise for us," I said.

"Oh, very well, but I like to know what is happening."

"Sometimes it is best not to, surely there is much more fun in that," I replied, and knew the truth of it even as I spoke. Until now I had been able in great part to anticipate events. Now it was as if I were about to open doors beyond which lay mysteries. The thought made my veins tingle. Adorning ourselves in white waist corsets and white silk stockings with rosetted garters - "For purity," as Pearl said - we made ourselves ready. Neither chemises nor drawers were required. Our gowns being of velvet, we felt the soft comforting of them.

My uncle did not accompany us nor did he ask anything about our venture. Perhaps Pearl had primed him, perhaps not. He would enjoy himself, I had no doubt, with some midinette in our absence. A leather case containing two bottles of champagne accompanied us in our carriage. The corks were popped before we had reached the outskirts of Paris. Pearl insisted upon our quaffing all.

"Oh, I shall want to pee soon," Elaine declared, for the jogging of carriages frequently made one want to do that in any event.

"Then you must hold it and wait until we arrive," Pearl said. I wondered not a little at that, for it was ever easy enough to slip out of a carriage in the dark and relieve oneself within its shelter in the dark. Elaine wriggled exceedingly, for our supper had been a light one.

"Please, Pearl, I must!" she begged, but the lady was adamant and afforded me a sly smile in the dark. I, too, tingled and burned to pee and fancied not having to ask our unknown hostess for the means to do so the very minute we arrived. When we did it was with rather puffed faces and tightened bottoms.

"Ask as soon as we get in," Elaine blathered, receiving the crisp reply that we would be seen to. I quivered and read some meaning in Pearl's reply, as well I might have done. Alighting from the carriage with our feet crunching upon the gravel, we viewed before us the dark shadow of a chateau no less large than that of the Comte. Endeavouring to walk daintily, I yet wriggled - as did Elaine - while we mounted the steps and entered a grand hall, there to be met by a lady of calm demeanour who immediately beckoned us forward along to what I imagined just to be a drawing room.

In that I was wrong, for it proved to be a large chamber of most curious aspect. The walls were covered in blue velvet all about. Chandeliers glittered upon cushioned divans much as those we had pleasured ourselves on at the Comte's. There, however, the resemblance ended, for in the centre of the floor were a number of posts and bars affixed and from these hung straps and chains, the sight of which sent chills of wonder through me. Indeed, I made to step back as did my cousin. I was all of a tremble, fearful that harm was about to befall us and that perhaps even Pearl had not foreseen this.

I was wrong, of course, and felt myself impelled forward by a gentle push in the back.

"Oh, Madame, I wish to...,"started Elaine, her voice quavering with more than a little apprehension showing in it.

"My dear, I know what you wish to do. Your tummy is all of a bubble with a surfeit of champagne, is it not, and dying to release it through your pretty cuntlips. Which is the daughter and which the niece?" our hostess asked. She was a lady of imposing stature, perhaps a year or two younger than Pearl. Her gown was black and artlessly simple in design, the front being ruched and forming revers. A broad band of black velvet with a single stone glittering at the front of it adorned her swan-like neck.

"This is the daughter," Pearl replied, indicating Elaine who twisted her hands together in wonderment and squirmed her hips in dumb appeal.

"Good. She knows the throbbing of a cock, then, as well as the other. Let us not delay matters, however. They desire to relieve themselves and I have two gentlemen here who delight in such spectacles. If either of them wets herself as yet then she will be whipped the more soundly. Bring the niece to a post and I will deal with the daughter."

"Madame!" shrieked my cousin even as I, receiving a light pressure from Pearl's hand in the small of my back, allowed myself to be impelled forward. Our hostess would have no nonsense. Taking Elaine by the back of her hair, she gave my cousin no quarter. "I don't understand!" cried she, "oh, I shall disgrace myself - I cannot hold it!"

"But a second or two," the lady abjured in a softer tone. The posts looked stout indeed, being set into the floor and with a small protrusion at the front of each, the purpose of which I was soon to learn.

"Oh, stop, please stop!"

The cry of course was Elaine's. I remained mute, though feeling all sorts of tinglings of apprehension course through me. Had Pearl misjudged? Were we to be put to torture? A gasp from myself and my cousin and our backs were put to the posts.

"Bend your knees a little, Arabella," murmured Pearl, quite ignoring the beseeching looks of wonder that I gave her. I was soon to learn the purpose of the command, for as I did so, a broad strap affixed to the back of the post was passed around my body and fastened tightly under my armpits. Therewith another secured my waist. Thus did I hang a little in a most curious posture, my legs being forced to part in order that I could better support myself.

"No, no, no, please!" Elaine babbled, but we were set to the posts with such calm and determined efficiency that ere we knew it our gowns were upped and tucked so well in that the lewdness of our enforced postures was on full display. Therewith I discovered also the purpose of the slight bulge that protruded from the front of the post, for it aided in the support of my bottom, my knees being bent and my feet splayed. Then were we both gagged with broad strips of velvet cloth, naked from the waist down save for our gartered stockings and the lower edges of our tight little corsets beneath which our navels twinkled.

Well satisfied that we were secured, our hostess then clapped her hands, whereupon two gentlemen of middle years entered, naked save for white shirts and with their cocks standing well up.

"Are they not a delicious pair? They are about to pee," laughed the lady, adding, "Maria, bring the bowls!"

I saw no one else, but then out from behind a screen scuttled a young maid who bore a white porcelain chamberpot in either hand which she placed one by one deftly between our feet and then disappeared. At that the lady smiled and, advancing upon us, tickled our bellies and cunnies together, for Elaine and I hung not two feet apart. I gasped within my gag and heard a splashing sound.

"Oh heavens, she has begun! Gentlemen, quickly!" exhorted our hostess, her place being quickly taken by the two males who stood one in front of each of us, rubbing their cocks as Elaine and I began to pee.

I could not help myself, in full sight of a male whose prick stemmed ready and whose balls hung with a heaviness that betokened the pleasure that must surely follow. I stared at him. My boldness perhaps surprised me. Our eyes burned into each other's. I was exposed. The lips of my quim ridged themselves slightly as a powerful jet splashed down from me to gurgle and hiss in the waiting bowl. His eyes lusted as I had never seen a man's do. He licked his lips and even stayed his hand upon his cock. The moment seemed to me one of wonderment.

My cheeks, deeply reddened, were already puffed. I wanted not the gag, yet understood it. In Elaine's case rather than my own it was a required precaution. A last, thinner jet wisped down from my cunt to be followed by a few golden drops. My eyes must have invited, for he then put himself to me. The purpose of my knees being bent became more obvious. He had but to flex his own and take my hips in order to impel his enflamed knob within me. I knew from the grunting sounds beside me that Elaine was being similarly accommodated, but I cared not of her in that moment. My own pleasure was rampant.

Well moistened as I was his thick, long shaft eased up within me as if oiled. Our bellies touched, his legs quivered violently. Tearing the gag from my mouth he applied his lips to mine. With that the last few inches of his pestle were squeezed desirously between the velvet walls of my sheathe. The sensation was divine. Our thighs trembled together. Groaning a little into my yearning mouth wherein our tongues twisted lewdly, he began to fuck me slowly. The sensation of being bound and helpless was one I found to my liking. The grip of his hands at my hips, though unnecessary, was masterful.

Naught was said. Standing to the rear of our stallions, Pearl and our hostess observed the spectacle with pleasure. I was nameless as was Elaine. His feet pressed against the chamberpot into which my offering had haplessly poured. It was a moment of obscenity and sweetness such as must be experienced to be known. Neither of our males was in any hurry about the matter, but pumped us steadily. Our breaths panted into each other's mouths. Perhaps more dazed than I, Elaine nevertheless received the urging shaft as greedily as I, else she would have whimpered and sobbed as I knew her sometimes to do.

The art of it was in the comparative silence, for the males were merged with us as surely as we were bound to the posts.

This I understood better later. For the nonce I yielded to the glory of the throbbing cock which I inundated several times before the pace quickened. My bottom bumped a little on the protrusion that helped to support it but I found no discomfort therein. Rather did the rubbing of its polished surface titillate me. Our lips and tongues worked the faster - then, gripping my hips more strongly, he expelled his sperm in long, leaping shoots that the inner squeezings of my cunny impelled. On and on the flow went until the last ecstatic shudders came upon us and we were done.

"It is good," our hostess said. Moving forward, she passed her hands under the men's buttocks and held them into us for a moment, as though all four of us were subject to her will. Then his tool slipped from me and he retreated, as did his companion, to the divan which immediately faced the posts. The maid reappeared and offered them cigars. Through a blue haze of smoke they regarded us lazily while we were released.

"They are more docile now than you," the lady laughed. I had expected petulance and cries from Elaine but she wisely desisted from any such silly displays. She knew not whether to laugh or cry, I think.

"They may bathe now?" Pearl asked. A gracious reply being received, we were escorted upstairs where we bathed at leisure and then returned down much more comforted, though this time to an ornate drawing room where cold meats, fish and salad were set out upon a low table around which we sat on cushions in the Oriental fashion. The two gentlemen were present, being attired in trousers again.

"A pleasant diversion, was it not?" Pearl asked Elaine and I. We were in company and there was to be no gaucheness.

"Quite amusing," I replied languidly while my cousin smiled over the rim of her glass. "But we have not been introduced," I added.

Such formalities were rapidly effected. Our hostess, it seemed, was one Mary Grey who had lived in France for several years. She had been a governess at one time and had come into money through the favours of her last employer who apparently had much good reason for being pleased with her methods. I suspected that was not the entire story, but let discretion obtain. By degrees she revealed all. Her employer had been a certain Lord L - who in pursuit of pleasures had purchased and set her up in this house that she might further their mutual amusements. He required her only to be as inventive as possible in order that he and such guests as he sent from England, or who accompanied him, would be fully entertained.

As might be expected, I bristled rather at this, feeling that we had been used as common whores. Though I did not have time to express myself on the matter, I was well anticipated.

"It is not as you think, Arabella," remarked Mary, "for only young ladies from the best families are themselves entertained here. It is a refuge for all sorts of games where one is perfectly free from interference or the knowledge of others. That you were a little roughly treated was part of your education."

"Oh indeed, but perhaps we did not need it," Elaine said tartly.

"Tut tut, my dear, we all do. Even an old dog may be taught new tricks. The gentlemen here expect to make no payment, nor the young ladies to receive any. Be not put out, for it was in fun. Have you not learned a little?"

At this, one of the gentlemen, who had so far taken no part in the conversation, leaned forward and spoke rapidly in French to our hostess who listened politely, nodded, and then regarded Elaine.

"The two gentlemen would like to enjoy you together, my dear. Are you willing?" she asked.

A quite comical expression passed over my cousin's face at that. She was clearly taken aback at this straightforward request. Being seated beside her, I passed my arm about her waist and drew her back upon the floor so suddenly that she had no time to resist.

"Yes, she will," I laughed and thereupon smothered Elaine's mouth with my own, clasping her body tightly beneath her armpits. "You will, will you not?" I asked her softly.

"I don't want to with both of them!" she gasped.

"Yes you do, you silly, you may suck one and have the other in your pussy at the same time," I said, observing out of the corner of my eye while kissing her that the two gentlemen had risen and were solemnly removing their slippers and trousers.

"No, no, no - you do it," she babbled and attempted to twist about in my arms whereat Pearl came and stood right over her, straddling her figure, so that she pinned her down by her gown with her heels.

"An end to this coyness, girl. Rise, Arabella, and leave her. All is to be voluntary. Up with your dress, Elaine, and prepare to put yourself to them. NOW!"

So abrupt and seemingly cold were Pearl's words that Elaine obeyed her more quickly perhaps than she had done anything before. Her legs being so delightful in shape, her bottom so round, and her cunny seeming to pout for attention, none could help but admire her as she lay pettishly waiting for the attentions that were soon enough bestowed on her. Expressing themselves with many words of praise which I could distinguish well enough, one gently skewered her thighs apart and lay upon her - deftly inserting his rampant weapon, while the other knelt by her head and brought her mouth up to his knob.

"How strange that she is still hesitant," I murmured to Pearl and Mary who stood with me watching.

"It is but her way. I believe she prefers it for it titillates her the more. We all have our little foibles and hers are not unattractive," replied Mary who was as fascinated by we at the manner in which Elaine took to the sucking of one stiff penis while the other sported back and forth in her slit. Her cheeks were pink, her eyes closed. Little puffs and pants of satisfaction came from all three.

"I do believe she likes being put on exhibition," I laughed, quite certain that in the rising miasmas of her pleasure Elaine would scarce hear a word. Coiling her stockinged legs up over the buttocks of the man who was fucking her, she began urging him on with her heels while drawing in her cheeks at the sucking of the other.

"There is a pride in it that a lusty young lady soon comes to know," said Mary, caressing my bottom as she spoke. "Your horizons are ever being broadened, Arabella. Once complete freedom is obtained in putting yourself to the cock, happiness is certain. In the summer here we have meadow fucks and they are very pretty."

"What then are they?" I asked.

"Picnics, my dear, with much wine and frivolity. Then two or three young ladies are fucked side by side in the warm grass. If there is not an extra prick to suck upon at the same time, one or other may draw upon the neck of a wine bottle and empty it even while she is receiving her other libation. Ah look, the devil is coming in her mouth!"

It was true. He who was receiving Elaine's oral attentions, withdrew his pulsing cock completely, twitched her nostrils between thumb and forefinger, and - thus forcing her mouth to remain open - expelled his long shoots of juice deep within, groaning much as he did so. This being apparently the signal for his companion - who waited until the last dribblings had been expelled - Elaine was then on her own under her stallion who wasted little time in pumping her cunny so well that she was completely inundated at both ends and lay in a seeming daze as his weapon in turn withdrew from between her love-lips.

Suffice to say that within the hour I was accorded the same dual salute and found enormous pleasure in sucking on a meaty shaft while the other was pestling me. The taste of sperm I found slightly salty but by no means obnoxious. It was the best possible thing for the complexion, I was told, and such surplus as remained upon both my pairs of lips was laughingly rubbed all about my face. After this, I required to bathe again, as Elaine did, whereupon - looking far more demure than we had upon arrival - we were kissed and complimented by all and took our departure.

At the hotel my uncle waited our return with obvious pleasure, though naught was said to him of what had passed. One rarely discusses such things in distant aftermaths. What is done is done. Such pleasure as had been taken is but to be renewed. Only when it is may confidences be exchanged. Reminiscences are best exchanged or conveyed in the heat of the moment, unless it be in immediate converse - such as at the Comte's - after several lubricious bouts.

I spent the night alone. Carried to bed by her Papa, my cousin uttered not a squeak of protest. I had no doubt, however, that she would find cause to struggle prettily on less private occasions.

CHAPTER XII

A few more days having passed in diverse sports, we returned to England, having learned more than pride would oftimes allow us to confess. That mattered not to Pearl who was wise enough to know that consent lies often in silence. Our general air of wellbeing was obvious to all. Having actually visited the Louvre, the Tuileries and other places of notable interest over several afternoons, we were able to talk about them and thus allay any doubts as to the official reason for our visit.

But a week after our return, when life began to seem unconscionably dull again and not a penis had pulsed its longing before my eyes, Pearl brought news that she said would please me. I was invited to a wedding.

Socially interesting as the prospect appeared to be, it hardly filled me with the sense of excitement that I needed. I was too polite, of course, to say so. Imbued with mischief and meaning to tease me, Pearl allowed me at first to think that that was all there was to it. Soon enough, however, she divulged such further news of the event as made my eyes sparkle.

The bridegroom was to be one Ewart Maudsley, an honourable gentleman of the realm, who had reached the prime of his life at the age of forty-two. His bride-to-be was a widow, Catherine, who counted her years four less than he, and had two charming daughters and a son.

After the ceremony, which by necessity would be a non-ecclesiastical one, since Mr. Maudsley was divorced, there would be a private reception, said Pearl who could well see that I was bubbling for her to get to the point.

"Well, then, I shall tell you, for I have teased you with mundane facts for too long, Arabella. There is a certain tradition in the lady's family which decrees that upon marriage or remarriage the bride is to be anointed."

"Oh, Pearl, you tease still! What does that mean and how does it interest me?"

"It will interest you muchly when I say that anointment is understood to be by means of a spouting penis well lodged in one or other of the bride's orifices! More than one, in fact, for it is decreed that the bride shall be mounted by all the male guests present and that the bridesmaids and others may follow suit."

"Good heavens, do you really mean that this is a family tradition!"

"In this case yes, my pet, rare as the custom may be. The bride's mother herself was so saluted many years ago, and two of her sisters have been. It is said to be a ceremony akin to those that take place along the lower orders at harvest time when the field women are stripped and take part in lewd pagan ceremonies. Have you not heard of such?"

"Indeed no. But wait! I do recall now that on the last harvest I wished to view the celebrations of the farmworkers, but that Papa forbade me to go. He said it would not be seemly for me to attend."

"Indeed, Arabella, for while the menfolk would not have dared draw you into the proceedings, you would have seen many a bottom or cunny tupped over the hayricks. Such comes from ancient times, I am told, when it was believed that with the harvest all should be fertilised again."

"Really, I cannot wait after what you have told me! Dear Pearl, you have always been my mentor, and indeed Elaine's. You have guided us along the paths of naughtiness to excellent effect. Tell me then how it will be and how it is that I am invited."

"You are invited by dint of my mentioning your divine talents most confidentially to Catherine. You may think it strange that she does not otherwise indulge in lewdnesses, but believes it her duty to follow in the tradition. It will not be a rumbustious affair for the guest list is very much hand picked and will be held in her future home which is being furnished now for the occasion. Catherine will not be the only one to be laid on the altar of love, as I have indicated. There will be two bridesmaids and they, of course, are already apprised of their fate."

"But surely this will break the circle of discretion and secrecy!"

"By no means, my pet, for the bridesmaids are her daughters. The older one, Grace, is eighteen and a proud young thing. She may not be easily put over. The younger, Susan, is but fifteen and as pretty a cherub as you could see. She has a mite more mischief in her, though is only to have her bottom breached so that her virginity as such may be conserved for a few years."

"Oh my goodness - and this is to happen in the sight of all?"

"How else? Otherwise the daughters would not be able to attend, and that would be quite unthinkable. As to our own role, you will be a Mistress of Ceremonies, if you wish, for Catherine is quite content to leave all such things in the hands of others. There is by tradition a curious formality about the affair, as you will see. The bride is not required to speak and must certainly not invite. Having herself chosen the due hour for her anointment - though I feel that the term were better expressed in the plural - she enters and offers herself quietly upon the altar which will be either a divan or a table, as her desire dictates."

"What a strange and wonderful affair! Yet will there not be an uncomfortable hiatus in it all, Pearl, for once the gentlemen have loosed their anointing sperm in her, the daughters may be restive in awaiting their own fate."

"Such also was foreseen in the beginning. It is said that the tradition in Catherine's family runs for many hundreds of years. The males attending will number no more than six, as also will the females. Each is to receive the prick in succession, but only the last one to mount is permitted to come. Any gentlemen who do so inadvertently or by becoming over-excited must quit the arena. The way is thus left free for any further enjoyment."

"Mr. Maudsley then - or perhaps I should begin to call him Ewart - will have a delightful harem of three after the event!" I exclaimed.

"As to that, Catherine opines that having been inducted, as it were, the girls are not to be further brought to pleasure by him thereafter, but I fear she is behind the times and may have to be content with a third of his offerings in the future. However, that is not for us to say. Catherine means to carry herself in a proud manner and not to indulge, as she says, in an orgy. What quaint ideas she has, for she has already been through it once when her Papa and her brothers anointed her dell. She had no passion for them, she says, though took their cocks dutifully. Being men of honour and in full knowledge of the rules of the affair, they did not attempt her thereafter."

"I can scarce believe what I am hearing, Pearl! Do you then believe her?"

"Only in part. Catherine is, I believe, a secret worshipper at the altar of Priapus, though she may well have persuaded herself of her goodness. There have been hints of anniversaries. I believe her drawers were taken down for them, though she denies it. It is said, in the tradition, that two 'strangers' must attend to see that all is done and done well, and we are they. Thus are we privileged! She is of an age, of course, at which she might want to break out a little and hence our presence could well provide the excuse for it."

"Indeed, that is doubtless why she is leaving any persuasions to us," I declared.

"Of course, Arabella, for then she herself may be seen to be guiltless. There is a fine element of farce about it, naturally. I have no doubt that she has hinted to Ewart that we are there to protect her daughters."

"Well, we shall then - against hypocrisy," I laughed and fell to dreaming much about the strange affair, as may be imagined. I said naught to Elaine and neither did Pearl. My cousin's occasional gaucheness - whether put on or not - would have proved an irritant much as it frets me to say so. I apprised her later of the event and she was very put out at not attending, though persuaded it was not possible.

Within two days I had met our hostess-to-be. Catherine proved to be a superbly-figured woman with slumberous eyes, a jutting bosom and a fine derriere. Of the daughters, Grace was a little over medium height, brown haired and with a slight coldness of mien which the heat of Priapus soon must melt. Susan was perfectly delicious. Such a rosebud mouth, such promise in her already-swelling titties, and such a tight, round bottom as would have bewitched the hand or the tongue.

Sensing that Catherine wished to be led rather than questioned, I made my own pleasure in the intended ceremony plain to her, though in the most delicate of words. Upon asking her what Grace knew, I was told that she understood that certain freedoms would obtain and that she should display not overmuch primness or the occasion would be ruined. To this she had replied a trifle sullenly, as I understood, that she would have preferred to keep herself to herself, but did not wish to spoil her Mama's day.

This conversation between us taking place in Catherine's private drawing room which led off from her boudoir, Pearl declared it was time that we cleared the air a little better.

"Do you doubt, my dear, that Grace will be mounted in the after-fray, even as you?" she asked our hostess who placed her hands in her lap, flushed a little and twiddled with her rings.

"I am a little jealous as to that, Pearl," she confessed, "for Ewart produces an erection whenever we speak of her."

"I have no doubt that you have nursed it well, as a result, and caused him to spout quite deliciously," smiled Pearl. "Sweet Catherine, the primitive nature of your ceremony cannot be dimmed. Your skirts are to be upped - and utterly divine you will look, too, with your wedding dress floating up around your hips - and you are to be put to the cocks of the males in tribute. A fine ceremony indeed and one that should be broadened in Society. Either I or Arabella will bring the males to you. None shall exceed more than a dozen strokes in your quim lest they froth too soon. It will then be the turn of the ladies present to satisfy the lecherous pricks more fully. You may be sure that Arabella and I will not be backwards in our duties in this respect. There can be no respite for your daughters. Their drawers must come down and they must be put under. There, you see you find in me naught but frankness, which I do suspect is what you seek."

"Oh dear, I cannot bring myself to think of it!" exclaimed Catherine.

"Then you must," I made bold to say, though softly and in tones which appealed rather than dominated. "I have heard that such ceremonies - rare and indeed precious - are many centuries old and must remain unbroken in the family line or bad fortune will befall. It is a time of fruition, of pleasure and of renewal of the bodily spirits, is it not?"

I had rehearsed my little piece well. Catherine gazed at me in a manner that indicated both her surprise and pleasure that I should be so well schooled.

"I have not had the courage to explain it so to Grace and Susan," she said with a somewhat doleful air.

"Why, there is no need," Pearl interjected, "A rehearsal of a sort is requisite for Grace at least. Dear, sweet Susan will lend herself more easily to the occasion and by my judgement and Arabella's will squeal little when being pistoned by her first cock. Even so, it would be as well for her to be broken in a little. Of this you need know nothing," she added slyly. "After all, we are but anticipating by perhaps less than a year in both their cases what they will otherwise be brought surreptitiously to enjoy by such seducing males as they encounter."

Catherine grew flushed at this, but nodded. There was evident relief in her at what Pearl had said last.

"Yes, it is true. I feel guiltless when I do consider that, Pearl - and, as you say, I shall know nothing of what might occur - in the next day or two?" The question in her voice being put so slyly was amusing, yet Pearl as I treated the matter gravely, as befitted the occasion in Catherine's eyes. I truly believe that she thought of it as a natural extension to the more formal one of the marriage service, for she said she had been schooled to believe by her mother and sisters and her mother's mother that it was in the true nature of things for such a ceremony to be indulged in.

"You will not be harsh?" asked Catherine after we had risen from a discussion of more mundane matters - as women are wont to - such as clothes, food and wine.

At this Pearl raised her eyebrows. "There are times, Catherine, when a girl must be put over. Indeed, it happens to some mature ladies, too. Have we not all known it?"

"Yes, it is true," Catherine acceded and bestowed on each of us a kiss wherein a seeming purity mingled prettily with a fine tang of voluptuousness. I perceived then how fiery she would become when unleashed and had no doubt as to the future happiness of Mr.

Maudsley who was plainly setting himself up a cosy little harem.

"Have no doubt, Arabella, that she will become a perfect queen of desire once the merry-go-round is in motion," Pearl said upon our exit, thus echoing my own thoughts. "Now we must set ourselves to the seduction of Grace and Susan. There is no need to delay the matter. Either or both may run to their Mama afterwards, but Catherine - being now prepared - will know how to turn their complaints and will feel the better for it that it is brought out into the open."

"What machinations are here!" I jollied her, "what are your thoughts about it and how do we begin?"

"No, my pet, I shall not let you take such an easy course in instruction," she smiled, "for I prefer to hear your plans. I am quite sure that your busy little mind has been most active during our conversation with Catherine."

Being much pleased at this deferment to me, I had no hesitation in answering her and said that we should deal with Susan first, for she was likely to prove the least intractable of the pair. I then went on to divulge my plan which Pearl listened to with many a pleased smile and finally nodded, saying that she could have thought of none better herself.

Within the passing of the day we had consequently made our acquaintance with Ewart Maudsley who proved to be a gentleman of much charm, being neither portly nor spare, neither tall nor short and of reasonably handsome mien. We, Pearl declared to him in the comfort of his mansion, were to be the Maids of Honour at the occasion of his nuptials, though in a manner which would be less conventional than otherwise. At this he laughed heartily and begged us to proceed with our plans, having taken quite an eye for me, as I could see. I then being the spokeswoman made few bones about the deployment of my ideas concerning Grace and Susan. Were I to say that he listened earnestly, it would be a statement of some truth. Were I to say that he listened in a state of quite alarming arousal, that would be no less the case for I was scarce halfway through my narration when his trousers evinced distinct signs of bursting at the crotch.

"To put no veil upon the matter, sir, both must be threaded before the ceremony," I told him, "and I am quite sure that dear Catherine -

though we have not broached every detail to her - would not have her two dears put to rascals."

"Quite right, my dear, quite right," he replied and - rising to refill our glasses - brushed his concealed erection against my arm in passing in a manner that gave me to understand fully its length and hardness. If he sought for a libertine caress on my part, however, he was to be disappointed for I wished him to reserve his forces for the immediate task in hand, as my demeanour plainly showed, and that task was first to involve sweet Susan. Having apprised him of exactly the manner in which he was to comport himself in order that all should pass smoothly, I then presented myself to him again that evening in the company of a rather surprised Susan who felt herself unduly honoured to be a guest at dinner with her future Papa and myself.

"How delightful to see you two together, for I am sure you will be the greatest of friends," he declared once coffee had been taken. The servants having been quietly dismissed, I sat with Susan upon a suitable sofa and remarked on the prettiness of her dress, she having said so little for the past hour that her tongue seemed tied in a knot. Occasionally when both our eyes were upon her a delightful blush would spread into her features which so enhanced her appeal that I made bold to kiss her upon the mouth, saying that she had such cherry-lips as were irresistible.

Having frequently since taken others of Susan's age in hand, I am prone to regard it as one of my favourite occupations for wriggling is quite natural to them in the years before they attain their majority and this gives an added pleasure to their seduction. Being too timourous to resist, she allowed me to press her head back while our lips sweetly merged and I was able to suck upon the delicious nectar they exuded.

Upon seeing this, Mr. Maudsley rose and silently retired for a few moments into an adjoining room - I having earlier so coached him to do. With his absence I proceeded with my fondling of Susan and felt the melons of her titties under her dress while she - all flustered - knew not how to comport herself.

"Is it not nice to kiss and be a little naughty?" I murmured, pecking at the corner of her mouth the while and feeling the small buds upon her breasts begin to stir under my fingers. "Your dear Papa

- when he becomes such - will want to cuddle and kiss you in this wise, Susan, so I must teach you a little. Part your lips now and let me feel your roguish little tongue."

"Oh, I should not!" she whispered yet was already in such a flush that soon enough the petals of her mouth opened to my urging and with the most electric of thrills our tongues were entwined. She, however, being nervous of the imminent return of her future Papa made attempt to resist the sensations that I knew were coming well enough upon her, for her bubbies had swollen a little and were pressing amorously into my palm. Bearing her down slowly and with all gentleness, I brought the back of her head to rest upon a cushion in the corner of the sofa so that she was supine and in perfect position for the second part of the play that was about to commence.

Then, while her warm face was concealed under mine and she received the thrilling stabs of my tongue, Mr. Maudsley entered silently - having observed all through the doorway - and knelt before the sofa where Susan's legs dangled. The faint sound that he made in so positioning himself caught the ears of the young Miss who then endeavoured to struggle up from beneath me. I, pressing my weight securely upon her, held her while making a quick motion to Mr. Maudsley with one hand.

A muffled shriek from Susan announced that he had passed his hands up beneath her skirt and in the process uncovered her legs."No, no, no!" she shrieked and would have twisted her face from side to side had I given her the room or opportunity to do so.

"Off with her drawers quickly!" I cried, for the little devil was truly wriggling like a fish.

"I shall tell MA-MA!" came then her wild cry, but I intend not to dwell overlong upon the seduction of Susan, for by careful degrees she was soon enough laid full upon her back to his cock. Once his hands had unveiled her pretty little cunny which he then proceeded to lubricate and tease with his tongue and lips - holding her legs over his shoulders the while - her tempestuous resistance soon resolved, as I knew it would, into bubbling sobs of surrender. I, having unbuttoned her corsage and laid bare the snowy mounds of her tits, set to sucking upon their quivering tips which in turn led her to yield her mouth more warmly to mine while her tight little bottom jerked in positive delirium as she succumbed little by little in such a hot daze as I had once known myself.

Finding her then limp and acquiescent, her cheeks rosy, her mouth moist and her nipples fervent from my lips, I made my gesture to Mr. Maudsley whose rigid penis stood ready and uncovered as I drew her to the floor upon a thick rug and there parted her lovely young legs while bidding her to be perfectly still.

Ah, how she bucked and whinnied when first he went down upon her! Such attempt as she made to close her thighs at the approach of his cock was forestalled by a few little slaps on my part, for never was there a time to be more firm than this. Even so, I then lay alongside her, supporting her shoulders upon one arm and bidding her work her tongue to mine while he entered her. Stroking her hot face I felt the febrile jerking of her hips at the first nosing of his crest between her puffy lips. A startled moan, a clutching at me from her hands, and he was within. Her bottom bounced and twisted upon his hands for long moments while his rearing prick made its first acquaintance with the silky interior of her cunt. A final thin cry from Susan and he was full within, her thighs widening more eagerly than I had imagined as her narrow bottle took his cork.

"Now, Susan, give him your tongue, for you will soon enough be doing it often," I whispered to her, and though she sought to hold me I knew it better that she should go under him freely and so released myself and knelt to observe the delicious spectacle while he took full possession of her and finally frothed so freely in her purse that his effusion trickled down the silky inner surfaces of her thighs and left her bubbling for more.

At that, while their bellies still quivered warmly together and his incoherent murmurings of pleasure filled her ears, I left them well enough alone. One must judge such matters as one finds them. Of occasion I have found it necessary to repeat such initial preparations, for some young girls like ever to be comforted by the presence of an attractive female in their first surrenders upon the altar of Venus. I sensed in Susan, however, a warm and giving nature and - while knowing that she would continue to be a trifle shy for a while - was well aware that he would be able to bed her properly that night with naught but a token resistance.

The breaking-in of Grace was of far greater interest to me, for she would prove less pliable. However, since I had taken Susan in hand, the matter of her older sister was left to Pearl whose own narration of events I have allowed to make my next chapter.

CHAPTER XIII

It was decided between Arabella and myself (so runs Pearl's narrative) that we would deal with the girls separately and not in visible concord with one another. Thus both Grace and Susan would each be left free to think what they wished of us, and I had no doubt that such would be the nature of their experiences that they would be unlikely to indulge in confessions to one another until much time had passed.

    I recognised in Grace - as did Arabella - a stubborn case. Being just above medium height and with long flowing hair, she had such a figure as would rival the statuary of any of the Italian master sculptors. Her legs were long and superbly tapered, her breasts like full-grown melons and her bottom a perfect peach of delight, being so deeply cleft that its springy cheeks could ensnare a stiff prick firmly between them, once she was taught and tutored.

    I intended to stable her - knowing that there was no other way to deal with her - though it took some persuading on my part to inveigle her to the stable at dusk, which I judged the best time for her initiation. Some bribery in other directions was requisite in the manner and I finally settled upon a farm worker of good aspect and sturdy loins who for a couple of sovereigns (and all the delight he was to have) would do as he was told.

    "What is to do in the stable, then?" Grace asked me as we

proceeded hence.

"There is a young filly who is restive. I thought between us that we might calm her and settle her," I replied glibly.

"Oh, I know little enough about horses," she made to say and would have turned back had I not insisted that someone must accompany me. Making further demur about the matter, she was nevertheless persuaded to. The stable at that hour had either a cosy aspect or a slightly forbidding one, according to one's thoughts at the time. Grace evidently having no heart for such a jaunt would have again turned back even as we approached the doors, saying pettishly, "Oh, I can hear nothing."

"There will soon be much to be heard," I rejoined truthfully enough and, taking her by the elbow, guided her within where my enlisted accomplice lay already in waiting. I do not doubt that she apprehended instinctively some danger then, but the very moment that the threshold was passed, her ensnarement was complete. To a wild cry from her, I pinioned her arms while the labourer, Fred, springing from the wall against which he had flattened himself, blindfolded her swiftly and then secured her held wrists with a strong binding of cord.

"Oh! what are you at? My God, what IS this?" shrieked Grace, being bundled now to a bale of straw which had been placed in readiness for her.

"Close the doors!" I snapped to Fred while bending Grace well forward so that her mouth was buried in the straw and her bottom reared well for our endeavours. Pressing down upon her shoulders, I then saw to it that Fred upped her skirt and wreathed it securely about her waist - all this to the wildest of cries from Grace who clearly had not even been uncovered to her drawers in the presence of a male before.

"You shame me! Oh, my God you will pay for this, you beasts, you beasts!" screeched she while Fred attended to the ties of her white cotton drawers. At their falling I shared his gasp of admiration, for never was a more desirable bottom unveiled - to say naught of the bewitching columns of her stockinged legs which supported her glorious moon. "I will DIE!" screamed she - her voice but partly muffled by the straw, and brought to a horrified halt as I accorded her a very sharp SMACK indeed on her bared bottom.

"Die, is it, Grace?" I laughed, "Why, my girl, your bottom is in full bloom to be unveiled and for what it is about to be accorded. I have no help for it than to put you to it in this way and will not regret it for a moment. Your dear Mama would have you inducted, my sweet, for there is no other path for you to pleasure than this. Fred - hand me that schooling whip!"

"AH! I dare you! Oh, you beast, your horrid beast, who is this awful man looking at my shame? I shall see you in prison if you whip me! Pull up my drawers - release me! Oh, help me, someone!"

"I am about to help you, my pet - I! Keep her shoulders well down, Fred, for the bale is at a perfect height for it."

And indeed it was, for with the upper part of her body laid across its top, Grace's long shapely legs were kept at full stretch and so her naked bottom with its alluring cleft and a peeping of dark cunt-hairs beneath, was orbed to perfection.

"No, no, no, NO!" came her wild shriek as I stepped slowly back and measured my distance. It would not be the first time I had used the schooling whip which requires a much-practised twist of the wrist to make it most effective. I intended only using the very tip of course - as Grace discovered in a matter of a second or two as the scorching of it made itself feel like a bee-sting on her bulbous right cheek.

"NEEE-OW-OOOOOH!" came her shrilling cry, but I gave her no time to recover from it than I had accorded the same salute to her left hemisphere. Fred - standing so close by her - was afeared, I think, that the long uncoiling whip would somehow catch him for he wore an expression of mingled apprehension and pleasure, yet he was in no danger whatever as soon enough he learned. I had judged my distance to the inch, as one must in such exercises and had given Grace only her preliminary. By moving just six inches closer I could so snarl the leaping whip that some six to eight inches would sear across her glorious bottom.

"STO-HO-OP it this MOMENT! Oh, my God, NO! Let me UP!" screamed she, all unaware of my insidious approach as I viewed the two pink spots which the first strikes had left and which other and more practised damsels would have received as a distinct pleasure for they produce a positively sparkling fire. Grace, however, was to receive more than that, as she now discovered at the first real laying of the plaited leather across her writhing orb which brought a shriek such as might have lifted the rafters.

"You BEE-EE-EAST!" she sobbed, "oh, you will kill me!"

"No, my pet, I mean to enliven you," I replied, remarking with my searching eyes the distinct protuberance which had made itself visible in Fred's rough trousers. I had already made it my business, of course, to examine his penis in a goodly and upright condition and knew him fair for his intended task.

"CRA-AAAACK!" Ah, what a satisfying sound a well-placed whip does make across a yielded bottom! It is to be remembered, of course, that I was still but giving her a small measure of it as regards length, for to have used the schooling whip in all its majesty would have been undoubtedly cruel. It might be said, of course, that by so indulging myself I WAS being cruel, but having years past taken the whip myself in such a fashion I knew full well how the cushioning effect of the female bottom absorbs the sting. True, its effect is felt for a moment or two as a fierce burning, but that diminishes very rapidly provided the required wrist action is used, for this causes the leather to skim the ardent female globe rather as a skier mounting a crest.

The cries and moans that emanated from Grace now as I proceeded swishing the long-reaching leather this way and that would have indicated that she was suffering the pangs of hell whereas - had she but known it - I was heating her up for the divine moments that were shortly to follow. As hot-eyed as any lusty male might have been as he held Grace pinned and observed the wild and salacious wrigglings of her hips, Fred had already managed to unveil his long thick pego in anticipation of its entry.

Within a further minute and to diminishing cries from the over-proud young lady, I observed that her nether orb was already sufficiently well-streaked and reddened to require such cooling as only the male organ can render. Her sobs and wailings were piteous indeed, for now and again I gave her a particularly sharp one, sweeping the coiling whip right under her bottom so that she was forced to reach up on to her toes while her cries rippled and spread all about the stable walls.

"I can stand no more - no MORE!" she shrieked, raising her head briefly while Fred's strong hands bore down upon her shoulders.

"Very well, my dear, then the moment of your salvation is nigh.

You know not who holds you - only his name. He is, however, furnished with as big a cock as you are likely to encounter in the next few weeks, and you are about to take it, my girl."

"I will not - I will not! How dare you whip me and then dishonour me! Oh, Mama, Mama, MAMA!"

"Were your dear Mama here, Grace," I said coldly, "she would wish you to comport yourself rather better than you are doing." So saying I dropped the whip and, signalling to Fred to hold her down as firmly as ever, stood immediately behind her and cupped her hot, wriggling globe as best I could in my palms. How silky and firm she was and how the cheeks throbbed! A gritting howl of course came from her which was rapidly choked-off by a firm SMACK that I immediately accorded her.

"Be QUIET, Grace!" I snapped above her mewings while her nubile hips endeavoured to swing her scorched derriere away from my encroaching palms. Nothing would avail her now, however. Resting my left hand upon her haunches - for the magnificence of her curves made them no less than that - I glided my other down and cupped the downy bulge of her nest which I found to be as moist as I had expected. "Put your hand over her mouth, Fred," I instructed, for I wanted no high screams at this particular juncture. Rubbing the heel of my hand suavely under the rolled lips of her quim and feeling the impending ooziness there, I withdrew it after a long, amorous moment and - wetting my forefinger in my mouth - I inserted first the tip within her resetted bottom hole and moved it about a little.

Grace's response was to buck wildly, but this suited her purpose little and mine all the better, for one slight rearward movement of her proud, hot cheeks sufficed to lodge my finger in her to the first knuckle, whereat her thinly-pitched squeals sounded even through Fred's clamping fingers. Allowing her no leeway whatever, I then pressed my left hand into the small of her back and so in the main prevented the attempted squirming of her hips while working my digit back and forth until she received in slow in-and-out motion its entire length. Tight indeed she was in that narrow, silky channel, but this mainly by compression of her muscles which she would learn soon enough to relax.

"Missus - can I have her that way?" whispered Fred hoarsely, for country folk as I well know are given to a good deal of buggery in the seclusion of their cottages. It provides pleasure without unnecessary fruitions, so to speak, and many a young wench's rosy complexion and bold bottom is owed to this ancient game of Venus.

"No, you may not, for it is reserved. Withdraw your hand slowly from her mouth now while I keep my finger up her, for if she howls again or protests she will know the whip's snapping twice over again."

"HOOOO-AAAAAR!" came then from Grace in one long bubbling moan as her mouth was freed and my finger remained inexorably tight up her delectable rear. "Grace!" I uttered warningly, and at that she clawed feverishly into the straw and moaned, but otherwise made no further outcry. I saw some future for her then and slowly withdrew my ensheathed digit while giving Fred the nod for which he had now long waited. Before Grace could properly sense our movements, I had quickly stepped to one side and he was upon her, his up-rodding cock finding immediately its intended haven between her rolled love-lips. Simultaneously I seized the nape of her neck and to a long, wailing cry of apparent despair, Grace received in one slow, upward lunge the entirety of his throbbing man-root until the hot bulb of her bottom rested into his belly and his big balls nudged her well-nested quim.

"Take it OW-OW-OUT! Oh my God, he cannot - cannot - A A A A A A R G H!"

Doughty stallion as he proved to be, Fred kept it a-throbbing full up her for a full minute the while that I had her secured. I knew this gesture to be of signal importance in the conquering of a proud young female, for her own inner nature would now in a short while overcome her scruples. Sobs resounded from her as Fred then at last began to ream her. His cock emerged glistening with her hapless juices at every long, plunging stroke which brought her nether cheeks to smack forcibly against his belly. I had counselled him in this also beforehand, for as relentless as I had been in my treatment of Grace yet I needed her now - and indeed wanted her now - to receive the full pleasure of his piston.

"No-ho-ho!" Grace continued to sob and endeavoured to jerk her hips all about, though I saw this as a disguise for the pleasure she was absorbing. With my free hand then I began to stroke her long soft hair, murmuring to her that this was but her initiation and that unbounded joys would follow. Perceiving that I was now being tender with her, she began to sob in quite another fashion.

"Still your hips a little and let him rod you - come, dear - take the pleasure - what a fine cock he has, has he not - your future Papa's is of equal merit, as you will discover. Ah, you are panting now! Does it not stir you? Are you not on the very brink of coming, my pet?" So on and on I talked all softly to her, bending my lips to her ear and even running my tongue within which in moments of amorous play can produce a delightful sensation.

Softer whimpers broke from her then and indeed she stilled the otherwise incessant rolling around of her hips and began to breath softly if fretfully as the most succulent sounds emanated from the conjunction of their parts, by which of course I mean the juicy, sibilant noises that produce those tiny squelches which are the very music beloved surely by all devotees of amorous combat.

Grace's shoulders then began to quiver and her face hid itself in the quick cupping of her hands, for though her wrists were bound she was free to move her arms. Sensing her thus at a peak of pleasure as Fred's pego rammed back and forth, I deftly untied her bonds while he, rasping out a grunt and a groan, worked his charger in her to the full and commenced pumping his sperm in her, jet upon jet, to which she wriggled wildly and freely until all was done and the sodden member - still proudly thick and long - was withdrawn and dribbled its tribute in a snail's trail down her thigh. In her turn, Grace quivered and was still.

At that, I thrust my hand within the pocket of an apron I had earlier donned, fished out the coins of his earnings and, thrusting them into his eager hand, motioned him to make a retreat. Perhaps fearing retribution from Grace whose blindfold I then began to undo, he fled, buttoning up his trousers as he went. She, hearing this, rolled over and would have slipped to the rough ground had I not caught her.

"Oh, who was that? Who WAS it?" she moaned.

"One of no account, my sweet, but one whose manly cock has served you well. Why, your lovely nest is pulpy with his sperm," I murmured, cupping it fondly and drawing her lips so swiftly under mine that she was taken quite by surprise.

"Oh, how you whipped me - I hate you," she sobbed to my lips, but I was not fooled.

"Young women such as you desire to be taken thus, however hidden may be your thoughts, Grace. Think on it and you will know that to be true. You wish to be made to do what you feel is exceedingly naughty to do. Had I not whipped you, you would never have surrendered, and certainly not to Mr. Maudsley's prick, as now you will."

"Oh, what? I could not! Poor Mama! No, never!" Standing up quickly though on the shakiest of lovely limbs, she managed to repair the fallen state of her drawers while gazing at me with a mixture of wonder and resentment such as I had well expected.

"You will do as you must and as the path of fate ordains. This your Mama knows as well as I. Should he come to you in your bed, you will raise your nightgown to him and be dutiful."

"I will not, I will not, and you shall not whip me for it either!" sobbed she, though I no longer heard any deep sorrow in her cry. From being totally stubborn and proud she had unwittingly become half willing and knew not in her mind whether to move forwards or turn back to her former state.

Taking her hair at the back in a sudden grip and so drawing her lovely face under mine so that she winced, stumbled and was forced to clutch me, I seized her chin with my free hand and breathed upon her lips such promises of libertine pleasures as she had never thought to hear. To each she endeavoured to shake her head, her eyes full wild, but my grip upon her was inexorable. Finally, I released her so suddenly that she fell back, which gave me a moment to retrieve the fallen whip and bring it smartly around the tops of her thighs. With a maddened shriek she leapt back.

"Into the house with you, Miss!" I thundered and at that she appeared to quail - or else saw thankful refuge there - and ran to the door, rubbing her thighs and I quick in her wake. It was by now dark and her stumbling figure preceded me across the paddock to where the lights of the mansion gleamed their yellow invitation. I had not finished with her yet, nor her hypocrisies.

She little knew, in any event, what awaited her within.

CHAPTER XIV

Arabella - now picking up once more my tale - must confess certain omissions in my narrative which shall now be filled in plain. Following fast upon the seduction of sweet Susan, some conversations between Pearl and myself brought matters to a head, as I shall explain, for they preceded in essence at least the nuptial ceremony. Certain theories had been formed in my mind and in Pearl's which I was minded to put to the test as much as she. Full knowing, therefore, what was afoot in the stable - from whence no cries could be heard through the doors and windows of the house - I waited within in the company of Catherine, Mr. Maudsley, and Susan.

    Susan, of course, was all of a guilty flutter at being put to the presence of both her Mama and her future Papa within but a day of her conversion, but this was an act of deliberation whereby in concord with Pearl I sought to burst the bubble, as it were. Naught being said Of the absence of Pearl and Grace, I saw to it as well as a guest might that Catherine was well filled with wine and that Susan had several tipples herself. This, causing the latter to giggle and become flushed, Catherine would have quietened her and sent her to bed. At this, however, I intervened.

    "May she not sit upon Mr. Maudsley's lap and kiss him goodnight first?" I asked. At this, Susan put her finger in her mouth to prevent more giggling, as I suspect, while as for Catherine she attempted to put on a worried mien.

"Perhaps not yet, for we are not wed," she averred, though hiccoughing a little as she spoke and appearing a trifle bleary from her salutations to the well-filled glasses which I had seen to.

"Oh, she must become used to it, for it will warm her nicely for bed," I declared. At that, Susan made as if to sidle off of her seat and perhaps escape to her room, but the little minx - knowing well enough what I knew - was stayed by my look and a crooking of my finger. "Come, dear, and warm your future Papa's lap with your nice little bottom," I declared boldly, whereat Catherine promptly reached for her glass again and uttered a sigh. Susan then hesitated again, having now risen and looking perfectly angelic in a white frilly dress with pink ribbons and her hair tied at the back in a matching bow.

"Come, Susan," I murmured more meaningfully. With that, her finger went back into her mouth and she approached him slowly as though butter would not melt therein, though his doughty cock had already twice melted in her cunny. Seated as he was upon a chaise-longue, he had ample room to accommodate her and indeed rather artfully swung her legs up on to it as she sat.

"Oh, really Ewart!" exclaimed Catherine, though not without a bibulous giggle which at last told me all I wanted to know.

"Really, my dear," he responded, adding somewhat coyly, "Her bottom is indeed nice and warm. May I not kiss her on the lips to say goodnight?"

"Why, of course he may, may he not?" I interjected to Catherine whose chair adjoined mine and both facing the pair so that we were as spectators.

"Well, I do not know really, I do not," blathered she while a colour rose high into her cheeks.

"Such pretty legs she has, too. Her thighs swell most agreeably for her age and I know must be as smooth as silk and as warm as a nest," I went on, accentuating the last word. "Really, Susan, do show them before you retire, for I am sure they must be as lovely as the outlines beneath your dress suggest."

"Oh!" squealed Susan who never thought to give an exhibition before her Mama, of all people. Ewart, however, having been primed as to Grace's fate that evening, gave her thereupon a hug which caused her blushing face to be buried in his jacket and raised the hem of her skirt a little until her calves and then her rounded knees were revealed. Flushing not a little, he then passed his hand up beneath her coiled-up skirt, causing Susan to jump and squirm.

At this such an expression crossed Catherine's features that it seemed she knew not whether to laugh or cry, but so softened had she been by her bibulous evening that she remained a trifle glazed about the eyes. Seizing then the opportunity of the moment, I rose and sat myself upon her lap, murmuring in a cooing voice,"Were you my Mama, I would kiss you most endearingly goodnight." So saying - and to her undoubted astonishment - I deftly loosed the buttons of her corsage and, dipping my hand within, encountered two glorious firm globes whose nipples quickly betrayed themselves by rising out to my delicate touch.

Catherine's mouth opened. Her head fell back against the chair. In a trice I had swooped my lips upon hers and felt the liquid yearnings of her tongue. Therewith also, as if in accompaniment, came a muffled squeal from Susan which was quickly suppressed - as I well envisaged - by the meshing of her mouth to Mr. Maudsley's.

"Haaar, what is he doing?" quavered Catherine to my lips while her full, creamy breasts seemed to swell the more to my caresses.

"He is feeling into her drawers, as he will shortly have the right to do, will he not?" I rejoined.

I have often wondered since what might have been her answer, but at that very moment cries sounded from without and into the drawing room burst Grace, crying,"Oh, Mama, oh Mr. Maudsley - Papa!" even before she saw clearly what was afoot. I then springing up and leaving her Mama's bared tits in full view, met the eyes of Pearl. Whip in hand, she followed quickly upon Grace's heels and closed the doors behind her. Needless to say, Susan slipped from Mr. Maudsley's lap with a startled cry. and tumbled to the floor, showing her stocking tops and drawers.

"OH!" screeched Grace, who clearly could not believe what she saw. "Oh!" echoed Catherine who would have risen had I not pressed her down again.

"Well, I do believe we have the truth of this little matter now," declared Pearl, brushing past Grace and gazing down with some approbation at Susan. "The ceremony has in part begun, I see, or at least a rehearsal thereof which I am sure will do much good to all. Catherine, you will now rise, please - and no! do not attempt to cover your breasts or you will feel the cracking of my whip about you. Susan, get off your bottom, dear, and sit by Mr. Maudsley who will put something very nice into your hand in a moment, I feel sure. Now, Catherine dear, we will have the truth, for Arabella and I are much put out by being made dupes of your occasion."

"D..d..dupes? Oh, I do not know WHAT you mean!" blustered Catherine while Grace uttered a howl of perfect despair and threw herself down into the very chair her Mama had just vacated.

"Be sure that I do not blame you in any wise for the pleasures you sought - and indeed shall obtain, my dear," said Pearl blithely to our hostess. "On the other hand, you have been extremely naughty in putting up such a cock and bull yarn to us about your supposed ceremonies. I have made a few discreet enquiries, you see - without of course mentioning any names - and nothing whatever is known of such things, whether by genealogists or by sociologists. Come - declare yourself to me truthfully and I may forgive you, though not without an appropriate penalty or two."

"Oh, Pearl!" Catherine's voice quavered and two distinct tears rolled down her attractive cheeks. "P...p...permit me to whisper it to you at least."

Pearl glanced at me, I nodded. Stumbling then towards her, Catherine laid one hand upon her shoulder and with deeply flushed face and the orbs of her tits protruding still from her gown, whispered for a full minute as it seemed to me, while all the while Pearl nodded gravely, swinging her whip at her side.

"My dear Catherine, what a foolish woman you are! Could you not have said? Can there be peace or concord now until all is known?" So spoke Pearl to a wail from Catherine who, like Grace, then hurled herself into a chair and huddled up as best she could as though in dire shame. "Tut-tut, what a silliness and a nonsense. Would you not have the truth come out, Ewart?" asked Pearl familiarly of the gentleman who had lifted Susan up again on to his lap. A grave nod came from him at that and his glance fell not without sympathy upon his intended spouse who sat crying into her hands.

"It were best," he declared solemnly, "for I feared for the

consequences of such a wedding party."

"Indeed? Though you were party to it - if I may make the pun," said Pearl crisply. "There is one here who is not at fault and that is dear Susan. Grace has sinned not of her own volition - not as yet, at least - but by virtue of her prim and stubborn behaviour she has brought her dear Mama a little way towards this contretemps. Rise again, Grace - and you, Catherine!" CRA-A-A-ACK! The leaping whip, though it touched neither, seemed to menace both and both jumped up much like Jack-in-the-Boxes.

"Oh, dear Pearl, I beg you!" quavered Catherine.

"You have no need to do any such thing, my dear, for the upshot of our conversation and the quite delightful consequences thereof will surely be the same as will result from your nuptials. But let us be a little freer in the matter. Divest yourselves of your clothes - yes, both of you."

"Oh MA-MA!" came then the expected shriek from Grace who would have run to the door had I not deftly barred her way. "You cannot shame us so!" echoed Catherine, though to no effect whatever, for Pearl's expression remained as impassive as my own was calm. Again then the whip cracked and again both leapt, though it touched neither.

"You have but two minutes, my pets," Pearl intoned. "Retain your stockings and your shoes for you will each preserve your elegance as lovely women thus."

"Ewart, dear! Oh, Ewart!" cried Catherine, while he sat as one transfixed. Tears then welled in our hostess's eyes as she saw no escape for herself but to obey and thus they loosed and cast off their dresses, chemises and drawers and stood trembling and seemingly downcast in their alluring nudity.

Of the two, Grace was naturally the most enticing, yet many an ardent male would - I felt - have veered to Catherine who possessed still such elegant legs and such imposing breasts and bottom that I experienced a twinge of envy for the possessor of any upright cock.

"You will approach me now - both of you," snapped Pearl who - just as I - could not but help see that the protuberance in Mr. Maudsley's trousers had swelled so alarmingly that he had been forced to place Susan's hand over the prominence as if to hide it. Having in view both her Mama's and her older sister's bottom, and they not seeing, the minx clutched it as might a baby its rattle.

"Oh, Pearl, what will you have us do," sobbed Catherine.

"Merely be truthful, my sweet - and please draw up your stockings tightly, both of you. Yes - that is better. Now, Catherine, I see no reason to conceal your secret any longer. You intended - and still intend, I trust - to let a delightful lustiness obtain after the formalities of your wedding ceremony were over. So be it. You intended also that both your lovely daughters should be inducted - if I may use a delicate term - but there is no longer need to wait for that now. Both have now been put to the cock and are fresh for more adventures. As for yourself, you suffered unduly from a lack of that very instrument with your former husband and so have lived in such dire frustration that you sought the forthcoming occasion as an outlet."

"Dear heavens, how can you say this in front of them!" wailed Catherine who made to cover her face but had her wrists slapped away. With a perfectly angelic smile upon her lips, Pearl then stepped full close to her and, before Catherine could resist, had cupped the furry mound of her bared cunt.

"Dear, sweet Catherine, you wanted cock. Is a woman to be blamed for that? Of course not. Confess it and your trials shall be all but over, for this is such a common desire among us all that one need have no shame whatever in uttering it. See how a blush sits so prettily upon your cheeks, and how warm and moist your cunny is in its longing, its state of deprivation. Fear not that your secret - as you think of it - shall be spread to the world. None shall know of our future pleasures here save those you wish to know. This is true also of you, Grace," Pearl murmured to the young woman who stood as one who knows not whether she is in a dream or not.

Even as she spoke, Catherine's breath had begun to come faster, for with every word Pearl had been so titillating her clitoris that her hips and bottom had begun to move in the most sensuous fashion.

"Mama! wh... wh... what shall I say?" cried Grace who then threw herself into her mother's arms as Pearl removed her sticky fingers.

"Speak but the truth - speak but the truth," moaned Catherine, thus slyly passing a box of eggs, so to speak, to her daughter to be broken rather than by herself.

"What dears they are, what perfect treasures," laughed Pearl, though without any malice in her tone and passing her hands as she spoke about their gleaming bottoms. "Come, Ewart, I see you are in a fit condition to embrace them both and make the peace here!"

No sooner of course had the invitation been extended, than the said gentleman sprang up from his amorous embrace with Susan and had his arms about their waists in a trice, this producing a shriek from Grace who huddled closer in to her Mama, their silken bellies and thighs meeting sensuously."S...s...save me, Mama!" came her broken cry, for Mr. Maudsley's rampant cock - now bared - was pressed in throbbing longing to the side of her thigh.

"Stand still, I tell you, stand still!" came then a bark, though not as might have been expected from Pearl, who flourished still her whip, but from Mr. Maudsley himself. "You will listen to me, Grace - and you, Catherine. We are but anticipating future events, are we not? Let us have an end to hypocrisies, as Pearl has said."

"My love, oh my love, I have been so wicked!" then cried Catherine who loosed her daughter and threw herself into his embrace, the better no doubt that she could feel his torrid weapon against her pulsating curves.

"My precious, not at all," he soothed, "for we are come upon the matter now more discreetly than might otherwise have obtained. There is naught between us now that shall spoil our future pleasures. You shall have cock in plenty as shall both Grace and Susan. We entertain ourselves as frequently as we wish and the ceremony shall be precisely as you desired. Each of the males will put his prick to you in turn. Grace! - you, too - do you hear me, girl? Come, slip your hand between us, your dear Mama and I, and feel my cock."

"B..b..but!" stammered she only to utter a resounding squeal as Pearl placed her slender fingers precisely where required. For a moment that seemed timeless then, Catherine uttered not a sound. Grace's knuckles pressed themselves to her Mama's belly as she grasped in a seemingly dazed fashion the massive staff of her future father, or as some might say her step-Papa. Then with a distinct quivering of her shapely limbs Catherine embraced her intended so that his charger was sensuously trapped betwixt all three.

"Oh, who will you have first, dearest?" she murmured in a choked voice.

"Grace, of course, for she must learn to go under him and you two will then pass the most amorous night together!"

It was Pearl, of course, who spoke and Grace who upon her words would have retracted her enclasping fingers had she not received from me a sharp SMACK on her bottom.

"No! Oh no!" wailed that maiden as if in deepest shock.

"Oh yes, indeed! Would you spoil everything?" responded Pearl who, by putting one foot behind the elegant stockinged legs of Grace, tripped her neatly to the carpet so that she fell crablike on her back - arms and legs waving - and then uttered a loud "PMFFFF!" as Mr. Maudsley promptly descended upon her.

"HOO-HOO-HOOO! MA-MA!" squealed Grace, but already the distended, purplish crest of his long thick pego was at the mouth of her cunny. Struggle as she might - and her desperation seemed not so great as it might have been had Pearl not "stabled" her - the throbbing shaft entered her with supreme majesty, being swallowed up inch by inch within her silken sheath until with a febrile cry Grace was pistoned to the full.

"Legs well open, girl ["commanded Pearl who accompanied her words by flicking with her whip all about Grace's ankles. Her own face suffused meanwhile, Catherine could only gaze down at the couple in what appeared to be awed curiosity which I soon ensured was further heightened by passing my hands lingeringly all about and beneath her bottom and cunt.

"NOO-NOO-NOO-NOO-AAAAH!" came from Grace. Her legs being positively skewed wide out now, so that Mr. Maudsley was pleasantly couched between them, her flushed and beautiful face then all but disappeared under his. Their mouths met, a whimper from her echoed in his throat, and then her silk-sheathed legs rose and wound tight about his manly buttocks as the motions of his virile tool commenced urging her to pleasure. Such small sounds as then emerged from their well-meshed lips indicated only her increasing desire while the silky, plump orb of her bottom rolled amorously upon his cupping palms.

Hot-eyed and silent as Catherine was, I turned her mouth to mine while Pearl, taken advantage of her freedom from action, went to tickle Susan's eager little cunny with her finger.

"Is it not nice? Is all not well now?" I softly asked our hostess while the pleasure moans of the enlaced pair sounded beneath us.

"The naughty man - he will have three now and I but one," murmured Catherine who was plainly enjoying both the watching and my fondling.

"Nonsense, my dear, for you are free now to do as you wish, and besides there is one who has yet to be introduced to the full pleasures of life - which is to say of course your son, Bertram."

At that, Catherine's knees quivered and bent, her legs opening. She appeared to be on the point of coming, as indeed she was - and as, a trifle prematurely perhaps, was Mr. Maudsley from his grunts and groans. He could be forgiven that, however, on his first foray into his future stepdaughter's warm and willing maw - a sentiment she appeared to share as with bubbling cries she received the powerful jets of his libation.

"No-ho-ho, I could not!" moaned Catherine, sagging against me.

I ignored her feeble objection, naturally. Bertram, after all, could scarcely be excluded from the marital ceremony, as well she must have known.

CHAPTER XV

There are two kinds of orgies as they are called, though I like not overmuch the term. The first are those which flare up spontaneously, as when a gentleman becomes exceedingly amorous with a lady during a private gathering - perhaps during dancing - and others are emboldened to follow suit. Alternatively there are those which are discreetly pre-arranged among carefully selected couples who are well aware, by virtue of being "accidentally" sent a copy of the short invitation list, what is afoot.

Of course, there may be well-founded moral objections to such occasions on the grounds that jealousies can result with consequent injury to relationships. Given, however, that one's fellow guests are primed in advance, all proceeds well and merrily and many a marriage has even been much enlivened in its future course by such introductions to the Priapic and Sapphic joys. It would be unfair of me to conceal the fact that orgies are also the means of introducing an untried young filly to several rampant cocks. Indeed, this is often enough a splendid means of softening her up to her future pleasures, and any foolish struggling that might otherwise have occurred is much diminished for she follows the example of others whose social standing is equal to her own, which is naturally of great importance.

Thus might it well have been with Grace and Susan, but with some caution - and not a little mischief - Pearl and I had now seen to it that they were thoroughly primed in advance. There remained only then to "introduce" Bertram - a fine strapping young man - to his Mama in order to complete the amorous circle. He was due to return on leave from his regiment three days before the ceremony and hence Pearl and I decided to surprise him.

This we did by saying nothing whatever to him of what was to pass - a matter in which Catherine and her little entourage were also counselled. I had more than a little admiration for the lady, for I knew no other who could have arranged for herself to receive the blissful urging of half a dozen pricks and more in the sight of all and under the comforting banner of "tradition." Her daughters now being given up to the same pleasures as she, Catherine felt freer to act in whatever way she would, but even so most intelligently played monitor to affairs, ordaining that Grace and Susan were to receive the accolade of Mr. Maudsley's cock but once a week.

I am urged by Pearl, who now and then looks to my manuscript to see what is appearing in it, to describe in fulsome detail the splendid orgy that Catherine's wedding day occasioned. As much might one attempt to detail all that happens in a circus when different performers are attempting to engage the audience's attention simultaneously! It has often occurred to me, indeed - since first taking up my pen - that even a single night's adventures between just two couples could well take up an entire volume were one minded to describe all in every small detail.

To my eyes, and I am sure to those of the others assembled, there was something noble and yet shy, bold and yet hesitant, in Catherine's entrance into the drawing room once the wedding party had assembled in the house. She wore still her wedding gown and veil of cream relieved by tiny roses, much lace filling and such a clever fashioning of her train that the raising of her skirt presented no tiresome problems.

Entering as she did, and appearing to gaze upon no one, she walked slowly to the altar of love that had been prepared for her. After due consideration among us beforehand, this consisted of a red velvet divan in the French mode - which is to say that it possessed no back and but one curving end over which she was enabled to lean. In this posture, the lower half of her body was fully presented, her back being dipped and the glorious cleft moon of her bottom raised to perfection.

Beneath her wedding gown, Catherine wore naught but a small white silk waist corset that gave greater flare to her hips, matching silk stockings that were drawn up tightly by the corset straps, and as pretty a pair of white silk shoes as one ever saw. Unveiled as she was by the loving care of Pearl and myself, a gasp of admiration sounded. The polished orb of her generous bottom gleamed, its pallor relieved only by a slightly gingery hue where the plump cheeks meet and rolled in one upon the other to form a deep and secretive cleft. Beneath the glorious and inviting orb showed clearly to all the well-mounded and thickly-furred nest of her quim whose rolled lips evinced their lascivious moisture amid the sweet curls.

All was then silent, the party of twelve having been split in two on either side of the Venus altar. Not being permitted to disrobe completely at this juncture, the gentlemen fumbled with the fly buttons of their trousers and in a trice presented as so many miniature flagpoles the rigid stems of their waiting penises.

"This present silence will obtain, for it is proper and seemly on such an occasion," Pearl announced. "The gentlemen will each enter the bride in turn and give her six successive, slow thrusts of their cocks. He who fails to do his duty and expels his sperm in the process will be excluded from the further pleasures that otherwise await us all. Likewise, he or she who utters a sound other than a murmur of pleasure during the ceremony will be sent out. The ladies now will remove their dresses and their drawers in readiness for the amorous combats to follow. Remember - not a word!" Pearl concluded while giving Grace and Susan a particularly warning glance.

The first to then "greet the bride" was, of course, Mr. Maudsley, since it was his privilege to do so. A particular strain of delight came over his features as - kneeling behind his Catherine on the divan - he slowly inserted his huge peg to several sighs of desire from the other ladies. Little by little it appeared to melt within the enclosing love-lips until - buried to the hilt - it withdrew majestically, already evincing by its gleaming the eager moisture that Catherine was already exuding.

Next came Catherine's brother, Albert, who - it was said - had long waited for this moment, though there were rumours enough that he had enjoyed the privilege before. Knowing Catherine, I did not doubt this to be so, though much enjoying every little detail of the event as he proceeded to stroke her cunt with his stiff prick, causing her mouth to sag prettily and her eyelashes to flutter.

I do not, however, intend a catalogue of events. How boring it would be (though it was far from so in reality) for one name to follow upon another. Particular interest was shown when - at the last - Bertram took up postillion at his adored Mama's bottom. Bending over him quickly then, as his eager young cock reared to its task, Pearl whispered something in his ear while guiding his enflamed knob not by the route that the other five had taken but so between the ardent cheeks that with a little push - and much flushing on his handsome features - his knob succeeded in overcoming the resistance of her bottom hole and surged up powerfully within. At that, Catherine might have cried out - so unexpected was this particular salute - had Pearl not slid her hand so deftly across her mouth that (all being engaged with the spectacle at her nether end) no one noticed. Catherine's eyes bulged and a distinct mewing noise escaped her. Then Pearl withdrew her fingers and Bertram manfully corked his Mama to the full so that his balls hung down at her well-creamed nest and there gently swung. Breathing deeply then, Bertram held himself so within her warm fundament for a long, long moment which appeared to hypnotise the entire assembly.

At that, Pearl clapped her hands. "The gentlemen upon the ladies now, but none to their natural partners for that would indeed be a waste of opportunities," she laughed. This, appearing to break the spell, all sank down upon the cushions which had been scattered about in readiness. Mr. Maudsley mounted Grace with no resistance from that lovely girl. Indeed, she fumbled between them eagerly, to ensure the swift and easy insertion of his pego. Simultaneously, Albert enjoyed the soft, tight crevice of his niece, Susan, for the first time, the little minx receiving him with such squeals and pretty moans as was proper to her youth, and as indeed she had quickly learned was all the more enticing.

Upon the divan, of course, dear Bertram then set to work to ream the glorious orb of his desiring. It smacked roundly at every stroke to his belly, the puckered rim of her rosette clasping and sucking upon his in-driving tool much like a baby's mouth. Raising her shoulders then, Catherine moaned and bucked her hips all the better to encourage this lewd assault. Then, twisting her neck about, she brought her tongue cow-like into Bertram's mouth whereat the smacking of belly to bottom sounded even louder and in perfect concord with the cries from all about that echoed now to the ceiling.

"How happy they all appear," laughed Pearl to me, for we had determined not to involve ourselves or otherwise interfere in the proceedings. In such a closed company, we had our reputations to consider, as she wisely observed, so leaving all to their bottom-thumpings we retired discreetly and quietly, having learned much of the ways in which people may be brought by guidance and persuasion to do what they really want. Grace, as it turned out, had proven less of a challenge than either of us had thought. Perhaps this proved the only disappointment.

"I had thought she would have to come several times to the whip first," said Pearl almost dolefully when once more we were ensconced in her house.

"What a streak of cruelty is in you," I teased, though only to provoke her to further speech.

"No, Arabella, you know me better than that. Had I accorded her as many as three dozen strokes in the stable with the schooling whip, not a weal would have appeared on her bottom, for my method of wielding it is all and I would not for all the considerations in the world have caused her harm. It is the weakening of stubbornness and not the infliction of pain - oh, what a horrid word! - wherein lie the pleasures of accomplishment. It is an art, is it not? With Elaine there was much amusement, but I am certain as you must be that she wanted it all the time and put up a great silliness about it instead of a genuine resistance. The latter is more exciting to overcome! In that manner many a young woman can be brought to the realisation of pleasures such as she will never achieve in a mundane marriage."

I confess that my ideas - which so closely mirrored hers - were much affected by my love of playing both voyeur and participant. As time progressed, however (and I speak of a year or two and no more than that), it was borne upon me that most of what Pearl said was true. For the fate of most young women of good social standing is not to enter into a happy, loving marriage wherein she may rely on the companionship and erotic pleasuring of her partner. To the contrary, she enters marriage knowing virtually nothing of what is awaiting her and is for the most part deflowered by one who is intent in thrusting his cock in her, jogging up and down for half a minute, and then experiencing what he is pleased to think of as his pleasure.

The discomfort and alarm that most young women experience under this assault - for it is no more than that and frequently causes them great physical discomfort on their wedding night - not only dulls their sensations but causes them the utmost alarm that such experiences are likely to be repeated throughout their married lives. In consequence their lives become a boredom of childbearing and their only close companions are women who have become as frigid as they. The majority of their husbands meanwhile disport themselves with women of the streets - or with whores who have set themselves up as "courtesans" in fine houses. Such females indulge in bottom fucking and sucking of the cock in their mouths such as no respectable young wife has ever been taught to do, which is more the pity Of it. Indeed - such is the environment in which they have been prone to find themselves - that the very thought of such "practices" would horrify them, which is even more the pity.

So it will be seen - since none can contest these facts - that Pearl and I consider ourselves Salvationists, and indeed still do. It simply will not do if women are to be taught the arts of embroidery and the niceties of social etiquette and yet be utterly neglected in the amorous arts, for these latter fulfil their minds and bodies far more.

Some may take this as a form of apology. It is not. I prefer to consider it an act of caring wherein my own profit is the fulfilment of a sense of mischief (this I confess to) and a greater one of achievement. It would not do, however, for me to be boastful in this respect for of occasion things may turn out other than we suspect.

Such was the case when a year later I made the acquaintance of Lord Cossington, then in his forty-fourth year and a man of noble aspect, kindly disposition, and as mischievous as myself when it came to the conversion of young ladies. He possessed two fine daughters, a son, and a ward. The last-named, Selina, had come into his care when in infancy and so was as much of the family as the others, her own parents having been shipwrecked. I suspected Lord C. of some amorous dalliance with her, for at twenty-two Selina was extremely attractive and had not the direct bonds of kinship with him that otherwise may inhibit erotic play.

I did not hint at as much, of course, for it would have been indiscreet to do so, but a turn of events was to uncover more that I might otherwise have learned, and in a most unusual way.

One fine morning, having ridden across to the house early, I encountered Emily, the older of the daughters whose age matched Selina's. Lolling in the garden with her was her brother, George, who was two years her senior.

"How thoroughly bored we feel today, Arabella, would you care to join us on a picnic?" Emily asked. Being fond of such occasions, I agreed on the instant, whereat she had much fun in loaning me a lighter dress than I had worn for my journey. "What a beautiful body you have," she observed while I - clad in but a chemise, stockings and drawers - made ready in her room. Being not unaware of a certain warm look in her eyes as she said this, I made such small, subtle movements of my body as frequently give unspoken assent to those of amorous whims. In a moment we were locked in a loving embrace, our lips meshing, tongues entwining, and our hands fervently appraising each other's curves.

Dipping one hand down within the low neckline of my chemise, Emily fondled the proud snowy orbs of my breasts while I, raising the skirt of her dress inch by inch, caressed her thighs and all about and under her drawers. Not a word was spoken for a long moment and indeed none needed to be for we were too busy at our mutual if unexpected salutations. There is an especial flavour about the unexpected, however, and this lent salt to the occasion, for I had not suspected Emily of such inclinations before.

The more our fingers sought, of course, the more they needed to and in a trice we were upon the bed with my drawers to my ankles as were hers.

"We dare not dally long, Arabella, but what fun to tease one another before we go, for I would dearly love George to be able to mount you today," said she to my uttermost astonishment while her hand caressed my cunt as mine did hers.

"Your brother? Oh, how bold you are!" I laughed, "and would you be party to this dalliance, then?"

"Why no, for that would be incestuous, would it not," replied she quaintly, though confessing with flushed features while our salivas mingled that she would love to watch such a thing, which she said she had rarely done. At that I reminded her that "rarely" meant "sometimes," to which she replied artfully that she had but used the term as a figure of speech. By this time, of course, our bottoms and hips were squirming merrily as we each sought to extol each other's juices which, with a fine gasping and a maddening of kisses, we soon enough did.

"Has your brother not done even this to you, then?" I asked, to which she replied that he had not, though had several times attempted to raise her skirts. Alas that I cannot write an essay on the Emilys of this world, for it rapidly became clear to me that her inclinations were to others of her own sex rather than males, but that she delighted in seeing a desirable maiden well rodded and then to enjoy her afterwards.

After the merry adventures I had already known, this intelligence did not surprise me as much as it might have otherwise done, though I was eager to know whether she had been fucked at all.

"Perhaps and perhaps not," she replied, with a strange admixture of both the prurient and the lewd in her tone which gave me to realise even more the complexity of her nature. "We must be careful, though," she went on, "for I believe that Papa intends to join our party and to bring Selina."

"Oh well, in that case it will not be possible, and besides I am not at all sure that I want George to mount me," I said with a great air of fussiness. She appeared to have read rather more of my character than I had suspected and for once I was caught off balance, as it were. Being agile of mind and wondering much about such a curious arrangement, I allowed myself to adopt the air of one who was both uncertain and a trifle naive.

"We shall manage, I am sure, for Papa will not stay overlong in our presence. He has a great fancy for Selina, you know," Emily said pertly and with all the apparent wisdom of the world. I will not, however, bore my readers with a further account of our conversation and will hasten forward an hour by which time the five of us found ourselves well accommodated in a secluded glade some five miles from the house. There we feasted and drank well and, being surfeited, lay back upon the sward and conversed idly of all manner of common things until I began to believe that Emily's ideas resided only in the realm of fantasy.

Upon that very thought entering my mind, however, Lord C. rose, yawned and looked all about him and then invited Selina to go for a "stroll through the wood," as he casually put it. She not demurring, the two set off, George being between his sister and I. Out of politeness, I had sat up at the departure of the two, but then sank back again whereat George leant over me and, placing his hands lightly upon my shoulders, kissed my lips.

"Oh, what are you at?" I murmured, adopting a role of mild timidity and surprise such as I suspected I was meant to.

At that, Emily cuddled into her brother from his rear and, clasping her hand to the front of his trousers, passed her fingers all about his penis beneath. With some inevitability it then began to stiffen so much that I could not help but glimpse its protuberance. Meanwhile George's kisses became so increasingly amorous that I allowed his tongue to enter my mouth and responded with my own.

"What a naughty pair you are. Why, she is playing with your prick," I murmured, for Emily's fingers were now even busier about the stanchion of flesh which his trousers still covered.

"She will do no other, for she ever teases me thus," replied he, delving his hand then up beneath my skirt so that in a moment my cunny was being toyed with in turn through my drawers.

Finding his kisses quite to my taste, while Emily lay mainly hidden behind him, I replied,"Then you should take her drawers down and let her feel the length of it. Why do you not? Oh, you are tickling me so, I know not what to do. Pray, do not take my drawers down or your Papa might return."

"That he will not, for he will be too busy with Selina," came Emily's laugh, and at that she tumbled right over both of us, half squashing me in the process so that I then found myself lying between them. "Be a good girl, Arabella, for George has a fine pego. I have known him come twice in a girl without even taking it out," she declared. Then, taking my face in her hands, she began to lavish kisses upon my half open lips while George deftly attended to raising my skirt to my hips and slipping the ties of my drawers. At that such a languid sense of desire overcame me, that I let myself be uncovered until my drawers lay at my side and George's not inconsiderable penis reared its rubicond head, he kneeling between my splayed thighs. Caressing them and soothing the moist lips of my love-nest he appeared in no great hurry, for he evidently enjoyed the spectacle of two young women kissing and caressing each other's breasts as we were.

"Let him do it to you," I whispered sensuously to Emily whose tongue made bold reply in my mouth before she spoke.

"Why no, that would be most improper, Arabella, for though I like to touch it sometimes - though only through his trousers - I could not permit otherwise, but I adore to see him working it in a girl's quim and bringing it to froth."

As many conversations as I had had with Pearl and others before, none was so strange as this, though I confess to enjoying every second of it."Exhibit yourself to him at least. Push your drawers down while he is doing it to me," I murmured and made to pull at her skirt as I spoke, though in a poor position to do so.

"Really, Arabella, what a naughty thing to suggest, to let my own brother see my naked bottom! Oh come, George dear, do not dally, for I am sure she is longing for it. Lift her legs up so that I can see!"

"Oh!" I ejaculated in apparent astonishment, for so bizarre was the situation that it mattered not what I said, and George in any event had already lowered himself - in apparent due obedience to his sister - upon my belly and inserted the crest of his charger between my cuntlips. The sensation, being as ever quite delicious - for he made the most slow and sensuous of entries - I raised my legs of my own accord and knotted my calves about his waist as the succulent rod of flesh buried its throbbing length full within my grotto and his balls couched themselves beneath my bottom.

Such an erotic pleasure al fresco is one never to be denied oneself should the opportunity arrive. The grass was soft, the earth warm, and the birds sang above. A glorious sense of freedom overcame me as he began to piston himself back and forth, thrilling me inwardly to the very core of my being.

Emily, of course, had slid down, the better to play spectator to the lewd and exciting view of our conjoined parts. It was a pleasure I knew well, for a sturdy, full-veined shaft urging back and forth twixt distended but tightly-clenching love-lips is at all times an enervating sight and one that never fails to stir. Even so, I did not intend to let her peer throughout the entire performance, so to speak. Reaching for her hair even as George and I panted and writhed on the first lap of our course, I drew her up in such wise that she was made to shriek at the suddenness of my gesture. Drawing her face alongside my own, I ringed her neck with my left arm and breathlessly commanded George to lavish as many kisses upon her mouth as he had been doing on mine.

"Oh no!" giggled Emily foolishly, but such were the electric thrills passing through him and I, that he would brook no refusal and delighted in passing his tongue into her mouth as I could see by the workings of their lips.

To attempt to describe such passionate moments by mechanical rote, as it were, is to destroy the very spirit of them. I began to come and jerked my hips more vigorously, being as I then felt more the mistress of the pair than their victim.

"Feel her cunny - push your hand up her skirt," I blathered. At that, Emily shrieked again, but since my hold around her neck was tight she could do no other than let him, at which George's passion doubled - if such were possible. Moaning and twisting beside us, his sister endeavoured in vain to avoid the very caresses which I could not see directly but could measure in their boldness by the movements of his hand beneath her skirt.

"Aaaaah!" Emily gurgled, for he had evidently found her spot and was rubbing it through the linen of her drawers. Her thigh - now all but uncovered - moved against my own. Our stockings rubbed. The moment was one of true delight, for where she had wished to see me struggling, the tables were turned, and thresh as might her legs she was unable to prevent herself surrendering to the opportunity of the moment. That there was no artifice in her attempted defence I could somehow tell, for she was most visibly between resistance and surrender. Turning her face, I brought then her mouth to my own and found it sweetly moist and open. This additional titillation proved however too much for George who, alas, spouted all his hopes then and there and in such abundance that I doubted not what Emily had said.

"He is c...c...coming in me! Oh, Emily, what a lot he comes!" I blathered against her lips which caused her to hug the more tightly to me while George expelled his powerful jets so that I was indeed all of a froth, the lovely easing back and forth of his cock causing it to spout with every stroke. Then with such a sigh and a groan as men usually expend in such moments of fruition, he fell more heavily upon me and lavished kisses upon us both.

All three of us might then have savoured a lingering aftermath for George's searching fingers had clearly found their way in some wise into Emily's drawers, as the moisture upon them clearly evinced. Scarce had we settled, however, with his cock pulsing prettily in my well creamed nest, than a crackling of twigs sounded to our rear.

Ah, what confusion followed! George uncorked himself and was first to his feet. Emily, making to rise in turn, caught the heel of her shoe in a tuft of grass and fell again, showing her garters. I - more practised in such events - was up in a flash, though not so quickly that all three of us were not come upon too soon by Lord C. and Selina.

What I expected either to say or do, I know not, for George had not time to conceal his weapon which - although it had temporarily exhausted its immediate resources - was still of impressive aspect. Selina neither blushed nor cried out, however, but regarded his efforts to conceal it with some amusement.

"It is what you suspected of your offspring, Papa, is it not?" she asked in such a languid tone that I was amused rather than otherwise by her coolness. Emily, blushing to the roots of her hair, was then up and pushing down her skirt while throwing upon Selina the most revengeful of glances, though daring not to respond in the presence of her father who first addressed George.

"You, sir, will betake yourself elsewhere! I do not doubt that Emily has again led you astray, though I find this no excuse for the disgraceful scene which meets our eyes. Should you return ere nightfall I shall take it much amiss. Off with you, sir!"

Few young men there are who could defy such a father's wishes, and George was clearly not among them. Buttoning up his trousers he was off at a loping pace towards his horse while I, taking care to preserve my demeanour, soothed my hair all about and returned to Selina a look as cool as any she bestowed upon me.

"Papa, we were only romping - it was but a playful thing," Emily declared in tones that would have convinced no one.

Such a feeble interjection was completely ignored. "Guide them back to the house, Selina," Lord C. announced grandly and then betook himself to his own waiting steed which stood tethered to a tree. As to ourselves, there was no hurry about the matter - Selina declared - for Lord C. would have his son gone before he dealt with us.

"He will DEAL with us?" I rejoined coldly. "Nothing of the sort will happen, Selina, for I am as ready to wield a birch or a whip as any and I count it not a sin to do as I wish, where I wish and when I wish."

Such a spirited reply took her back. She recovered her poise, however, quickly. "Did he fuck you, then, or was it Emily?" she asked in a tone of apparently disinterested curiosity while Emily herself let out a perfect wail of horror at the suggestion, causing Selina to laugh. "Well, then, at least I have an answer to my question," she said, "but I have no doubt that you are the naughty one, Emily. You have not gone totally unobserved, you know, and your behaviour has caused your dear Papa many a fretful moment."

"Indeed? Well, at least he is MY Papa and not yours," responded Emily, endeavouring to regain her poise, though to no effect upon Selina. "At least, not yours really," she added lamely.

"That is as may be, but since I count him my kin as much as yours, we must all obey him, must we not? Come, let us return at a slow canter, for I'm sure he has nothing too unpleasant in mind for your misbehaviour."

I allowed Selina and Emily to mount their horses first and then moved indolently enough towards my own, intending no hurry. Selina wisely said nothing at my deliberate sloth. No doubt she felt she had met her match in me.

As for my part, I was indeed interested to see what might be Emily's fate.

CHAPTER XVI

Upon our entrance into the house we were met in the drawing room by Lord C. who to my surprise, if no one else's, offered us each a glass of port in order, as he politely said, that we might settle ourselves for a few moments after our ride and discourse upon what had occurred.

"Oh, Papa, may I not go to my room and rest?" asked Emily.

"You may not," was the brief rejoinder, whereupon a glass was put in her hand and all four of us stood about as if meeting casually at some reception, his lordship remarking upon what a pleasant day it was and appraising me much with his eyes as he spoke. This was clearly not to the liking of Emily who both wanted to be the centre of attention and yet not, so knew not how to comport herself. Then, moving closer to her, Selina put an arm about her waist and said in a perfectly normal tone, "It is not the first time you have handled George's cock, of course, is it?"

"I cannot believe my ears! Of course I did no such thing! How can you bring yourself to say such a horrid thing in front of Papa! Oh, Papa, tell her to be silent!" came Emily's wail.

"You knew it not, but you were observed, Emily," replied he coldly. "Indeed, you have been so observed on other occasions and, while I freely admit that you have never been seen to release your brother's member from its proper place of concealment, your desire to be exceedingly wicked has been known to me for some time. Surely you merit punishment for that?" he concluded in the mildest manner.

"Wh...wh...what will you do?" quavered Emily.

"You are to receive a lesson, my sweet - it is as simple as that," rejoined Selina. "Do finish your port, Emily, or we shall be all day about it."

Again Selina's tone and attitude amused me, and I now saw her worth. Taking Emily's glass from her hand - for the young lady drained it in one nervous gulp - she faced her and took on a severe look which hardly became the attractiveness of her features.

"You will now come upstairs with me, will you not, Emily?" she asked, though the manner of her speaking suggested a command rather than a question. At that Emily threw a wild look to Lord C. who however stood impassive for a moment but then, seeing her hesitation barked once "EMILY!" in such a tone as sent her scuttling out in the wake of Selina.

We being then alone, I asked him quietly, "What is now to happen? Shall she be birched?" Thereupon he smiled and embraced me with such closeness that I distinctly felt his member standing stiff up beneath his vestments against my dress.

"No, Arabella, she will not be birched but strapped. It is a far more effective instrument as you shall see."

"As I shall see? I intend not to taste it myself save perhaps by way of amorous play."

"That you may have as well, if you want," he laughed, "but as to seeing, there is no problem, as I shall show you in a minute. What adorable lips you have - so perfectly formed for kissing!" So saying he moved his mouth all about mine and then slipped his tongue between my teeth while passing his hand down my hip and inching up my dress.

"You naughty man, you are hard enough already at the thought of it," I murmured, feeling an ineffable thrill as simultaneously I grasped his erect member through the fine cloth of his trousers while he, finding that I wore no drawers (for I had thrown them behind the tree upon being discovered) made free with the warm, naked bulb of my bottom. Then ensued such whisperings between kisses and caresses as delight all sensuous partners, I freeing his upstanding cock the while. Did he enjoy strapping? Had he strapped Selina? Had he really seen Emily toying with her brother's prick? Had he himself had her drawers down?

His excitement rose with every question, while his skill in avoiding direct answers was - in the passionate circumstances - excellent. Did he not want to fuck them both, I asked, as from above came the most distinct cracking sounds of leather meeting bare flesh."Perhaps," he taunted, "but would you have me do such a wicked thing?"

"I might and I might not," I replied in equal measure to his coy evasiveness, "but what of allowing me to see poor Emily receiving the strap."

"Oh, poor Emily, pouf! Selina knows well how to wield it in such a manner as will cause her no great pain but rather stimulation. Come - for I believe we shall arrive at an opportune moment."

Following him then into the hallway and up the winding staircase, he let us into an ante room that adjoined Emily's bedroom. There, while I watched and stood as silent as I knew I must, he removed a small painting and disclosed to my eyes two small peep-holes which gave on to her bed. He taking the one and I the other so that our shoulders nudged, what a sight met my eyes!

Kneeling upon the bed was Emily, bereft of all save for her stockings and shoes. Selina herself had cast off her dress and stood sensuously attired in a small black silk corset that left her fine, full breasts uncovered and - below - framed with its lacy fringe the bold dark bush of her cunny. Her snowy breasts, each jutting boldly forth, looked so luscious with their pointed brown nipples that I longed there and then to caress and kiss them.

How many strokes of the broad leather strap the sobbing Emily had received I knew not, but the smooth orb of her bottom was already a bright pink and with every new CRA-AAAACK! of the tawse (as it is properly called) splatting across her nether cheeks, a bubbling cry broke from her and she jerked her hips forward.

"Are you not a bad girl?" asked Selina a trifle breathlessly.

"No-ooooh! I am not! Oh, I am not!"

CRA-AAAACK! and SPLATT! sounded then the tawse again in a full double salute that raised the pink tinge on Emily's bottom to a brighter hue.

"Emily! I will ask you again! Are you or are you not?"

"Yes, yes, yes, I am - oh, please stop!"

I was already now quite beside myself, for Lord C. had cupped one hand beneath my bottom which he was tickling most rudely while his free one played the devil with my moist cunny. For my part, I frigged him gently. "Is she not ripe for it now?" I dared to whisper.

"Yes, my love, but watch - watch on," breathed he even as Selina swathed the broad leather from side to side bringing ever more bubbling cries and howls from Emily whose head hung down as she squatted on all fours, presenting not only her hot bottom but the luscious fig of her slit to our view. The sight, of course, was causing my companion's rod to throb ever more fiercely in my hand until I was afraid that he would spill prematurely and so spoil whatever immediate fun might follow - hence I toyed with him more lightly.

Then it was that Selina silently let the tawse slither to the carpet and quickly seized something from a shelf which had all the aspect of a penis and was in fact a velvet-covered dildo. Being unaware of this movement and rather tensing herself for a further swathing, Emily remained perfectly in position, turning her head rather too late as Selina mounted the bed behind her, ringed her waist with one arm and nosed the head of the dildo smoothly up between her love-lips.

What a shriek sounded! What a wild twisting of both Emily's head and hips! But there was no escaping now the simulation of the act which she most clearly desired but could not bring herself to otherwise surrender to. Moaning and sobbing within the tight ringing of Selina's arm, she received inch by inch the doughty imitation penis until just over half was buried sweetly up within her.

"OOOH-OOOH-OOOH! you cannot!"

"Oh yes, my dear, I can, for you are now in training, Emily. I have strapped you before with your Papa's permission, but have never put you to the cock before, albeit that it is not a real one - though it soon will be."

"AHH-OOOH! I can't St...St...stand it! Take it out! Oh, it's going too far up!"

"No, my pet, you have but seven inches out of nine. Ah, you little devil, how juicy the strapping has made you," chortled Selina who leapt from the bed and - while holding the dildo in with her left hand

- gripped the nape of Emily's neck with her right and pushed her head down. Then to further bubbling cries from Emily she commenced moving the dildo suavely in and out.

What a delicious sight that was! Emily's hot bottom weaved and jerked, her sobs resounding, but even so I could see by various subtle movements of her hips that Nature was responding to the call, as indeed I feared Lord C.'s prick would at any moment. To his great dismay I therefore desisted from rubbing it and instead couched his swollen balls on my hand.

"Suck it!" he groaned, quite beside himself.

"No," I replied pertly, while certain that dear Emily was beyond all hearing now for her breath was positively gasping out and her hips working more eagerly to the steady shunting of the dildo. "You have seen enough, sir - how rude of you," I taunted him and then fled on tiptoe to the landing where he was forced to follow. There being bedrooms all about along the corridor, I ran to one with his lordship in hot pursuit and cast myself down on a bed smiling at him. Falling as one berserk upon me he attempted to ruffle up my skirt and so get at me but I prevented him - in part, I confess, by digging my nails into the back of his hand which caused him to yelp and look woebegone.

"How crude you are - let us undress and do it properly," I said at which, of course, he leapt up and began to divest himself of coat, shirts, trousers and all else while I had merely to remove my dress, chemise and boots. Then would he have mounted me on the instant, but lying upon the bed with him I clipped my thighs close together.

"Pray wait. You are in too much of a lather and will come too quickly for my pleasure. What lovely bottoms and titties they both have. Tell me truthfully, have you not sheathed this fine prick of yours in Selina?"

He, kissing me all about, nibbling at my risen nipples and rubbing his monster to the side of my thigh, replied that it must be the greatest secret, but that he had and for several years past for she had learned to bounce her bottom early to his desires.

"Excellent! At least we have come to that point. Now pray tell me what Selina meant by the training of Emily."

"Ah, as to that she has a penchant for it and would have had her way earlier had I not forbidden it. She desires to bring sweet Emily to such a point as will bring her to imitate herself. What little Emily has learned has induced her so far to toy with George's cock and to watch it being done to others. Or, at least, so Selina tells me."

"In that Selina spoke the truth, my dear, for Emily is a veritable cock-teaser and one who needs to be brought to the rod. Had you entered her bedroom upon the right moment then Selina would have had no need to recourse to the dildo. Why did you not?"

"Because, my love, that would be incest," Lord C. replied with such amusing solemnity that I opened my legs to him at last and allowed him to roll upon me. His body, being firm and muscular, pleased me.

"You f...f...fool," I stammered at the proud nestling of his cock within my slit, "that is a description and not an excuse."

Thereupon, however, we entered into such a rage of lust that naught was heard save for our moans as his long, thick pestle worked back and forth in my silky channel. I tightened the lips and squeezed my muscles within, all the better to feel the ridging of his knob. I yielded, I came. Scarcely was such a moment ever more delightful. Knotting my stockinged legs tightly around his waist I spurted out my tributes in a seemingly never-ending stream, my bottom cupped so firmly on his hands that the lower half of my body was all but lifted in the air.

"How superbly you fuck! Come! Come in my cunt!" I breathed, and though given little to such utterances could not help myself on this occasion, having seen what we had seen and enjoyed ourselves already in a long preliminary. Indeed so abundant was his jetting that my bush and thighs were lathered and I felt myself swimming in delicious sin. Tingling sweetly within me, his fervent cock withdrew at long last and rubbed itself amorously in a last salute against my sticky lips.

"We shall do it again later," he husked, falling rather limp beside me.

Thereat I leaned up and kissed his nose. "We may or we may not, for I am sure Selina will be in a hot state to receive you, and as for Emily - must not her training proceed a stage further now?"

"No, my dear, for as much as I wish it and indeed would love to probe her quim, I cannot. They are such fair creatures, both. What a pity - in such a sense as you will understand what I mean - that she is not my ward, as Selina is."

I answered him not, having my own thoughts upon such matters. A stiff cock in the night is worth two spent ones in the day, whoever it might belong to and I sensed that Selina would share my view. She was, after all, very much akin to Pearl in nature and close to myself in age. How well she had dealt with Emily was plain from that young lady's quiet demeanour for the rest of the day, Selina making no bones about asking me whether I had enjoyed my time with Lord C. and whether he had watched the whole proceedings.

"All was viewed and all was done," I replied succinctly, "but tell me Selina of your ideas about training Emily."

"Do I really have to tell YOU?" she replied in a manner intended to be complimentary. "The issue is simple, Arabella. Soon enough she will go on to her brother's cock, for she will not be able to resist it, but she is still backward in this respect and hence I have to ensure that she does my bidding. It is very pleasant, indeed thrilling, to see a girl kick and struggle a little while she is being brought to pleasure, is it not? I believe that you yourself know this more than you tell. I intend no evil in dear Emily's respect, of course. It is simply that she must learn to obey. When she does, the freedom of pleasures shall be hers. A girl who did not want to be strapped would start up and struggle - even fight, perhaps. She bends not to my will because her Papa ordains it, but because the heat and the stinging of the tawse lure her even against her will. It is an erotic pleasure that she will not admit to. I began by smacking her bottom quite gently with my hand - as Lord C. did to me years before. She spilled her juices several times upon my thighs before I knew her ready for the leather."

"There are great pleasures to be gained therefrom, it is true," I replied, "but what do you intend next with her, for I am sure she has been exhibiting herself before you in toying with George's cock when she must have known you were watching."

"Today, of course, she was really caught out, Arabella. During the picnic, that is. But as to the rest, I agree with you. If therefore she wishes to flaunt, she must do it properly, as you will see this evening."

Disclosing no more to me of her plans, Selina made me wait until the hour for dinner approached at eight that evening, at which time Lord C. complained of Emily's lateness in coming down. To this

Selina replied simply that Emily had already eaten in her room and would be brought down later after coffee had been served. To this his lordship replied "Aah" and gazed at her in wild surmise, but Selina's expression was such as brooked no questions. The meal then passed in its usual leisurely fashion after which - the servants having been dismissed - we took coffee and liqueurs in the lounge before Selina absented herself, saying she would not be long and would bring Emily down.

"Seat yourselves both on the chaise longue. A kiss or two between you will not go amiss," she smiled.

"What on earth is to do?" Lord C. asked me in astonishment, while I - taking Selina rather beyond her word as I guessed she intended me to - made bold to lay my hand on his crotch and offer my lips to his.

"But... but if they come down soon...!" he expostulated, little knowing the rare mood that had come over me.

"Kiss me, you fool, and show me your cock. Did you not promise to do me again?" I wheedled, so caressing the back of his neck with one hand and his penis with the other that my ardour soon overcame his scruples. Indeed, I had his prick out - stiff and rubicond - and my tongue in his mouth at the very moment that the door-handle rattled slightly, a squeal sounded, and Emily was brought into the room with Selina holding her ear very much as a schoolboy might be led to the front of the class.

Seeing her Papa's stiff penis in my grasp and my bodice full unbuttoned to show my breasts, Emily shrieked - as well she might have done in any case, for her attire consisted solely of black patterned stockings, bootees that buttoned up to her well-rounded knees, and a translucent pink robe that floated full open to display the superbly rounded figure beneath. The jellied mounds of her snow-white tits jiggled as she was pushed into the centre of the room, the springy curls of her Venus mount showing dark against the pure silky sheen of her lower belly where her thighs dipped in enticingly. A groan from her sire announced that he had seen all. His cock pulsed in my palm.

"Oh-woh-woh!" sobbed Emily, vainly endeavouring to keep her shapely legs together.

"The naughty girl - I caught her playing with herself. She is naughty beyond compare. I smacked her bottom well, I can tell you. Turn around, Emily, and show it."

"NO!" Emily shrieked, but of course to no avail whatever, for Selina's grip on her ear was as strong as a clamp and in a trice she was whirled about to show the delicious cleft moon which Selina's palm had rendered a most enticing pink. "Arabella, will you not save me? Oh, the shame of being exposed so in front of Papa!"

"Is she not lovely?" came my sole response, addressed of course to Lord C. who sat in wonder at this spectacle, seemingly feeling that now that he had exhibited himself to her, he might as well go on doing so. Indeed, the more he saw as Emily was turned about and about, the more his cock reared, if that were possible, she making time and again to cover her face and each time having her hands smacked away. Led to a further corner then and facing into it, so she was made to stand.

"Do NOT move, Emily, or your bottom will be the worse for it," Selina announced, giving those bouncy cheeks an extra SMACK which brought a howl from her. Then, moving suavely across the room, she sat upon the opposite side of Lord C. and nestled her head against his shoulder. "She is not a bad girl, really - merely mischievous," she said in a tone which might have done something to assuage poor Emily's feelings as she stood all huddled up.

"Herrumph! I, yes...," stammered his lordship uncertainly while - bending over him then - Selina gave the stiff cock that I was fisting a pretty kiss upon its purplish nose.

"Oh-oh, I want to DIE!" screeched Emily suddenly, "Selina, I HATE you!" and therewith she made a sudden rush for the door only to find that Selina had not only turned the key but pocketed it.

"You see, she is still wilful," Selina observed in a voice of great apparent sadness and gave then Emily's bottom such a loud SMACK that the young lady leapt a full two inches from the floor and danced all about, holding it and wriggling in the most enticing manner. "EMILY, you may go to bed. To bed, Miss!" snapped Selina. Producing then the key - no doubt to Emily's vast relief - she unlocked the door, whereupon that young lady moved so fast that but a blur of her shapely legs and well-rounded bottom was seen before she was heard scampering up the stairs.

"Well, then, I think we shall to bed, Arabella," then said Selina to my surprise, for it was comparatively early yet. Even so I caught the signals in her eyes and, giving his lordship's pecker a little peck, I rose and went to her.

"But here, I say!" came his immediate and rather plaintive cry.

"Perhaps you would settle Emily down - would you?" Selina asked him beguilingly and then drew me out, suppressing her uprising giggles as best she could. Seeing my expression caused her even more mirth, though being as quick-witted as she, I understood well what was about. Besides, I wanted her and well she knew it. Her room, having a double bed - for the most obvious of reasons - we were soon ensconced naked together between the sheets, our erected nipples rubbing together.

"You thought us all to have an orgy together, of course," she murmured, "but I am quite sure that Emily would have felt shamed in the aftermath. One must consider the sensibilities."

"Indeed, one must ever do that. An orgy in such circumstances would have been most unseemly, Selina. Let me tongue you," I added for good measure, slipping my face down between her lustrous thighs while she jiggled her hips and pressed the moist rolled lips of her quim to my mouth.

"Ooooh, how nicely you do it - give me more - work your tongue," she moaned while I, manoeuvring myself sensuously around and slithering all upon her, finally impressed my bottom over her face so that we indulged ourselves in a long and delicious soixante-neuf and in this and various other ways passed the most fulfilling of hours so that the trials of Emily were all but forgotten. Only when we lay at last in liquid languor, having refreshed ourselves through numerous libations so that our bodies throbbed most agreeably, did I remember.

"Shall we go and see if she was well settled?" I murmured while Selina's long eyelashes tickled my cheek and our arms enfolded each other warmly.

"I wonder if we are not all of a kind - you, I and Emily," responded she obliquely to my question, "for while a good stiff cock is to be savoured at all times, so even more in some respects is a woman's tongue. But yes, let us slip along to her room for a moment."

So, donning each a light robe, we made our way silently to

Emily's bedroom, there to find her lying on her back, naked to her stockings with the bedclothes just below her knees and her eyes closed. Upon our entrance, she opened her eyes, gazed at us in bleary-eyed surprise and then immediately doubled herself up and turned to the wall with a little mewing sound that so caught my heart that I was the first to fall beside her and gather her into my arms. There being but one oil lamp lit, I could yet see and feel the flushed nature of her velvety cheeks. Presenting her bottom to me as she was, I sensed the delicious palpitations she was still evidently experiencing and - passing my hand swiftly under the lustrous cheeks - felt a betraying pulpiness and creaminess all about her cunt.

"Let me feel, too," laughed Selina softly and, while I withdrew my sticky fingers, felt Emily all about her quim while she squealed softly and attempted feebly to smack our fingers away.

"Oh-oh, do go away - how naughty you both are!" Emily moaned.

"Oh, listen to who is talking! 'Tis you who have been naughty, have you not, and have had the best of it into the bargain. A good spanking, my sweet, is ever the best preparation for young ladies in taking the cock for the first time."

"I don't know what you mean! Oh go away, do. I hate you, Selina, you know I do."

"Stuff and nonsense. You love me dearly, as do I you. Give me but one kiss now and you can cuddle your creamy pussy and have a lovely sleep."

"No - won't, I won't," mumbled Emily, but having her face turned by Selina and I cuddling her from behind, she surrendered her lips as might a young girl being kissed for the first time. As she did so, I passed my hands up beneath her marbled tits and cupped them fondly. Peaking ardently to my thumbs, her nipples quivered as I caressed them, causing her lips to splurge more fondly beneath Selina's who, sitting upon the rather crowded single bed, leaned over her.

"Was it not nice, being naughty? You have had your legs opened at last and a good stiff cock working in your cunt at last. You see what good my training did for you?"

"D...d...didn't! Oh, the naughty things you say! Go away!"

At that I rose and drew Selina up. "Come - she has had her fill. Let her but dream upon it," I whispered, to which Selina nodded and drifted with me to the door, casting one look back at Emily who hastily covered herself and turned her face to the wall.

Upon the dark of the landing we stood then for a moment, I casting open my peignoir and pressing my warm belly to Selina's. Our tongues met. Our hands passed beneath each other's moist quims. "How I would have loved to see her bottom bouncing to it," I murmured thickly. The passion of the dark upon such occasions always arouses me. Our thighs spread lewdly as we caressed one another.

"You shall, my pet, for she will have to be put up to it again tomorrow. You are more sensuous a girl than I have ever known. What delights we shall have!"

CHAPTER XVII

All does not always proceed, of course, as one would have it. On the morrow I had cause to return home, for Mama was unwell and Papa was uneasy at my long and constant absences. Being of a tactful and kindly nature, he ventured few questions of me, however, for which I was grateful, giving me pause to consider how different indeed was my own domestic environment from the many I had experienced.

There is naught to be wondered about this, however, as I have long since learned. Each house, each residence, each manor, and indeed each lowly cottage and "model home" - as the phrase now is - becomes unto itself an island to which visitors come and from which they go, their intrusions leaving all unchanged, or slightly changed, or much affected. Within our enclosures we are all as natives who speak a different private language even to that of our neighbours. I have been into many a house where all outside seemed identical or much of a muchness, and yet within there reigned such varying degrees of decorum, dullness, boredom or loose and wanton living such as constantly intrigues and bemuses me.

I would kiss Papa frequently and he me, but never would his hands stray to any part of my person nor mine to his. It is not so much that such acts between us would have been unseemly as merely impossible. Such is my homily, about which I have been given occasionally to philosophising to Pearl.

"Oh, people are different," is her sole response, and indeed I have good cause to know that there is not much to add to that save by way of extrapolation and repetition. There arose between she and I a private language, if such it may be called. Thus upon sight of a comely young lady one or other of us might say, "There goes a possible one," or "What a nice bottom she has," or indeed, "How I would love to take her to bed or have her put to a lusty male."

Such remarks stirred us constantly, though to the outer world we were but two well-dressed and undoubtedly attractive females who went the ordinary way of the world.

"Tell me then what is sin?" I asked her once.

"Why, that is simple, Arabella, darling. Sin is the causing of pain or grief, mental or physical, to others, by whatever means and in whatever way. That in my simple view is all one can say of it. Naughtiness is not a sin, but is merely mischievous. Do you count us as having committed a sin, or caused such to others?"

I thought deeply upon this question and decided we had not. For this I shall doubtless be labelled by prudes and those of great stuffiness as a hypocrite. So be it. There is a lewdness - a mischief of lewdness - that dwells in all, whether it be the schoolmistress who takes her satisfaction from birching the bottoms of young ladies or the gentleman who merely wishes that he could follow her example but does not dare to. We who obtain the leisure accorded to us by wealth fare better by far than others. The wife left bereft of a husband who has turned to whores descends perhaps into poverty, which I count a most terrible occurrence. Both are at fault, of course, for she knew not how to entertain him, nor he how to be entertained. There is no solace, as I have often heard men declare, in the arms of a gay girl who lives but to fill her purse from each cock she receives. Better a warm hearth and several warm bottoms than a cheerless home or the over-rumpled and generally tawdry bed of a whore.

So much, indeed, I said most earnestly to Pearl who laughed at my then attempted earnestness.

"Come, dear, the truth of it is that we love fucking and equally love watching others at the game. For what else is it, if the truth be told? Not a girl we have ever put up to the cock has since regretted it. Indeed, she has become all the merrier for it and has blossomed out no end."

"True," I laughed, though for all my philosophising I would often ask of such a maiden afterwards, "Was it nice? Did you enjoy it?" Not all give truthful replies, of course, for they wish to be thought demure still and are taken frequently by surprise at their own lubricity - the pleasures of which they have been brought to realise. All temper their desires, too, for that is the way of woman. Such meagre adventures as I have recounted did not all take place within the compass of a month nor even six. The writing down of them but compresses them. I have frequently gone without a cock or another woman's tongue for a month in order that I might then enjoy the next encounter the more. Those who write of endless orgies are fools and charlatans who know no better than to constantly invent what they have never experienced, nor have the wit to bring about.

However well settled she may appear to be, a woman must ever look to her pecuniary advantages, not immediately but as they extend into the future. Thus Selina in her wisdom saw to it that Lord C. - who was widowed - was sufficiently well furnished with entertainments as would make him look no further for a spouse who otherwise would enter into the benefits of his Will. Such schemings, which may be thought ruthless and immoral to the world, are better understood between women than by men who have ordained for themselves the laws of property and seen to it that they alone own the spoils.

A writer of such meretricious novels as men secretly acquire from the bookshops in London's Holywell Street - and which, as I happen to know, are also hawked by vendors at the back doors of country houses - would have it that such as Elaine and Emily were rodded by their sires each day, or some such nonsense. Having enjoyed the fruit of the cock, such girls are wiser and intend not to become helpless hens to the strutting cockerel, but ration out their favours in due course as whim, desire or opportunity takes them.

Mr. Maudsley was such a one whose ebullience was rather more quickly subdued than he had anticipated. Within a year, Catherine saw to it that her elder daughter was married off and that Bertram was accorded no more favours, for to have permitted such would have created unwanted complications in her view. As to Susan she remained a perfect little houri - an arrangement that suited Catherine well as regards her own dalliances and kept Mr. Maudsley happily chez lui.

What a cold-hearted view this may be thought to be, and yet what a practical one! All were happy thereby, as were Emily and Selina, for both could flirt and dally as they would while dear Lord C. dare make no wrong move or he would soon have been brought to heel and forbidden entrance to their beds.

I myself by the age of twenty-three gave thought to marriage, but discarded it as unnecessary, at least for two or three years, by which time certain stocks and bonds that Papa had set aside for me would have matured. Pearl gave no thought to marriage nor ever had, though making numerous acquisitions from various gentlemen who greatly appreciated her reputation for "arranging things" to their desire.

"Some would call me a procuress, but that would be a nonsense," said she, "for I procure, introduce or persuade only such as would be persuaded and who are, of course, of equal social rank to the gentlemen. Some ladies arrange marriages, but I arrange pleasures. The latter is most often preferable to the former!"

In this she was right, for it takes neither wit nor sophistication to procure a girl from a dancing troupe, or such as parade upon the stage in Tableaux Vivantes when they appear, under cunning lighting, to be naked but are of course wearing flesh-coloured tights which cause great delight to gentlemen who see thereby the exact conformation of their tits and bottoms, not to say their often fulsome thighs. Young servants may equally be seduced, and frequently are by the masters or sons of households who slip a sovereign into their hands for their favours.

Such "adventures" Pearl and I ever considered tawdry and of no merit, interest or excitement whatever. We preferred some ceremonies or mischiefs such as are not obtained by merely paying a girl to up her skirt. I wished frequently that I had myself first been mounted in the manner of Elaine or Emily.

"Why? Would you have had it so?" Selina asked me when I confessed this to her some months after the seduction of Emily. I had put Selina to the tawse since then and she much enjoyed it, as did I, for in moderation - or some would say a shade beyond - it causes the bottom to burn delightfully and to arouse one's ardor.

"Why, do you not know? I mean Priscilla and Kate," came the

reply, and one which meant nothing to me until it was explained to me that the two young ladies in question were twins and in the care of an uncle who, so it was rumoured, had several times endeavoured to invade their drawers without success. Worse, it seemed, the two had run to their aunt who was a woman of prim ways, so that she in turn had berated her husband and nagged him constantly upon the matter.

"They must be put to the cock, then, not only out of reasons of wilfulness, but disloyalty," I said immediately since I knew somehow that it was looked to me to say it first. "Of course they must be well-strapped first," I added, to laughter from Emily and Selina.

"Be in no doubt that I have thought of it already," said Selina, "but the problem, my sweet, is that Esmeralda - the aunt - keeps the girls ever within her sight for fear that her husband will get his prodder to one or other."

This problem - such as it was - I considered for but a brief moment. "The solution comes plain to me," I declared grandly, "for there must be many a lusty young man would as soon poke a mature lady as a younger one. We must deal with all three of them, must we not?"

Becoming quite excited at the prospect, Emily all but clapped her hands. "Oh, but who? Who is to be the young man and how may we set about it?"

"A touch of some opiate, Emily, in Esmeralda's wine. That will quieten her sufficiently to make less or little ado about what happens. Moreover, she will then be so compromised herself that naught will avail her to protest about it afterwards. By the sound of things, we have a fair task ahead of us and must consider the details earnestly. Listen and I will tell you what I have in mind."

CHAPTER XVIII

If I gained a full conquest in what was to occur, I also gained a fervent admirer in Selina with whom I had up to this time been the passive rather than the active companion. How carefully my steps were taken shall be seen, for I first needed to make acquaintance with the uncle. He, being under the watchful eyes of his wife as much as his nieces were, I chose to represent myself first as a charity worker and so inveigled myself into the house by way of inviting donations, receipts of blankets and old clothing-all such as one normally collects in doing good works.

The pious are ever anxious to please, believing perhaps that in so doing they encourage to themselves the greater admiration of their Creator - a philosophy I take to be a nonsense. For though I bow as all do to our Creator, I can never bring myself to believe that such mundane deeds as the giving of a few sovereigns or a couple of old blankets would be singled out as meriting the donor a better afterlife than others. How unkind this would be upon the poor who can give nothing by way of material things!

Such thoughts lessening my conscience ever, I found Esmeralda much as I expected to find her, which is to say in the middle way of life, neither fat nor thin, and possessing still a reasonable attractiveness as well as a goodly, large bottom. The fact that the last-named was itself to receive "donations" caused me to smile inwardly while being entertained by her, promised gifts, and introduced to Priscilla, Kate, and Herbert - as was the uncle's name.

Priscilla and Kate were twins indeed, of elegant slimness, pale of features and with large eyes. That they seemingly had good legs and were a mite above middling height pleased me, for so a girl should be who is destined to be bent over to receive her future gains.

Thus having made covert entrance to the house, as it were, I needfully gained the attention of Herbert who by good chance was a master builder. I needed his advice, said I, upon the enlarging and converting of a small house into a refuge for the homeless. My manner of speech being ever soft and my general appearance made utterly demure by deliberate choice of the most unfetching dress and bonnet I had been able to find, I thus utterly dissolved any suspicions that his wife might have had of my enticing him away from the house. By making my request hesitantly, and ever seeking an eager nod from Esmeralda, I soon enough won the day and arranged to meet the good gentleman at an address I gave him.

Two days later our rendezvous was made, and no greater delight ever appeared on a man's face than when he saw me arrayed modishly in a dress that more freely offered all my curves to his view. Moreover, the address I had given him was one of a hostelry - much to his astonishment - though not for long when my purpose was made plain.

I was not of course so indiscreet as to rush into explanations immediately. I did confess to a certain subterfuge in entering his residence, though at haste to point out - most truthfully, I should say - that I frequently did collect on behalf of charities for the needy. Utterly intrigued - and not a little bewitched by me - he hung upon my every word as we sat lunching in an upper private room of the hostelry.

One of my lesser-known charitable works, I softly informed him, was in assisting gentlemen of the first rank (a phrase that made him flush with pleasure).

"In what way, may I ask?" he enquired.

I shrugged as if the matter were really of no great moment. "There are deeds of giving and deeds of love, are there not? They appertain mostly, of course, to works of charity, yet within one's own domicile there are deeds of love to be performed also. What beautiful nieces you have! I trust they are of my mind," said I smoothly enough while he - mouthing for the bait, as it were - caught it nicely.

"They are - er - that is to say - er, backward. A little perhaps," he said with consummate politeness.

I clucked my tongue at this and appeared to consider the matter. "They are not beyond redemption? Have you endeavoured to convert them?"

At this he gaped a little - for which I could scarce blame him. Taking advantage of his momentary confusion, I rose from the table and sat upon a small sofa, motioning him politely to follow. This he did, whereupon I laid my hand comfortingly on his knee. "Let us not be coy about the matter," said I, "for as I saw it both Priscilla and Kate are worthy girls who well deserve pleasuring. They are close upon eighteen are they not?"

Seeming a trifle distraught or excited, he nodded, being feared perhaps to speak for the moment. Then, gathering himself under the questioning look in my eyes, he said as if with some attempt at self-excusing, "They are prime to be mounted. Dare I say that?"

"You may of course," I laughed, "since it is true. They have not yet learned that charity is giving and hence they must be taken. You have the wherewithal to do this, I imagine?" Saying this with quite a sparkle, I passed my hand up his thigh and discovered an expected eruption that felt sufficiently hard and long to please any maiden.

"Ah then, you mean what you say!" he exclaimed and, casting his arms about me, donated many a fruitful kiss upon my lips while I deftly unveiled his rigid member.

"What else? They are fair to be put up to this, but once they are in position and ready to be saddled, as it were, you, sir, will have to learn constraint." Being asked then what I meant and his hands already in course of raising my skirt, I responded that in what I was pleased to call the ethic of the matter, only his own cock must first make entry into their sublime bottoms, for to permit another so to do would be a coarseness. "On the first occasion at least," I added.

"By jove, I see the sense of that. A purely domestic occasion, what?"

"You may see the sense of it, but can you do it, for as I see it they must be put up to you side by side. Come, let me demonstrate, for you are in fine fettle and I ready to receive your charge. Give me first a little room that I may kneel up - so." Thus saying I uncovered myself to the waist and to his supreme delight exhibited the fact that I was wearing no drawers. The sofa creaked a little, but by bending his knees and pressing them to the edge of the seat he was enabled to present the nose of his cock to my rosette.

"Dearest, what a bottom you have," he exclaimed hoarsely while causing me the most pleasant of sensations as the rubbery rim of my most secret aperture yielded slowly to his nudging.

"That is precisely the sort of compliment I wish you to pay Priscilla and Kate. Oh, but enter it slowly for the first three or four inches, then ram it up me to the full. Oh, you brute, what a monster of a prick you have! AH! OOH!"

In such circumstances I am not always given to lucid conversation. His prodder was indeed thick and doughty and was expanding my narrow channel deliciously so that all the breath seemed to be being forced from my body. Unbuttoning my corsage as best I could, I allowed his hands to delve within and cup the pendant gourds of my tits as the last three inches of his throbbing penis split my bumptious cheeks.

"Hold there!" I gasped, "oh, hold!" for like most males he needed tutoring in the art. "Imagine for a moment that you are thus in Priscilla's bottom, Herbert. She will churn her hips greatly and may cry out, but you must hold her as one does a nervous filly. Above all, keep your prick well up her for a long moment as you are now doing. Remember, too, that dear Kate will be also positioned in readiness for your amorous assault alongside her. You may thus fondle her quim and bottom while reaming Priscilla. In and out now, but not too fast and take care that you do not come, for that is the discipline you must put upon yourself in your first exercising of them. Ah yes, in-out, in-out, slowly, so!"

"My God, I want to come," he groaned, whereat I snapped at him that he must not.

"No, sir, for that will spoil the whole affair. If you emerge from Priscilla with a limp cock, poor Kate will be utterly cheated. You must delve your tool in and out of them alternately until you are truly fit to burst. Each must receive at least twenty strokes of your fine weapon before you spill your juice."

"Permit me this time, at least!" he groaned.

"No! If you do, I promise you nothing further! Take it out NOW - yes, already! Out, I say."

Downcast and throbbing mightily, he obeyed, I feeling the loss no less than he, for his penis was so thick and long that one was truly corked, and gloriously so. My bottom felt bereft with the final exit of his knob, but he - as I told him - had to exercise his willpower as much as I. Seating myself quickly, but with my skirts full up, I cheated any further endeavour he might have made, though clasping his weapon tenderly and assuring him that he had done well.

"They will not let me have them, though," he groaned of a sudden, as might one who has inhabited a realm of fantasy and now finds himself returned willy-nilly to the harsh world of reality.

"Will not?" I laughed. "We shall see as to that. I give you my word upon it that they will - and freely after their first or second trials. As to your dear wife - for I am sure that she will be the next subject of your objections - have no fear upon that score, either. All shall be seen to if you will but trust me. Will you?" And with that I bent and sucked his swollen crest so nicely - my mouth neither loose nor over-tight - that he groaned out his agreement immediately and began thrusting his throbbing member back and forth between my lips as smoothly as though it were in my cunt. Enchanting as the exercise was, however, I gave him but half a minute of this and then left his steaming rod to quiver in the air.

"What a tease you are!" he groaned.

"I have been known to be, but am not on this occasion. You, too, are in training, sir, for your balls must be full for the manly task that awaits you. How firm and eager it stands, and must do so on the day. However much Priscilla may squeal, protest and wriggle when you first cleave her cheeks, she will also know the first pangs of jealousy when you withdraw and afford her sister the same salute."

"Ah, I cannot believe that it will happen! Pray do not keep me waiting long, I beg you. But may I not fuck them also, for I long so to do."

"You fool, of course, but their first exercising must be disciplinary and a cock in the bottom is by far the best means of ensuring their future obedience, for it is a sensation neither will forget and indeed will come to cherish. As to your wife, she too may seek some further licence after the event and that I am sure you will allow her."

"What is to do with her, though? You have not told me!"

"Have I not?" I answered with great innocence. "There is a farm lad whose acquaintance I have made. It is not my fashion normally to bring a lowly male to such a lady, but in this case the means are justified. You will come upon her in the act of congress with him, and you must ensure that your nieces are also witnesses to the event, for I would wager that they have not so much as seen a rigid penis yet, or have you perhaps had an opportunity to display your fine appendage to them?"

"Almost but not quite. My wife came upon me too soon," he confessed dolefully.

"As I thought - but no matter. They will have fair sight of it soon enough. You may then begin to exercise them regularly. Your dear wife may even prove a convert to the cause once she has been able to view the proceedings, for few women can resist the sight, nor indeed the accompanying and most luscious sounds, of a nubile young girl wriggling to a man's embedded cock. But enough of such talk for you must conserve yourself for the great event. Let us say in two days time, on Sunday, for it will be a most appropriate day for your good lady to be kneeling while receiving the pestle."

Thus in the most bizarre but amusing fashion was the scene set. Upon the appointed day and hour I presented myself anew to Esmeralda, bringing her - as I " said - some fine wine for all her kindness. Being a ready tippler as she was, the bottle was soon enough open, I delaying with apologies through a pretended fit of coughing my own partaking of it while she tasted it and found it - as she said - much to her liking. In but a moment her glass was drained, whereat a most peculiar look of dreaminess came over her as the opiate took effect. She leaned back and with eyes half closed made feeble attempts to clutch at the air and then subsided with a sigh, her eyelashes fluttering and her cheeks full rosy.

I waited then a long minute before rising and stepping over to her quietly. From the garden I could hear the voices of Herbert and his two nieces as they played croquet - for he was of course under my instructions what to do. Esmeralda sat back on the sofa as one dreaming pleasantly - as I am sure she was. In order to test the depth of her slumber I began cautiously to unbutton her corsage and, proceeding little by little, finally brought out to view two large firm tits whose thick brown nipples looked at any moment ready to rise into even greater prominence.

Esmeralda stirred not but moaned a little as I passed my palms all about and beneath her mammalian beauties and saw to it that her nipples were well erected before then going quietly to the front door where I let in my accomplice. He was a young fellow of no account, a strapping twenty-year-old who could not believe his good fortune that he was about to fuck a lady and be paid several guineas into the bargain.

I had spun him such a yarn, of course, as he believed, telling him that the lady most enjoyed it when she was in an apparent state of dreaminess and that he might get no words from her but would receive plenty of encouragement. I will not however dwell too long upon the preliminaries that followed, for that which was to succeed this little orgiastic scene was of more importance. Within some five minutes - for it took at least two to wrest Esmeralda from her dress, chemise and drawers - the doughty lady, moaning much but encouraged by our dual caresses - was upon her hands and knees on the sofa with her bottom well thrust up and her anonymous champion ready to dip his lance.

So ready indeed was he that he all but thrust it up into her cunt on the instant, but being apprised by me that if he hastened too soon he would neither be paid nor asked to give a repeat performance, he entered but his knob and half his shaft within her hairy maw while I, throwing open the French windows on to the garden, tripped quickly outside and ran as in an alarm to Herbert and his nieces.

"Oh, you will not believe what is about! Come quickly!" I implored in such a tone that the three were upon my heels as I re-entered the drawing room there to find the youth well and steadily at work while Esmeralda, rocking her hips and squirming her fat bottom, was no doubt in the belief that she was dreaming it all.

The cries that rose from Priscilla and Kate upon viewing such a lubricious scene, with the youth's balls smacking at every stroke beneath their aunt's resplendent derriere are better imagined than described. Both covered their eyes, uncovered them, and then covered them yet again.

Such a cacophony of sounds then ensued as would have delighted any stage manager.

"What is about here?" cried Herbert, whose cry of apparent alarm did not delay the youth's activity for a moment since I had forewarned him of events and indeed had told him that the young ladies in particular were most desirous of seeing his doughty prick in action - "such being one of their strange foibles," as I had said and which he in his ignorance was ready to believe.

"AH! Oh!" screeched the nieces simultaneously. Bang! Bang! came at the front door.

"Oh my heavens, who is that?" came with apparent wildness from myself while simultaneously rushing to open it upon the arranged arrival of Selina and Emily who, crowding then into the room, made a perfect theatre of it all.

As for the youth whose cock was literally steaming back and forth in Esmeralda's tunnel, he grinned vacantly all about, believing himself utterly king of the castle or cock of the roost and ready to tread all the females about him. Finding no other resort, Priscilla and Kate then fainted, or so well appeared to do so that they each sank to the floor and there lay inert, which suited my plan to the hilt.

"Upstairs with them quickly and I will follow," I charged Herbert, Selina and Emily, being quite convinced that the girls had not really fainted at all but had sought refuge in the pose of so doing and hence would have to keep up appearances until they were got up to a convenient bedroom. Thus did they themselves act as accomplices to my scheme, however unknowingly, while in the next minute I saw to it that Esmeralda was as well pumped and spermed as a woman might be. Indeed, as the flushed youth withdrew at last his cock, several heavy drops of sperm fell from its enflamed nose, which spoke well for his virility.

"Have her upon the floor now and keep her occupied in such a way as suits you, for you will not be disturbed now for a long time," I advised him and thrust such coins upon him as he had earned. Dumb as any ox and no doubt as bewildered as he was pleased, he pocketed the money in the smock he wore and which served as his single upper garment. Not until I reached the door and prepared to close it upon him did he find words.

"I never knew the loikes of this, Missus," he declared.

"Nor will you again, my lad, unless I so summon you. Do your work well and you may be further rewarded."

With that I made my way up feeling such a sense of elation in me as I had rarely before experienced. Several shrieks from the girls had reached my ears in the short passage of time since they had been taken up. Their recovery from the vapours had been seemingly instantaneous, but now their cries were so muffled as to be scarcely audible beyond the bedroom door.

The boudoir chosen for the scene of their "donations" to the best of causes had a large, high bed which promised well for the postures they had already been made to take up. The drapes of the bed had been drawn back and all was in view. Most importantly Selina and Emily had gagged them, for this we had agreed on beforehand lest their initial cries sounded too loud and spoiled the merriment.

Both Priscilla and her sister lay uncovered on the bellies - by which I mean that their skirts were drawn to their waists and their frilly drawers removed. Such splendours of feminine allure are rarely revealed in perfect twinship, side by side. Their legs were long and slender, save where their prettily rounded knees gave way slowly to the rich swelling of their thighs. Their bottoms were as round and polished apples, deliciously pale in aspect. I would have preferred them naked, but knew the haste of the matter in getting them down first. Each lay with her face buried in the quilt while Selina sternly "lectured" Herbert, as had also been pre-arranged.

"You have seen what these naughty girls were prepared to witness and may well have encouraged their aunt to do while you were inveigled into the garden," declared Selina to muffled squawks from both. "It is for you, sir, to punish them that they might thereby know your authority more than they appear to have done heretofore in this house. Are you not of the same mind, Arabella?" she asked as I closed the door.

"Indeed. Esmeralda hinted to me that she might have a secret visitor and even made so bold as to ask me to absent myself for a while. I did so, of course, out of politeness, yet you can well imagine my horror when I saw what she was about. This poor man has suffered much between the three of them and hence retribution must be immediate."

I had brought with me a small valise in which I had carried the wine. Also within lay a tawse which I now produced - out of sight, of course, of the girls. Herbert, meanwhile, having uttered such remarks about the whole matter as justified the scene to his listening nieces, prepared himself for the event by rapidly doffing his attire until he stood ready in his shirt - a look of perfect glory on his face and his standard raised for Selina, Emily and I to see.

Some feminine instinct then warned both his nieces to turn their heads as best they could. Indeed, their foreheads bumped together rather comically as they did so and observed, standing immediately between them and behind them, their uncle with his raised cock. Not unnaturally their eyes bulged and two thin screams were emitted from behind their gags. Too petrified to move until now, they made to do so as one but were immediately thrust down by Selina and Emily and so held by their shoulders while I awarded each of their tight bottoms a warning flick of the leather. Their hips jumped, as might be expected, but I entered not into an immediate strapping of their nether glories as perhaps Selina and Emily expected. Instead I began to lecture them quietly, underlining each telling phrase with another flick and another until faint pink spots appeared on their otherwise flawless cheeks.

I pride myself on my ability to lecture young ladies, though I was then scarce six years their senior. "Your aunt has thought well to protect you so far from the approach of the male organ but feels she can do so no longer and that you are both ripe to be put up to it. Neither of you are to fear the event, nor are you to struggle overmuch when your uncle is put to you."

My voice at such times tends to a monotone which I am told is quite hypnotic. How much of my words the two absorbed I know not, for they had buried their faces in blushing shame at my first phrases and were besides jerking and writhing ever more to the snapping and taunting of the strap while Selina and Emily both firmly held their shoulders down, their eyes glowing not only at the manner of my "preliminaries" but showing every excitation themselves at the flowing of my words which washed - as they said afterwards - like erotic waves over them.

As I continued now with my softly-spoken peroration, so I began to stir the tawse the faster and the harder. Priscilla, being the first to receive a really doughty stroke that seared full across her polished orb, leapt like a fish, her howl sounding through her gag, as next did Kate's.

"Hold your legs well open, both of you," I snapped, "or you will get it harder. Now, my pets, you are to receive a full dozen each to heat your lovely bottoms for the fray. Hold them well, girls!"

CRA-AAAACK! and SPLATT! the tawse then sounded, though for the unlearned who may be among you I find I need to explain that the sound of the tawse is far worse than its bite. The leather is thick and heavy. It falls lazily rather than swiftly, but due to its width - almost some five inches in this case - the whole area of the bottom feels heated and quite deliciously stung under its broad impact. The sensation it accords is different to that of the whip, for while the tawse indeed does sting it also impels a glowing heat into the derriere which builds up slowly. One who is to be truly punished might receive three of four dozen strokes at the least, but this was not the purpose of my present exercise. I required only to bring the girls up to such a fervent state of readiness as would make their tight rosy holes more receptive to the glowing penis that awaited them.

His cock quivering, Herbert could scarcely wait for the denouement and stood ready to lunge. I hastened the affair not, however, for a tawsing crudely done and over-hastily effected will do no good whatever. Only when both his nieces' glowing bottoms - writhing and tossing madly as they were - were in my view ready to be cleft did I step aside.

Herbert approached then within but a few inches of Priscilla's squirming orb, his heavy balls swinging and his cock a full nine inches in its majestic uprising. At the first touch of hands to her hips, Priscilla seemed to sense that they were his and made a wild attempt to rise, this being however forestalled by Selina who leaned all her weight upon her, observing merrily, "No, Miss, you are about to be exercised now!"

Quivering visibly with lust, Herbert palmed her hot orb as if in a dream and then parted the tight cheeks to expose the puckered rim between. At that I found it necessary to aid Selina by placing my own two hands in the small of Priscilla's back as her muffled, rattling cry announced that his penis had begun to effect its inexorable entry.

CHAPTER XIX

I have bewailed before - I trust not to the boredom of my readers - the despair I have sometimes encountered in endeavouring to recapture the divine moments of amorous combat in all their subtle, fleshly details. Would that I could do so of the moment that was upon us - or rather, upon Priscilla and her uncle.

His face positively lustred with lust and happiness and his loins straining mightily, he effected the majestic entry of his cock into her bottom with the initial caution and slowness in which I had instructed him. Priscilla's head twisted madly from side to side and had it not been for the strong clasping of his hands to the fronts of her stockinged legs, she would I am sure have evaded the rude prodding of his prick.

"Slowly, my dear," I murmured within her hearing, seeing the tendons on her neck straining and her eyes full bulging while a series of whimpers issued from her throat. As for Kate, she had turned her face the other way and lay sobbing under her gag while Emily restrained her would-be movements gently.

"HAAAAR!" gasped Herbert then for the tightness of Priscilla's rimmed orifice around his stiff, veined penis was well evident from the expression of wonder and excitement on his face. Indeed, I understate the look on his face. It was in all truth one of delirium. He, however, mastered himself well and a full minute passed before he achieved the full lodgement of his prick in the silky and succulent tube which was destined to receive it.

"Remove her gag," I then instructed Selina quietly while Herbert with flushed and quivering features kept himself embedded so that his balls brushed the nested haven of her quim.

With the removal of the cloth from around Priscilla's mouth came her expected howls, cries, entreaties and sobs. "NO-WOH! NO-WOH! Do not let him! Oh, take it out, take it out, take it OUT!"

I motioned Selina aside and slid my face so quickly beneath Priscilla's, with my arms tightly clasped under her armpits that her howls sounded full against my ears.

"Shush, dear, shush, it is but for your own good," I soothed while tasting the appealing saltiness of her tears and feeling the vibrant sobbing of her lips to my cheek. Then - "Herbert, do not move yet - refrain yourself as you must so that this little darling will best feel its throbbing and its length," said I.

"Oh no, he mustn't, he mustn't, he mustn't!" babbled Priscilla, though I, more knowing than she and sensing well the sensations she was enduring, caught such a slight change of note in her voice as encouraged me mightily, for by a deep instinct well known to well-corked females young or old, she now held her hips more still and was privately savouring, as well I knew, the exquisite sensations that his fully sheathed prick was producing in her.

"Kiss me - come, darling, kiss me and be a good girl," I whispered beguilingly. For a long and fretful moment while issuing the prettiest of moans she sought to evade my seeking lips, I laughing meanwhile with full understanding while she did so.

"Now, Herbert, now!" I commanded and with that I drew her quavering, sobbing mouth upon my own while his big corker withdrew slowly and then majestically rammed in again.

"DOH-DOH-DOH-DOH!" yammered Priscilla meaningless into my open mouth, our tongues being now touching since she could no longer elude the sensuous moment. Well at her then, Herbert began to shaft her deeply, each forward stroke of his penis bringing an ardent quiver from her. "WHOOO-AAAAARGH!" gurgled Priscilla, flooding my mouth with her breath in a manner that I found as exquisitely exciting as all the rest. Seeing naught, I could yet hear her flushed bottom cheeks smacking into his belly with every stroke, the slimness of her waist and the bulbous conformation of her adorable derriere rendering each second one of utter beauty and sensuousness.

Indeed, I all but lost myself in the moment and would have let him eject his boiling sperm within her. Yet mastering myself and striving to rise up through a perfect dizziness of delight, I managed somehow - while still enfolding Priscilla tightly - to sound out the single cry, "To Kate! To Kate!"

Little was I aware that overcome by the spectacle, Selina and Emily had both taken it upon themselves to lavish every possible caress upon Herbert's other niece and thus - as I sensed his slow withdrawal from Priscilla's bottom and hearing her final, surrendering moans - I slipped from under her only to see Emily's tongue well dipped up into Kate's sticky quim while Selina lavished kisses on her swollen tits and mouth.

"Kiss me - come, darling, kiss me and be a good girl," I whispered beguilingly. "Ah, you devils, let him get at her," I laughed, for so far from struggling Kate held her shapely legs wide open and was clearly enjoying the event. At my cry, however - and upon the quick rising of Selina and Emily - she uttered the inevitable shriek upon seeing her uncle's massive cock in full erection above her.

"NO!" screeched she and would have leapt up in turn, but Herbert with commendable speed was on her in a flash. A wild wriggling of Kate's bottom, a threshing of her legs and arms, and in a trice the nose of his enraged penis was well buried in her muff. "AUNT-EEEEEEE!" came then her wild cry, for while it was evidently one thing to enjoy the lewd caresses of Selina and Emily, to have her uncle upon her was quite another. Fiercely and sweetly did she wrestle, her face quite adorably flushed as inch by inch the rampant protrusion that stemmed above his sperm-laden balls parted her already well-moistened love-lips. more and more until he had her to the full and her throbbing but diminishing cries told well that her future pleasure-rod had got home at last.

All strangely quietened then in the boudoir, as happens from time to time upon such occasions. The bedsprings squeaked a little as he fucked her - and as well they might since all five of us were upon it. Priscilla being dazed and unfulfilled, I gathered her into my arms.

"What a good girl you have been," I murmured whereat she began to cry a little, as was expected, and appeared to hide her face against my breasts, though slyly endeavouring to gaze at the same time upon the now hotly-threshing pair who, as I well knew, would not now be long about their business. Hearing the quick in-hissing of breath through Kate's nostrils, I knew her to be coming. Herbert's excited grunts and small animal moans told me also that he was fast approaching the peak of his pleasure.

"You, too, my love - soon enough," I whispered to Priscilla into whose eyes a glazed look was coming. Dipping my forefinger under her sticky slit, I rubbed her gently. Her lips parted, her tongue drove into my mouth, a fierce quivering shook her and then came the divine spurting of her love juices over my fingers even as with a long-shuddering groan Herbert expelled his fierce, warm jets into the now receptive nest in which it was rodded. Ah, what fervent, trilling sounds of pleasure rose, and then all was quiet, only the deepness of each partner's breathing betraying the endless depths of our pleasure.

Thus did we all linger for a long moment until, stirring myself first, I rose and clapped my hands, saying, "Come, girls, up with you! Priscilla, you, and Kate, too. You will both be good and obedient girls henceforth, you understand?"

A great silliness reigned between them then, as I well understood it would. At one moment they blushed and at another giggled, knowing not where to put their eyes, though both evinced a sly interest in their uncle's heavily dangling prick as I could see from their darting glances.

"Oh, but I cannot face Aunty now!" bemoaned Priscilla first, and being echoed immediately by her sister.

"What nonsense - it is rather she who may not be able to face you," I replied truthfully enough. "Come, we shall all go down and see what is about."

In part, such affairs as this are always a pantomime. In part, I say, for all things are also quickly enough smoothed out. Esmeralda, as might have been expected; lay naked to her stockings on the sofa, the silk of her hose being streaked with dried sperm. Her champion - or perhaps mine - had absented himself, having fucked her well twice and thinking it better, perhaps, not to face "the master" again. The opiate I had put into her wine had evidently worn off, or almost so, for she sat up at our entrance and made with a screech to cover herself.

"Oh, Herbert, what have you been at! I have been most cruelly attacked and ill-used," declared she with supreme hypocrisy, while Priscilla and Kate ran as if to hide in a corner and appeared perfectly witless.

"Ha! Cruelly attacked, indeed. My dear, we know the better of it, so let us have no nonsense in the matter," responded her husband boldly. " There was a certain wisdom in your actions, however, and our dear nieces have benefited well from your example which I found them eager enough to follow and would have done before this had it not been for your foolish meddling. Observe how neatly they are dressed again after the amorous bucking of their bottoms while you, my pet, make bold to display yourself in nudity to us!"

"Oh, you have not done it to them, have you?" cried she with all the inconsequentiality that some females possess when put to a question.

I felt it timely then to make an interjection myself while Esmeralda was still reaching wildly for her fallen clothes. "Priscilla and Kate - come here!" I barked whereat - and with memories still of the tawse at their bottoms - both scuttled to me like nervous rabbits.

"Has your dear uncle not taken pleasure of you both upstairs and did you not permit him to at last?" I asked pointedly of both. There were hesitations, of course, but a single gesture of my hand which was no doubt again reminiscent of their most recent experiences brought at last a whispered and half-giggling "Yes" from each.

"Oh, my God!" screeched Esmeralda theatrically at that and rose, clutching her gown in front of her." You have done it with them, Herbert, you have!"

"Be quiet, woman!" he thundered, as much perhaps to my surprise as her own while Selina and Emily stood as amused spectators of all. "They have learned obedience and the pleasures that stem therefrom, Esmeralda, as you never have. I am prepared to give you time to learn, however. Shall we say one minute?"

"Oh, Herbert!" Her cry was indeed one of apparent despair, yet few women are at a total loss even in such a situation. Throwing herself into his arms, she clung to him and began to ooze forth such tears as to her seemed requisite to the occasion. Her spouse, however, remained unyielding.

"Well, Esmeralda?" he demanded, the while that his hands

reached out to soothe the bottoms of his nieces. It was a gesture that Esmeralda clearly did not miss despite all her well-acted appearances of grief.

"Yes, Herbert," came then her muffled reply. It was enough. Priscilla and Kate bit their lips and smiled, though endeavouring to appear not to. What hidden jealousies, what secrecies of desires, what previously concealed thoughts were momentarily revealed therein! Such moments are food for reflection indeed.

I said naught but turned, went from the room and gathered up my bonnet and cloak in the hall as did Selina and Emily theirs. The occasion was not one for further interruptions by ourselves. The front door closed upon us quietly. The carriage in which they had arrived stood waiting still, I having dismissed my own upon arrival. A reflective silence fell upon us as we rumbled down the drive and made into the lanes.

"Quite adorable were they not?" ventured Selina then.

I smiled at her, for she was echoing my own thoughts. I would have fain had Priscilla and Kate abed with me that very night, as well she would have done. "Not only adorable and so sweetly curved, but at a most interesting stage, too," I replied, not gazing at her directly but smiling to myself through the dust-hazed window of the carriage.

"Go on, Arabella, tell us what you are really thinking," urged Emily, stroking my arm fondly.

"How brief such adventures can be. We are there one moment and then gone," I mused. "Of course, if one had a house of one's own, how pleasant it would be to continue exercising Priscilla and Kate - in the company of gentlemen, naturally - and not only the twins, for there are several other likely young ladies in the neighbourhood who would much benefit from our attentions as we thereafter would benefit from theirs."

I allowed my voice to die away and waited. The idea of having my own centre of pleasures without ever wandering afield began to enchant me the more that I thought on it.

"If one had one's own house, yes," ventured Selina and threw a questioning glance at Emily who, however, cast her eyes down and seemed not to know how to respond. At that very moment, however, fate took a helpful turn about me, for the carriage began to slow down at the approach of three riders in the narrow lane. I knew them vaguely, and - calling to our coachman to stop - waved as they approached. The first to do so was a girl of twenty with such long golden hair that she seemed as a perfect goddess. Coming immediately behind her was her younger sister whom I knew as Maude. Their companion was a handsome gentleman who introduced himself as Robert.

"We are at home tonight. Would you perhaps care to come to dinner?" I enquired after we had exchanged the usual pleasantries. Robert's eyes met mine more deeply than they had before. A shimmer of understanding passed between us such as can sometimes occur to people who meet for the first time. He, accepting for them, there was a further small flustering of voices and then all was agreed. With a wave and a gentle jingling of the harness of our horses, we were gone. Peering then quickly from the window, Selina noted well the pertly-rounded bottoms of the two sisters in their riding. Then, settling herself again, she awarded me a huge smile.

"If we had a house of our own - as you were saying," she remarked.

"Such as Lord C.'s, yes," I responded, whereat Emily appeared to wake up.

"You do not mean it? Oh, you could not possibly! What will Papa say? Besides, you have invited those three to dinner," she said wonderingly as if she had just fallen upon the fact.

"Not only to dinner, my pet, but to stay the night, if they but knew it," I responded, holding my eyes full in her own so that an understanding flush began to appear upon her cheeks.

"Oh, but...wh...what will Papa do?" she asked, her mouth most prettily open.

"Emily, you are the last person to ask that question now," laughed Selina, whereat we all burst into giggles, though my own veiled such continuing thoughts as I was then having. Lord C. would soon be persuaded. I knew that well. On the morrow we could invite Herbert, Priscilla and Kate to join us. Although he knew it little now, Lord C.'s mansion was soon to become a veritable house of pleasure.

THE END